T0147952

I'VE LOVED BEFORE

I'VE LOVED BEFORE

MATRINNA WOODS

I'VE LOVED BEFORE

Copyright © 2014 Matrinna Woods.

All rights reserved. No part of this book may be used or reproduced by any means, graphic, electronic, or mechanical, including photocopying, recording, taping or by any information storage retrieval system without the written permission of the publisher except in the case of brief quotations embodied in critical articles and reviews.

Certain characters in this work are historical figures, and certain events portrayed did take place. However, this is a work of fiction. All of the other characters, names, and events as well as all places, incidents, organizations, and dialogue in this novel are either the products of the author's imagination or are used fictitiously.

iUniverse books may be ordered through booksellers or by contacting:

iUniverse
1663 Liberty Drive
Bloomington, IN 47403
www.iuniverse.com
1-800-Authors (1-800-288-4677)

Because of the dynamic nature of the Internet, any web addresses or links contained in this book may have changed since publication and may no longer be valid. The views expressed in this work are solely those of the author and do not necessarily reflect the views of the publisher, and the publisher hereby disclaims any responsibility for them.

Any people depicted in stock imagery provided by Thinkstock are models, and such images are being used for illustrative purposes only. Certain stock imagery © Thinkstock.

ISBN: 978-1-4917-4048-4 (sc)
ISBN: 978-1-4917-4050-7 (hc)
ISBN: 978-1-4917-4049-1 (e)

Library of Congress Control Number: 2014912557

Printed in the United States of America.

iUniverse rev. date: 08/15/2014

Dedication

I would like to dedicate this book to my entire family and all who played an integral part in shaping the person I am today. Some of those people are my mom, dad, brothers, my younger sister, my grandmothers, my grandfathers, and my close friends. I definitely want to send a special thank you to all of the Milwaukee Public School teachers who invested their time into my education. I also would like to thank the wonderful staff at University of Wisconsin-Milwaukee who helped enhance my education experience through their dedication to their work.

Lastly, this book is dedicated to all of the intriguing people whom I have had the pleasure to cross paths with in this life (in the community, at work, and out and about) who have inspired, encouraged, and influenced me and my writing. Thank you, all.

*In memory of Thomas Jasper Buchanan III
(February 8, 1987–November 11, 2009) and
Earnestine Hughes (May 29, 1943- July 18, 2006)*

SPECIAL THANK YOU TO THE EDITING
DEPARTMENT AT iUNIVERSE SELF
PUBLISHING FOR HELPING TO IMPROVE
THE QUALITY OF THIS NOVEL

editorial.board@iuniverse.com

Chapter 1

Working in the Big House Kitchen

"**B**ertha, quit playin' around with them potatoes before Massa come in here now." Mattie yelled at Bertha from across the kitchen.

Bertha was standing at the scrub bowl in the big house kitchen, fumbling around with the potatoes that she was supposed to be peeling as part of the evening's dinner.

"Mattie, why do I gotta do this all the time? Why you never let me do the fryin'?"

"Look, Bertha, you know Sue in charge of the fryin' today."

"But she did it last night and on Wednesday, and Pearly did it on them other days. I never get to do the fryin'."

"Look here, girl, don't give me no lip. You do the potatoes, and that's the end of it unless you wanna be back out there in the field in that hot sun. You lucky that all you gotta do is them potatoes. Now get to peelin' them!"

"But I'm fifteen, and I only used the stove to do the fryin' once," Bertha insisted.

"Look, girl, I said get to peelin' them potatoes, or I'll tell Massa to put you back out in the field to work in that sun. Goodness sakes, this child drivin' me mad!"

Bertha looked out the big window in the kitchen and saw the Mississippi sun beaming down. It was hot outside, and the air was dry, but inside the kitchen the moisture in the hot atmosphere seemed like a cocoon that held Bertha captive. Even so, without further protest, she picked up a potato and started peeling it. As she proceeded with her duties, she wiped a gloss of perspiration from her upper lip. Mattie was the head of all of the servants in the kitchen. She was a robust woman who often ate a couple of meals at the same as managing the preparation of all of the meals for Master Jackson and his family and whatever other guests they may have been expecting at the time. When Bertha proceeded to peel the potato in her hand, Mattie turned around and popped a dumpling into her mouth and started chewing.

"Mattie, why you always get to eat whiles we in this kitchen? Nobody else get to eat in here, Bertha asked."

Mattie took two steps forward and grabbed a fried chicken leg that was in a basket sitting on the counter. After taking a large bite from it, she quickly charged at Bertha and pointed the drumstick in her face. With her jaws bulging from the portion of chicken in her mouth, she confronted Bertha.

"Look, girl, you ain't but fifteen. I been runnin' this kitchen before you got to this here plantation, and I was runnin' this kitchen before you was born. I eat when I please. You hear me?"

"Yes, ma'am."

Bertha could sense the rage underneath the forced calmness in Mattie's voice as she spoke through a tight jaw and a mouth full of chewed chicken, so she wisely decided to back down.

"That's what I thought," Mattie said. She then

turned around and stormed out of the kitchen, letting the door slam behind her.

"Fat hog," Bertha mumbled softly when she was sure that Mattie was through the door. She started laughing quietly as she grabbed a small piece of cornbread and chucked it into her mouth in defiance of Mattie's rule.

Sue was beaming with sunshine that day, and she entered the kitchen with a bounce in her walk. She tossed a bag that she was carrying on the counter.

"Hey, how you doin' today, Bertha?" Sue asked.

"I'm always fine," Bertha answered. "I can't help it; just look at me."

"Girl, you mighty high of yo'self, ain't you? Now be quiet and peel those potatoes like I know Mattie told you to do. We know that you can't do nothin' else."

"I wouldn't be so quick to talk, Sue, because you always take forever fryin' that chicken. If that was me, I'd do it way faster."

"Yeah, you might do it faster, but that bird would be burnt up just like when Myrtle tried to cook for the first time. Bertha, Masta don't need to be wastin' on burnt up food."

"Pshh," Bertha hissed at her.

Sue and Bertha worked silently for a moment, and then Bertha turned to Sue, still upset about not being able to cook.

"I don't know why Mattie won't let me do none of the fryin', Sue." Bertha placed a knife up to the potato in her hand, applied an excess of pressure, and scraped off the skin, fumbling it because of the distraction of her anger.

"Well, you know that only women get to do the fryin' in this kitchen, and you ain't a woman yet. You's still a li'l girl Bertha." Sue laughed, walked over to Bertha, and softly patted her on the head. Bertha stood there with her jaw dropped. Then she quickly fired back. "Little girl? I'm a full-grown woman. And if I gotta be a old, wrinkled-up woman like you to cook, then I don't wanna cook at all."

"Old woman? Bertha, I'm barely six years older than you."

"Well, I am a woman, Sue. Can't you tell?"

Bertha accentuated her hips and other parts of her figure, imitating a seductive woman. They both laughed loudly at the ridiculous body movements that she had demonstrated. Sue went back to her station and started to prepare the frying pan and other cooking materials for her portion of the day's dinner. As Sue was setting up her area, Bertha quickly popped another piece of cornbread into her mouth. This time, the piece was too large to be easily hidden. Bertha began to chew as quickly and as quietly as possible without being noticed.

Sue was still busy getting to her assigned kitchen duty. As she looked over all of the cooking utensils that she had just laid out on the big wooden cutting board near the firewood stove, she realized that she was missing the large black cast-iron frying pan that she needed. Sue looked around the kitchen and spotted it right next to Bertha, who was still busy peeling potatoes with her back to her.

"Bertha, can you hand me that fryin' pan hangin' up there right next to ya?"

Bertha was trying to finish the cornbread that she was still chewing and pretended not to hear Sue.

"Bertha, hand me that pan over there."

At that moment, and in the most suspicious way possible, Bertha reached up for the frying pan without responding to Sue. Holding her head down, she blindly felt around for the handle of the pan that she knew was hanging on the wall right above her.

"Bertha, what in the world is you doin' over there?" Sue questioned.

"Nothing."

Bertha's muffled response was barely audible as crumbs fell from her mouth and hit the floor.

"Are you over there eating?"

Sue had become frantically suspicious because of Bertha's behavior.

"No," Bertha replied quickly as more crumbs fell from her mouth.

"Bertha, stop yo' lyin'. Are you outta yo' wits? Do you wanna get us in trouble with Masta, and that's only if Mattie don't come in here and beat us dead first! You know that if one of us gets in trouble while another is in here, then we all gets in trouble. I'm not gettin' a lash on account of you!"

"Mattie ain't aimin' to do nothin', Susan. She just likes to scare us into following her rules."

"Child, you hardheaded! That's why don't nobody like you in the first place. And don't call me no Susan. Everybody know I don't like that name. My last masta wife was Susan, and I ain't nothin' like her."

"Well, I'm done now." Bertha finished up the cornbread that she had swiped. She swallowed it and opened her mouth to show Sue that there was nothing inside.

"You better be done."

In the middle of their spat, Mattie walked back through the kitchen door and startled the two of them. "Nobody likes who?" she asked with a tone of curiosity, suspecting that the girls were in the middle of a fight.

The two girls turned to Mattie and automatically straightened up their postures as if Mattie was their drill sergeant. Bertha quickly wiped the crumbs from her face as Sue stood next to her.

"Oh, nothing. Me and Bertha just havin' a li'l girl talk," Sue answered. "You know how we young'ns do."

"Oh, all right." Mattie suspiciously eyed the both of them from head to toe, but she couldn't figure out what was going on.

"Well, why ain't nothin' cookin' in here? We don't have much mo' time. Y'all know that. Bertha, is you done with them potatoes yet?"

"No, ma'am, not yet." Bertha clinched her mouth and bit her tongue to keep from back talking.

"Well I'm gon' need you to hurry up. We ain't got all day."

"Mattie, it's too hot in this kitchen," Bertha said.

Bertha never missed an opportunity to whine and complain. Mattie stared at her in a moment of contempt for her complaining. She was already fed up with Bertha for the day. She put one finger to her head and stood there, silently thinking of a solution that would shut Bertha up.

"You know what, Bertha, why don't you go outside to the garden and pick some tomatoes for tomorrow's dinner?"

"But Lucille was supposed to do that yesterday," Bertha protested.

"Well, it was too hot out yesterday."

"But, Mattie, it's hotter today than it was yesterday!"

"Just go. Right now! And don't forget this." Mattie walked over to the large hand basket, which was always kept on the kitchen counter just for picking vegetables in the garden, and gave it to Bertha.

"How many do you need me to pick?" Bertha gave in without protesting.

"Oh, about twenty."

They really didn't need any tomatoes at all, but Mattie had found a magic number to pull out of thin air.

"Twenty? But this basket only holds about ten or twelve!"

"Well, make two trips, honey," Mattie suggested. She gave Bertha a sarcastic pat on her shoulders and shooed her out of the door. "Now getta goin', sweetie."

Bertha took the basket and stomped out of the back door of the kitchen leading out to the yard. The slam of the door echoed behind her. Mattie and Sue watched her exit with smirks on their faces. Bertha kept up her quick walking pace all the way to the garden while maintaining her anger the whole way there.

Master Jackson's garden was about eighty-eight yards west of the house in eyesight of the cotton fields, where the men and women were still working their daily picking duties. It took Bertha about ten minutes to reach the garden, which was about five minutes quicker than the time it took her to reach it on foot the last time that she was on garden duty.

The sun was still beaming down on the dirt fields even though it was almost six o'clock in the evening.

Bertha was extremely hot, and sweat was dripping from her forehead. She knew that she should probably take a second to grab a drink of water from the water well that was only a few feet from the garden, but she was hell-bent on completing her task so that she could get back to her duties in the kitchen.

When she reached the patch of tomatoes, she stooped down to a squatting position and began to pick them and place them into the basket. She managed to fill the basket with twelve tomatoes, but that was eight short of the twenty that Mattie had asked her to bring back. She stopped for a second to think of a way to bring the twenty tomatoes back in one trip.

She looked down at her sweaty shirt and thought that she could probably use it as a carrying tool. She didn't think that was all that good of an idea, so she tried to think of another option. Stumped, she decided to go forth with fitting the eight tomatoes into a fold in her shirt despite the sweat. She folded up the base of her shirt and created a little pouch. She managed to get five tomatoes inside it. She realized that she was still short three tomatoes and decided to place the remaining three tomatoes on the top of the basket that was already full to capacity.

As she bent down to pick up the three tomatoes, one of the tomatoes stuffed into her folded shirt fell to the ground. She ignored it for the moment. She concentrated heavily to balance the tomatoes that were stuffed into her shirt, while trying to intricately place three more tomatoes on top of the overflowing basket without knocking any of them out. As she was bent over with one hand trying to softly and strategically place the tomatoes in the basket while the other hand cradled the tomatoes in her shirt, another tomato fell from her shirt. This one landed right on the top of the basket, knocking four tomatoes to the ground. In a show of frustration, she kicked the basket over and cursed at it. All of the contents of it went spewing around the garden, near her feet.

Next to the garden was the tool shed that the men who worked the field used. The wooden shed was old and decrepit. The large doors on front of it always seemed to squeak of rusted metal door hinges, and this was usually very audible in the open air. However, in her frustration, Bertha did not notice the sound as the door slowly opened. Emerging through the doors from the inside of the shed was a tall figure who approached the area in the garden where she was. She felt a presence coming close to her and looked over her shoulder to see what it was. Her frustration was clearly visible through the tightness in her facial muscles. Her attitude was not the least bit welcoming, and her hair was blowing into her face because of a swooping gust of wind that further agitated her. As she looked up, her caramel-colored face had a glistening shine from her continued perspiration. When the approaching young man got close enough to her, she got a quick look at him and returned her focus to her task.

"What do you want?" she responded, still crouched down.

"What you doin'?" His voice was deep and pointed.

"I'm mindin' my own affairs." Bertha snapped back and continued her efforts to refill the basket. Her former master's wife, who taught her to read, would often respond to questions in that manner. "Well don't you need no help, li'l, missy?" He pretended as if she hadn't been rude to him. "My name ain't Missy; it's Bertha." He stood back and smiled as he folded his arms. He was amused by her feistiness. "Let me give you a hand." In his deep and distinctive voice, he insisted on helping. Bertha could nearly feel the bass of it rumble through her.

"Who are you?" she asked. Bertha decided to stand up and get a better look at the young man who was hovering over her asking questions and offering to help.

"My name's Bubba Spokane."

"Bubba? Dat yo' real name?" Bertha was as condescending as she could be.

"Well, yeah. I have another first name, but I don't care to use it, and I don't care to share it either. Now do ya need some help or what?"

She got a long look at the stranger who was standing in front of her. This was when she stopped focusing on her frustrations and realized how stunningly attractive he was. Bubba had broad, shirtless shoulders that protruded out from under the straps of his denim overalls. He was a hardworking young field man, and his overalls were all covered in dirt and oil. He stood about six feet, four inches tall and had large, well-defined muscles. His eyes were compassionate and brought out the beauty in his handsome face. His skin was nearly perfect, and he had an infectious smile that showed his straight white teeth. He had a handsome set of teeth for a field Negro.

"Well don't you have work of yo' own that you

should be doin', Bubba?" Bertha questioned. She was still intent on demeaning him.

"Well, missy, I got a early start today so I finished my pickin' a li'l early, and Masta Jackson had me put on tool duty for the rest of the day."

"Tool duty? What's that?" she asked.

"Cleanin' and oilin' the tools. Don't you know nothin' about workin' in the fields?" Bubba developed a condescending tone of his own.

"Well..." Bertha scrambled to think of a rebuttal, but she couldn't think of anything clever to say. "I don't work there very much these days. Listen, Bubba, I'm grateful for yo' offer, but all I'm doin' is tryin' to take twenty tomatoes back to the kitchen for Miss Mattie. I think that I can handle that on my own."

"Oh, Miss Mattie in the kitchen?" Bubba had met Mattie before.

"She somethin' else, ain't she?" Bertha noted.

Bubba smiled a great smile in remembrance of his last interaction with Mattie. "That's a good woman, though."

"Yeah, somethin' else ain't the only thang I would call her."

Bubba paused and took a look at the basket and then at the tomatoes that were spilled all around Bertha's feet. "They won't fit," he noted.

"Huh?"

"Twenty ain't gon' fit in that there basket. Let me help you."

He bent down and grabbed six tomatoes with his large hands. He easily placed three tomatoes in each hand and stood there waiting for Bertha to finish stuffing the other tomatoes into the basket.

She repacked the basket with twelve tomatoes and realized that with Bubba's help and her fitting the twelve into the basket, she only needed to carry two more tomatoes in her off hand. She realized that carrying the basket in one hand and only two tomatoes in her other hand was much easier than her original plan. Then she reluctantly showed her gratitude.

"Well, thank you for yo' help, Bubba."

"That's mighty fine of you to say." He shrugged and looked away in his confidence.

If Bubba wanted to or had to, barely breaking a sweat, he could have gathered the dozens of tomatoes in the garden that day and carried them all back to the big house before anybody from the field even noticed that he was gone.

"Well, lead the way, missy."

"Look, Bubba, if you call me Missy again, I'm gonna go across yo' face with this basket of tomatoes. You hear me?"

"Yes, ma'am." He replied quickly but with a slight smirk as they both headed in the direction of the big house with Bertha leading the way. It was almost seven in the evening, and the sun was finally starting to set. Bertha and Bubba were halfway back to the house when Bubba suddenly stopped them.

"Hold on for a second, Berda," he said with a high level of authority in his voice.

"Ber-tha," she corrected him, but without the venom in her tone that she'd had before.

"I'm sorry, Ber-tha. You look mighty worn out, and you ain't sweatin' right. I think you need some water. We gotta get some liquids in you."

He placed the tomatoes that he was carrying

on the dirt ground in order to free up his hands. Then he reached in one of the pockets of his large overalls and retrieved a small glass container filled with water.

"Here, have a drink." He twisted off the black bottle cap. Bertha's hands were full, and he held the bottle to her face until she accepted it.

"Oh, all right. My mouth sho' is dry."

With Bertha's hands still full, Bubba gently poured the water into her mouth, and she drank, slightly spilling a bit of water down the side of her mouth. Bubba took a handkerchief out of his pocket to wipe the water off of Bertha's chin and from the side of her mouth, but before he could reach her face with the handkerchief, she quickly turned her head away and stopped him.

"Whoa, whoa, don't come near me with that thang," she announced with a laugh.

The handkerchief was dirty and covered in filth. Bubba looked down at it in his hand. He had been using it for months and had not washed it. It was once white, but now it was gray and brown from filth.

"Yeah, you right. I probably should clean this thang soon."

"I'll let the wind dry my face."

They both started laughing.

"What a field Negro like you know about not sweatin' properly and whatnot?" Bertha questioned.

"The wife of my old masta always told me to drink plenty liquid whenever I was workin' outside in the fields in the heat. She said it was good for the body. Good for strength and energy. Well, I'm a pretty smart guy. And besides, I heard one of them otha white folks say it too."

He had another smirk on his face that showed a deep dimple on his cheek. They both laughed again. Then Bubba put away the bottle and the handkerchief. He bent down and picked up the tomatoes, three in each hand again, and they both resumed walking.

"So how old are you, Bubba?"

"I'm nineteen years old, but I'll be twenty soon. How about you?"

"You' ain't supposed to ask a lady her age."

"I know, but you just asked me first."

"Well, if you must know, I'm fifteen years old," Bertha finally answered.

"Only fifteen?"

He looked down at her while admiring her figure. This made Bertha blush, and she placed the basket of tomatoes in front of her body to block his view.

"Well, you look mighty fine for fifteen."

The compliment turned her caramel-colored cheeks a faint shade of pink.

"Yeah, well thank you again for helpin' me."

"No problem on my part."

They made it back to the house, and Bertha stopped Bubba before he could help her carry the tomatoes into the kitchen where Sue and Mattie were now busy serving dinner.

"Hey, Bubba, I'll have to stop you right here," Bertha said." Mattie don't allow no men folk in her kitchen. I wanna thank you for makin' this a bit easier for me."

"Well, I'm glad I could help you," he responded.

"Even though I woulda done just fine on my own, I'm thankful for yo' help."

"No you wouldn't have.'

"Huh?"

"You woulda had to make two trips." He winked his eye at her in his cockiness.

"Well I'll be doggone. Thank you anyway. You can take off now."

"Well, all right," Bubba agreed. "Bye now." He backpedaled away from her as quickly as he could to get back to his duties before turning around and jogging back to the fields. As he jogged, he yelled out to her. "I hope I see ya around again, missy!"

"My name is Bertha," she yelled back at him, furious at being called missy again.

"All right now, missy!" He yelled back with a few yards of distance between her and the basket of tomatoes that she had threatened him with. She scrambled around and quickly picked up the first pebble on the ground that she saw and threw it over a distance, aiming at his head. He was able to avoid the pebble that landed a couple feet behind him as he kept jogging away with a smile.

He hadn't stopped running when he yelled out without turning around to look back at Bertha. "You missed!"

She snatched the basket of tomatoes from the area on the porch where she had placed it and burst through the kitchen door, frustrated at Bubba. As she walked over to Mattie with the tomatoes, she had to stop herself from slamming the basket down on the counter. Mattie noticed a few less than twenty tomatoes in the basket.

"Where da rest of them at?" Mattie asked.

"They outside on the back porch," Bertha told her.
"How you manage to get them all with one trip?
"I had some help."
"Help? Who helped?"
"Yeah, this big, tall, stupid fella helped me, but he headed back to the field now."
"Tall fella?"
"He must be stupid to help you with that attitude," Sue chimed in.

Mattie looked out of the window in the kitchen to get a good look as Sue also ran over to the window and stood behind her to get a look herself. A distance away they saw a tall young man, who had stopped jogging and was now walking back toward the fields. Mattie strained her eyes to get a better look and recognized that the tall young man was the handsome young Bubba, whom she'd met in the fields a couple of weeks ago while doing a special duty for Master Jackson. Sometime during Mattie's interaction with Bubba, she told him jokingly that he was mighty tall and handsome, but he wasn't too old or too big for her to put him over her lap and give him a spanking if he got out of line.

"That's Bubba, ain't it?" Mattie questioned.
"Yeah, Mattie, he said that his name was Bubba."
"Oooh, look at them shoulders," Sue announced to the other two.
"Oh, that Bubba is a nice young man," Mattie told Bertha.
"How you manage to get him to help you with that attitude of yours?" Mattie asked as she looked at Bertha with a facetious grin. "I'm surprised you didn't scare the poor fella away, Bertha. Did you thank him?"

"Yes, ma'am, I did."

"Well good."

Mattie was pleased to hear of Bertha showing gratitude, but she was still focused on getting their work done and finishing up serving dinner.

"Now you all get back to work." Mattie directed. "Both of you get back to work."

Chapter 2

Bertha and Bubba

It had been two days since Bubba helped Bertha carry the tomatoes to the big house. She thought about him periodically throughout each of those days. She was upset that she did not have a strong enough arm to reach him when she had chucked the pebble at his head because he kept calling her missy just to annoy her. Every time he crossed her mind, she became upset, but her thoughts would always lead her to his chiseled cheekbones and infectious smile. His good looks always ended up giving her butterflies.

Sue was the oldest and most experienced young lady in the kitchen. She was the first to expect that there was love in the atmosphere with Bertha, because she sensed that Bertha was not her usual self. She was not popping food into her mouth in an act of defiance whenever any of the other girls or Mattie turned their backs. She was not as sassy with her back talk when she was asked to do something or even when the girls intentionally made wisecracks about her appearance just to get her going. They knew that if they got her going, she was a beacon of entertainment. In her unfocused mind, thinking about Bubba, she didn't pay the girls' insults much attention. Sue picked up on this and knew exactly what was going on. She recognized the behavior revealed by Bertha's constant daydreaming, but she tried to get Bertha to refocus anyway.

"Hey, you silly fool! Are you gonna finish choppin' them carrots anytime soon?" Sue asked. "Is you just gonna stand there all day lookin' out the window up in the clouds? You probably thinkin' about that Bubba boy. That sky ain't goin' nowhere, and none of them clouds gonna come down and help us finish up this meal. So move ya fanny!"

Bertha was standing there in a daze, still lost in her thoughts. She had forgotten to keep chopping the vegetables and didn't even recognize that Sue was talking to her.

"Bertha, Bertha!" Sue raised her voice in an effort to get Bertha's attention, and finally Bertha snapped out of it and turned around and looked at Sue.

"What? What you hollerin' at me for?" she asked with a displayed annoyance.

"Finish up with what ya doin' over there!"

"Oh. Oh, I'm sorry, Sue. I guess I'm not feelin' too good today. It's probably because of the weather."

"Oh my goodness! Bertha, I know that look anywhere. You thinkin' about that Bubba boy. Ain't ya?"

Bertha was completely caught off guard, because she thought she had been hiding it well. She almost could not get the first word out of her mouth to explain. "Pshhhh, huh? What? No I'm not!" Bertha uncomfortably raised both eyebrows as four wrinkles created by the expression stamped her forehead.

"Well you better get yo' head out of yo' tail, 'cause we gotta get this preppin' done."

"Sh-sho' thing, Sue!"

Bertha was annoyed that Sue had interrupted her train of thought within her daydreaming. However, she and Sue would finish up cooking duties that day. Mattie was sick and had been in bed the whole morning and part of the afternoon. Soon, dinner would be served to Master Jackson's and Sage's pleasure. As Master Jackson's daughter and around the same age as Bertha, Sage was not hard to please with the cooking. She hardly ever complained.

As the sun began to lower in the southern sky, it was time for Bertha and Sue to clean up the kitchen with the help of the other girls. At dinner's end, Bertha was happy that the meal had turned out good. She was proud that she even got to help stir the gumbo, which was a big deal for her.

The kitchen was nearly spotless except for a few pots that were soaking in soapy water, and Bertha volunteered to finish cleaning those. The girls were standing around in the kitchen lollygagging because their day of work was almost complete. As soon as Bertha finished cleaning the cookware, they could all be released from their duties for the day. Just as Bertha headed over to wash the pots, Sue gazed out of the window while the other girls heckled Bertha in the background.

"Hurry up with them pots so we can be done for the day. You over there movin' slow as molasses," Myrtle yelled out to Bertha.

"She just tryin' to hold the moment, because she happy that she got to stir the pot. Girl, you ain't did nothin' worth much. You still can't get the stove lit, and ya been workin' here for eight months already. You's a sad, black monkey." Beatrice harassed Bertha as Lucille stood off to the side in her own world.

Lucille was a couple feet away from the girls, picking cotton balls off of her shirt, scratching her head, and picking her nose occasionally. Lucille was always discrete with her weird antics, and most of the time Bertha was the only one observant enough to pick up on them. Sometimes Bertha would even catch Lucille tugging at her undergarments when she thought that no one was watching. They never seemed to fit her quite right.

Bertha looked at Lucille long enough to make eye contact, and Lucille looked back. That's when Bertha reached down and discretely tugged at her undergarments quickly to imitate Lucille, who smirked. Lucile turned away and tried to hold back laughter. None of the other girls had seen Bertha's silliness, because they were all focused on what they were doing. Lucille looked over at Bertha and stuck her tongue out before any of the other girls could see. She knew that Bertha was mocking her, and they both proceeded to hold in their giggles.

"Who is that out there by that tree?" Sue blurted out, gaining everybody's attention. She had glanced out of the window while Bertha made her way over to wash the dishes and saw something that caught her eye. "Is that Bubba?" She was surprised to see Bubba so soon because he was a field guy and they rarely saw field guys on their side of the plantation. He had been the topic of conversation earlier, and she did not expect to see him that day. Neither did Bertha.

He was outside sitting under a tree many feet away from the kitchen window that Sue was looking out of. Bertha walked over to the window to get a look for herself.

"Yeah, that look like him for sure," Bertha mumbled, trying to be nonchalant about the sighting.

"I can tell that's him by those overalls he wearin'. He had on the same ones the other day, all ragged and torn," Bertha told the girls.

"And dirty," Sue added as all the girls laughed and scurried over to look out of the window. When Lucille got a look, she was surprised at how handsome Bubba appeared even from the distance. "I don't care how dirty he looks. He sure is handsome." Lucille just had to say what she was thinking. All the girls turned and gave her an intimidating stare like they would always do Isabelle. Isabelle was the most timid girl who worked in the house and the other girls would often push her around.

"What in the world ya lookin' at me for? You can't shoo me away like you do Isabelle."

Lucile was not going to take any of the girls' flack. She stood up for herself and put her own sassiness and toughness on display as her blue eyes became filled with rancor. The girls all took heed and turned back around.

Outside, Bubba sat in peaceful solitary, seemingly unaware of his surroundings. The warm summer air breezed, and the leaves on the trees dangled inside of the breeze, creating a very relaxing ambiance of nature. He sat on the ground with his back against the tree trunk and his knees propped up as his arms rested on them. He quietly peeled the skin off of an apple with what looked to be a small knife. Suddenly, he glanced up and saw all of the girls crowded tightly around the large kitchen window. They were all staring out at him. He had extraordinary eyesight and could clearly see the faces of each of the girls. Flattered that they were staring at him, he chuckled and gave a slight smile without bearing his pretty white teeth. He waved to them amused, but he was used to getting extra attention from women. The girls in the window were all giddy and overtaken by his attention, and all of them, except for Bertha, giggled and waved back to him, mesmerized. Bertha stared back, not impressed. That's when he found her face in the crowd, and their eyes connected from afar. Nobody noticed this interaction between the two of them except for Sue. After calming down from being overtaken by Bubba's good looks, all of the girls scampered away from the window, dispersing like cockroaches in light. Bertha stood there awhile longer than the other girls and then slowly walked over to the dishes, finally breaking eye contact.

Sue stood back and glanced back and forth. First she looked at Bubba through the window, then at Bertha who was over at the scrub bowl washing pots and pretending that she was indifferent about seeing Bubba. Sue got a bright idea and decided to give Bertha a pass on doing the dishes for the day.

"Bertha, it look like that rain storm will be settin' in soon," Sue announced. "Go on and take off a bit early today. I know it takes ya a good walk to get back. You might as well get goin' now. I'll finish up those last two pots."

Bertha was confused by her early dismissal. It was highly unusual, but it was music to her ears. She dried her hands, grabbed her bag from the closet, and then took off for the door. That's when she remembered that she would have to pass Bubba as she headed home. He was still sitting under the tree. That's also when she realized what Sue was up to by letting her go early. She thought that Sue must have wanted to see her and Bubba trade greetings and pleasantries from the window so that she and all of the other girls could tease her about it the next day when she came back to work in the big house. She was sure that they would all label the two of them as lovebirds or some other ridiculous phrase, so she headed out the door and tried awkwardly to pass Bubba without greeting him or making eye contact. She was not successful at doing this, because as her immediate path home led her closer to where he sat, he jumped to his feet and ran over to her.

"How you doin', Bertha?" he asked as he started walking alongside her. "Did I get it right this time?"

"Yes." Bertha let out a blatant sigh of disappointment.

"This weather got you down?" Bubba had picked up on Bertha's demeanor. "Did Mattie work you hard today?" He was trying his best to spark up a conversation.

"No, today went good, Bubba. Look, I thanked you for helpin' me out the other day. I don't believe I owe you much else. I'm just tryin' to get back home to rest my feet."

"Bertha, you work inside the house, but you live near the field folk. Why is that?"

"I don't know. Bein' the first dark girl workin' inside the house is already a big change around here to most folk. I guess Masta didn't want to cause too much more of a stir around this town. Plus, I got family on this land. Most them girls was bought without kinfolk. That's how masta likes it. That way he can be they masta and they momma and daddy. I'm not sayin' I agree with it, but that's how it is.

Now, you gon' bother me the whole way home? I normally like to walk in peace."

"Oh, oh, oh. Well I am mighty sorry to go out of my way to interrupt you and ya peace, Miss Bertha." Bubba let out a confident laugh. Bertha's resistance did not break his persistence in trying to get her to engage in a conversation with him. "Now I ain't seen ya in two days, and I didn't think I'd ever cross paths with you out in the field. Since work been slow these last couple of days, I thought my chances to see you would be better if I came on this side of the land. You know I could get in trouble if they catch me over here? I ain't worried about it, though."

Bubba was still carrying his apple and knife in his hand. She looked down at the apple that was halfway eaten and starting to turn brown from missing its protective skin. Then she turned away and looked straight ahead.

"Is this how you treat the kind of fella who put that much thought into seein' you?"

Bertha continued to stare straight ahead and did not reply. Inside she was charmed, but she did not want to give it away. She was fighting it the best way she could. She never felt so flattered, and she was quite uncomfortable with the feeling.

Bubba took a glance at Bertha and could sense that somewhere inside of her she was enjoying his company, so he proceeded to walk alongside of her in silence a short while. That's when the dark clouds gave way to the weight of the water that they had been holding, and a bolt of lightning crossed the sky. Thick and heavy raindrops fell and landed on top of the two of them, drenching them in seconds.

They both quickened the pace of their walk in order to take refuge from the rain.

"How far you want me to go with ya?" Bubba asked. He desperately wanted to get out of the rain as he closed in tightly with Bertha on their now hurried walk. They each used the other for makeshift shelter by huddling up and putting their arms over their heads to protect themselves from the rain.

"I thought that bein' a man in a time like this meant you suppose to offer me yo' shirt or somethin' like that to keep me from the elements. I know a big, strong, tough guy like yaself ain't afraid of no rain, is you?"

"No I'm not, and besides, I think that you look better with a little rain in yo' face."   He   strongly objected to being afraid and understood clearly that she was mocking him. Right then, as they were continuing on their path to Bertha's cabin home, he gave her that smile of his that was sweeter than honey. Then he looked directly into her eyes with those soft eyes of his that were the color of roasted pecans, and Bertha had to look away. She was stubborn and still not ready to give in to his allure.

"Matter of fact, will you hold on for a second?" Bubba asked. He abruptly stopped Bertha, and she looked at him as she stopped walking, assuming that something was wrong.

Before Bertha could figure out what he was up to, he placed his knife on the ground and put his apple into his pocket. Then he started to unbuckle the straps of his overalls and pulled off his shirt, bearing his toned upper body that he had developed and modified from lifting machinery and other unwieldy loads doing hard labor in the field. Just as soon as he got his dingy white shirt off, the rain came down harder, and Bertha stood there looking at him through squinted eyes that she could not keep open because the rain was blowing into her face with such force. With the shirt in his hand, he rang it out to rid it of some of the water that had soaked it. Then he came closer to her, who was standing a couple of feet away. He raised his arms up and stretched the shirt out over both of their heads to block the falling rain. They were huddled close together, and she could easily smell the scent of his body. To her surprise, it wasn't a foul scent, and it wasn't a strong scent either. It was a neutral scent, the scent of Bubba, and she became immediately comfortable with it. They continued on their path down the narrow dirt road that led to Bertha's house. Bertha, in her appreciation of what Bubba had done, decided to soften up her attitude toward him.

"Thank you for lending yo' shirt on this walk," She told him with a slight smile.

"I figured that that was the best I could do." He had to talk over loud raindrops, but he smiled, never turning off his charm.

"I certainly appreciate it, Bubba."

There was silence for a few moments. Bubba pulled the brown apple from his pocket and took a bite as he stayed huddled up with Bertha. Then, he tossed the partially eaten apple on the ground.

"Why'd you peel that apple? You know the skin of apples is good to eat?"

"It's a thang I do." He suddenly and genteelly pulled her to the side and under a tree that was immediately off of the dirt path.

"Uh-uh. What you doin'?" Bertha was suddenly frightened. She immediately thought that Bubba was up to no good. That's when she looked up and saw the huge carriage headed their way on a collision course with where the two of them had previously been walking. They were now safe under the tree, and the tree leaves and branches provided a break from the constant rhythm of raindrops pounding their faces. They stood under the branches until the carriage had passed. The intoxicated driver of the carriage saw the two of them scramble to get out of the way. As he speeded past, he cheered them on for their swift efforts to retreat.

"I never seen niggers move so fast without a whip behind 'em!" The driver shouted back at them as he pumped his fist with a big smile.

Bubba snickered a bit, while Bertha was still in shock from almost getting pounded by the carriage.

"So you help me to do my duties, you save me from the rain, and you keep me from getting smashed to death by a drunk cowboy driving a carriage. What I owe you?"

Bubba knew that he was in control at that moment, and his persistence would shortly pay off. "Well you don't owe me nothin' except to let me to see you to ya door just in case another carriage come speedin' by. But if it fancies you, you could meet me by the pond this time tomorrow and say we even."

"Will do." She displayed that shy smile of hers and obviously had given in to his persistence. "Now can we get to goin'? My feet tired."

"Allow me to lead the way," he demanded with smooth, Southern confidence.

"How you gonna lead the way? You don't even

know, quite frankly, what shack you headed to." Bertha giggled at his overconfidence.

There were dozens of scantily built cabin-like homes in the field slave living quarters. There were nearly one hundred of them that all housed three to five family members.

"I know the area we headed," he said, confident that he would lead them home. "You just point out the place."

Chapter 3

Romance at the Pond

The next evening when Bertha finished her house duties, she took off for home. She had been teased and verbally battered by the girls all day about her and Bubba walking home together. She could still hear them in her head as she walked home with every intention to skip the meeting at the pond with him. She was a bit embarrassed by what had been said about the two of them.

"Oooh ohh, you and yo' love have a good walk home?"

She replayed Sue's teasing in her head. Then she could hear Agnes: "That good lookin' man don't want you. He wants me. I may be ugly, but I don't sweat and stank like you."

She could hear Beatrice pile it on: "Yeah, just as soon as he get a whiff of that stank, he gon' wish he wasn't born yet."

Then Bertha could hear the girls all burst out in laughter. She had laughed with them, and she laughed on the way home as well. She was not too affected by their teasing because she had a high self-esteem. Besides, she knew that her issues paled in comparison to the issues they all had. She would usually find the girls' ridicule entertaining, even when she was the target of all of their gibes.

When she thought about not showing up to meet Bubba, she began to remember his smile and how attractive he was. She knew that she would feel really guilty if she left him there alone. When she arrived to the point in the road where she had to make her decision, she decided to make the left turn toward the pond instead of taking the right turn to head home, where she knew that Aunt Lola and Cousin Zeke would not be waiting for her. She told them before she'd left that morning that she would be working late. She knew she wouldn't be working late, but she did not want her aunt and Zeke to worry about her meeting up with a young man they hadn't been introduced to yet.

That evening's walk was much more kind to her than the previous day's. Had it not been for a slightly damp ground that had been drying all day from the heat of the bright sun, it would have been impossible to tell that it had rained so heavily. The day was near perfection, besides the nag of a few mosquitoes, but even that was more tolerable than yesterday's rain.

She made her way over to the pond and saw no one there. There were a few birds hanging around the water looking for food, but that was it. She spotted the brown rope tied to the tree that she and Sage would swing from when they were younger, right before they would let go of it and dive into the pond. The pond was now used by the slaves for many purposes. However, Sage never saw a reason to separate herself from the Negro slaves, and she was comfortable being there even when there were other Negro slaves there besides Bertha. Sage enjoyed their company and watched with great curiosity as the water rolled off of their hair. As a young girl, Sage never understood the wonder of Negro hair.

As Bertha reminisced for a split second, she could

not figure out where the heck Bubba was. She was known for being a tad impatient and was ready to turn around and head home. Before she could take a step away from the pond, she heard a big splash and turned to see Bubba bopping out of the water in the middle of the pond. She could not help but smile when she saw this, even though she tried hard not to. She watched as he swam to the edge of the water and got out wearing shorts that were soaked and soggy, outlining every nook and cranny of his lower body. Bertha made an effort not to look down at his swim trunks, and once again, she smiled.

She stood there speechless. As he walked toward her, he flashed a smile himself. It was unlike his normal smile that he always so effortlessly flaunted. It was a smile that Bertha had never seen before in her life. It was a picturesque representation of human joy. It was the quintessential embodiment of happiness, and it overtook her. Somewhere inside of her she felt her knees on the verge of buckling, so she stood up straight and poked her chest out in a very masculine way that felt very unnatural to her. Bubba was unaware of how Bertha was feeling as he stopped right in front of her.

"I just wanted to see how long I could stay under there. I'm up to about six and a half minutes."

Bubba wasted no time starting up a conversation with her so naturally. Bertha did not hesitate to respond either.

"That's pretty good."

"Yeah, I been increasin' my time ever since I was a young boy. Never know when I might need a skill like that in life—you know, if I ever have to take off from this place and duck them dogs in the water."

Bertha's demeanor quickly changed. She was vexed. "Don't tell me you one of those make-it-to-the-North kind of folks. Is you one of those niggas who think that they gon' be the lucky one to get away? If you is, then I'm wastin' my time here with you. Even if you do get away, runnin' away ain't never solved the problem for us folk. Only time will save us—time and prayer. These folks will come around one day and realize what they doin' to us ain't right. I just hope it's one day soon, so I can see it in my life with my own eyes."

"Ain't sayin' that I am one of those niggas. I'm just sayin' that I might be. My daddy was a slave, his daddy was a slave, his daddy was a slave, and his daddy was a slave. Maybe some of us don't got that much mo' time to wait."

Bubba looked Bertha right in the eyes, displaying his passion about the issue and for the first time showing Bertha the defiant and serious side of himself. This strayed a bit away from his usual unruffled side, but Bertha did not feel threatened. She quickly changed the subject.

"So I'm here to pay my due now," she said.

"Thank you for comin'. You look mighty fine as always."

"What would you had done if I didn't show up today? I had a good mind not to come."

"Well then, miss lady, I guess I woulda been waitin' for you when you got done in the kitchen tomorrow... to get a sorry and a reason why you didn't show up. But I knew that a good one like you was gon' keep her word. Plus, yo' word is all we niggas got. What do you have without it? Now come over here and let's sit down and watch these birds.

I find it quite settlin'. I have some sweet drink over there in the bushes for us. I brought two canisters so we don't even have to share the same one. Made it myself from lemons and melons. It's a little somethin' that I learned to make at the last place." Bubba was excited to spend time with Bertha.

"That's mighty thoughtful of you, Bubba."

Bertha was now starting to calm down and relax so that she could make the most of this time with Bubba. He ran over to get the two drinks that he had stashed off in the bushes. Then he ran back over to sit next to her. She had made herself comfortable on the ground. He had pep in his step and could not control his energy. Through this, Bertha saw the little boy in him, and her heart fluttered.

He returned with the drinks and sat down and looked at her. He had eyes full of adoration. He was proud that she was spending time there with him.

"It's a mighty fine day, Bertha."

"Yes it is." She calmly stared out at the surroundings, focusing mainly on the water. Bertha found it impossible to hide the smile that was beginning to appear no matter how hard she tried.

"You seem very happy to be here right now, Bubba." Bertha looked at him from head to toe.

"That's because I am. I feel like I'm here with somebody important. You's the talk of the town and around this plantation. People think you Jacko's pretty li'l pet. Shoot, bein' the only brown-skin Negro in the town to be allowed to work inside, you should know that the word would get around. Some people think that you and Jacko got somethin' goin' on."

"That's just fool's talk. I been here since I was a

girl. And since then, I've never heard anybody call him Jacko befo'."

"Yeah, that's 'cause they don't say it around you. They know you his li'l pet. We field niggas don't call no white man masta when he ain't around. Me, I don't care what I say around nobody. You can go back and tell him if you like."

"Look, I work inside the house, but I ain't no tattler," Bertha said. "I can't believe that folks around here care so much about me workin' in the house. It just really ain't that big of a thing for me. Besides, I don't sleep there like them yellow girls. I'm still one of y'all whether ya like it or not."

"Yeah, you one of us, and you the prettiest thang I've seen since I been here and you work in the house," Bubba replied. "Being a handsome fella like myself, I gotta have the best. Maybe that's why I like ya so much."

"So that's why you like me so much? Because I work inside the house? What, you must wanna taste a fresh piece of bread every now and then? Will I have to sneak into Jacko's candy jar and bring some back for you?" Bertha quickly became defensive at the thought of being used. This side of her came out when she was worried, as a shield to protect her. It would usually scare off most guys or simply rub them the wrong way, but not Bubba. He just rolled with it.

"Naw that ain't it, Bertha. I'm more concerned about tastin' those lips than I am of any bread or candy."

The butterflies soon returned in the pit of her stomach. Bubba always had a retort no matter what she said to him, and this intrigued her because no one else she had ever met could hold their own in a war of words with her. She had finally met her match and found herself speechless as she got caught once again in the web of his gaze. She could not break away. Bubba turned away from her and looked straight ahead for a long while as his arms rested on his knees, which were propped up. They sat there in silence and watched the water. Then he broke the silence.

"You know, when I was a boy around four or five years old, I had real bad teeth. It would hurt every time I would chew on somethin' hard. So no matter what I ate, my mom would cut it up for me so I could eat it. If it needed to be chopped, she would chop it. If it needed to be sliced, she would slice it. If it needed to be peeled, she would peel it. She did that for all of my food."

Bubba gazed straight ahead as Bertha sat next to him and listened intently. After a short pause, he continued. "She did all of that for me. She even peeled the skin off of my apples. I don't know where she is now. One day she went out to work in the field at the old place and never came back. She just disappeared. I was only around ten at the time."

Bertha sat there, and her eyes began to water, not only for Bubba and his pain but because she could relate. She missed her mother greatly too. She barely even got to know her. She was so young when she was taken away, and as each day went on, her mom became more of a figment of her imagination than a mother. She found herself speechless again until she reached over and placed her arm around Bubba. That's when his walls broke down, and for a moment, his strength faded away and he was overcome by his sorrow and started to cry. At that moment, he was no longer a young man filled with anger and rebellion. He broke down and sobbed like a broken warrior with the weight of the world crushing him. Bertha was there next to him to witness it all. She hugged and squeezed him tight as his muffled sobs became louder. She held on until the sobs came to a halt, and when he stopped crying, he looked up at her and saw tears flowing from her eyes.

He was embarrassed that he had broken down in front of her, but he regained his composure and was soon wiping the tears away from her eyes as she silently cried without any sobs. His hands touched her face and could not be controlled. The moment was thick with emotion. The pain and sorrow soon turned into affection. With each of his large hands on her cheeks, he slowly pulled her face closer to his, and they shared a kiss. They shared a kiss that seemed to last a lifetime but ended all too soon. They shared a kiss that solidified their unity in time for forever. It was their first kiss. It was the kiss to end their day at the pond.

Soon thereafter, Bertha was working out in the field as much as she could to be near him. She would ask Mattie if she could help out in the field, and Mattie had no problem letting her go because she thought that's where she should be working in the first place. Master Jackson seemed to have no problem with it, and if he did, he kept it to himself.

The Negros out in the field were the most oppressed people on the land, but they always found a reason to laugh. They were always joking around and singing and talking loudly all day as they worked. Bertha took a lot of flak from them initially, and it annoyed her. But after a while, it was all in fun, and she dished it as well as she took it.

There was Francis who was the oldest woman in the field. She knew about everything that went on around the whole plantation. She was always so nice to Bertha.

"Hey, Bertha, you comin' out to work with the folk who keep this plantation goin', or is you gonna stay cooped up in that house all day with them other folk?" she'd ask.

"Naw, Ms. Francis, I'm comin' out here to work with you darkies," Bertha would joke back. "Now where is that hooligan Bubba? I came to work aside him today. Nothin' much to do in that house. I need to get some fresh air anyway."

"He over 'round there foolin''round with them otha young boys. You betta get 'round there and see about him befo' one of them field girls get a hol' of him."

"Sho' thang, Ms. Francis."

There was Tiny-Toe Tim. He was born with an irregularity that caused some of his toes to be abnormally small. Even so, he was one of the best workers in the field.

"Oh look, Bubba, here come yo' woman. You better straighten up before she go back to her real man Jacko and have you shipped outta here." Tiny would always tease Bubba when Bertha was around.

"Oh, you hush before I have Masta to ship you outta here." Bertha would always defend Bubba.

That's when they would all laugh out loud. They were always laughing. In the field, the rule was you had to laugh. They all laughed and laughed at whatever they could laugh at. Their motto was you must laugh to keep from crying, because times were tough.

There was Peter who played the banjo in the evening or at night when work was slow. They would make a bonfire and sit around it, telling stories and drinking moonshine while Peter played. Peter would sing songs that he had made up. He'd sing in his husky tenor voice to a slow rhythmic beat:

When ol' man river come washin' ashore,
I'mma be waitin' in my boots, ready for
    more.
I'mmal be sittin' in the sun, waitin' on
    the Lord,
Prayin' that the Lord don't leave me no
    more.

Everyone would sing along with him once they caught on to the impromptu lyrics. The girls in the field began to open up to Bertha even though they wouldn't talk to her much. They would all watch her and imitate her when she wasn't around. Sometimes this was done mockingly, and sometimes they imitated her because they admired her. She was funny and pretty, and Bubba adored her. They were proud to see her with Bubba, who was one of them. After all, they used to think that she thought she was too good to associate with them.

Betsy Lawrence was around Bertha's age, and one night when Bubba was off wrestling with some of the guys, Bertha was sitting alone by the bonfire and Betsy got a chance to talk to her. Even though Betsy was around Bertha's age, she was already married. She had two young children and was seven months pregnant. She sat down next to Bertha, and her pregnant belly poked out beyond what Bertha thought was possible.

"Bertha, how you doin' this evenin'? You know, awhile ago I didn't think you would ever hang around with the likes of us folks. I sho' didn't think I'd ever see you around here with no field nigga either." Betsy dove right into a conversation with Bertha.

"I neva thought that I was better than any of you," Bertha responded. "That is what was said about me. You can't believe everythang you hear."

"Yeah, what about that time you told Vander that he was so ugly that he wasn't good enough to sniff the cushion you sat on?"

"He said that my chest was flat as a board. I ignored him, but he kept at me."

"How about when you cussed poor ol' Tom out when he tried to walk you home?"

"I was havin' a bad day. Besides, that was the old me."

Bertha looked at Betsy, and they both laughed.

"You know what, Bertha? You got a lot of spunk. Most times I don't blame you. I can only dream about how you got treated by them girls in the house when you first got there. We thought for sure that you'd be back workin' in the fields in no time when you first went in. I know we used to think that you were the enemy, but Lord knows them yellow house girls are the enemy!"

Bertha laughed. "Well, I guess you get used to them crazy folk after a while. They just like y'all."

"Like us?" Betsy shouted back and reached up to feel Bertha's forehead with her chubby fingers.

"What you doin', Betsy?"

"I'm checkin' to see if you feel warm 'cause you must be ill if you think that them girls in that house anything like us out here."

Betsy was joking, but she was slightly appalled. In her coolness, Bertha shrugged her shoulders with a smirk on her face but did not respond. Betsy felt the conversation was hitting a dead end, so she decided to talk about something else.

"That Bubba sho' is somethin' to look at," Betsy said. "I guess it make sense that he would be the one to get to ya. Bubba enjoys workin' out here in the thick of it. He a special kinda man. If I wasn't with nobody, I'd be breakin' my neck to be with him just like all these other girls around here. I guess you can consider yo'self lucky, Bertha, 'cause you the only one he wanna look at."

"I'm lucky? No, he the lucky one." Bertha corrected Betsy, trying to hold in her laughter.

"That's what I mean about you, Bertha. You got some nerves." Betsy smiled as she looked at Bertha.

Soon, Bubba came back with a few of the guys, and their girl talk was over for the night.

Bertha knew that she was lucky to have Bubba, and she had to be near him all the time. On the days she wasn't allowed to work out in the field with him, he would meet her by the house at the end of her day and walk her home. They found happiness through their circumstance in life, and this provided hope and got them through many trying days.

Bubba and Bertha became closer over the next four months, and during this time, Master Jackson's drinking became more frequent. He would hardly leave the house, and sometimes he wouldn't leave his office. He would request that Bertha personally bring all of his meals up to him every day. He said that it was to give the other girls a break and that it was Bertha's price to pay for being the darkest Negro in the house. He was soon finding more and more work for her to do around the house, which limited her time working out in the field. Bertha did not understand what she had done wrong and why she was being burdened with extra work, and neither did the other girls. However, as he ordered her to do certain tasks around the house, Mattie enforced his orders to Bertha's displeasure.

Most of the time when Bertha would bring Master Jackson his meals, he would be working on something, and she would leave swiftly. Other times, however, he would pull her into a conversation and make her laugh. He was a very charming guy. He could always make Bertha laugh if he tried, and most of the time, he was surprised at how often she would make him laugh.

"Come right in, Bertha." Master Jackson was behind his desk reading a book. Bertha was standing at his office door with the day's lunch made for him on a tray.

"Place the food over there," he directed. "I'm not quite hungry yet, but I will be very shortly."

"Yes, sir."

Bertha was in a good mood because Bubba had placed a bundle of daisies on the back door steps for her that day, and the other girls were teasing her about it. She didn't care about the teasing, because she was flattered at his effort and thoughtfulness. Master Jackson felt her lighthearted vibe, and he did not want that out of his presence too soon.

"Why don't you have a seat, honey? I know that I've been working you a lot lately. I just want people to know that I'm not easy on you, and I expect just as much, if not more work, from you as anybody else."

"I understand." She reassured him that she was fine. She had previously let go of any animosity that she had about doing all the extra work. With her busy all the time, the girls began to feel sorry for her and didn't bother her as much, and she was happy not to be bothered. Because of the sincerity in her voice that day, it put Master Jackson at ease. The truth was that he hated to work Bertha so hard, but he felt that it was necessary for a multitude of reasons.

"Good," he acknowledged.

"Yeah. First I was wonderin' why you's workin' me so hard, but then I knew that with me stayin' busy, I don't have to put up with the sisters of Satan and old, ugly Agnes. The longest I can stay away from them, the happier I'll be," Bertha noted.

Master Jackson laughed a bit. "The girls giving you a hard time?" he asked as if he could remedy any problem that she had been having.

"They always give me a hard time, but I can handle myself."

"I know you can, honey."

Master Jackson looked up at Bertha and gave her his complete attention. He had a smile on his face and stared at Bertha for a few seconds as if she were the most beautiful thing he had seen in his life. Bertha was standing a foot or so in front of his desk the whole time, and he asked her to have a seat again so that they could talk for a while. Bertha sat down on the small sofa located near his desk.

"Now, Bertha, you know everybody isn't as pretty as you are. Some people might give you a hard time just because of that."

"I know, sir. I'm used to it."

"Now I want you to hang in there, because I know you're doing a really good job down there in the kitchen and around the house. I'm very proud of you," he said.

"Thank you, sir. I try my best every single day."

"I know you do. Now there is something else that I want to talk to you about. Bertha, I see that you are growing into a very lovely young lady, and I know that you're getting to the age where you're having certain feelings. I just want you to know that I think that you should wait a while before you get involved with any boys around here. It's just not a good time. You're not ready for all of that. And the country is changing, and there are things that are going on. I don't want to have to ... I mean, you don't wanna worry about having kids right now, sweetie."

"Kids?" she questioned. "I haven't even thought about that. There's a boy I like, but I wouldn't dare think about kids or nothin' like that, sir. Not yet."

"That's good to hear. I just think that you should give it a rest with this boy. He will be there when the time is right."

"What do you mean, sir?" Bertha became slightly upset. She could not fathom the thought of not seeing Bubba. "I enjoy bein' around him, that's all. We real good friends."

"I hope that's all it is, honey. Besides, none of these niggers around here are good enough for you,

Bertha. You're beautiful, and you're a very smart girl."

"Awww, thank you, Masta Jackson."

"Well, I think you better get going before Mattie come looking for you and give you more work than I could ever think of."

"You know what, sir? That's about the truest thing I heard all week."

They both laughed again as Bertha exited his office. When she was gone, he sat there with a feeling that he hadn't felt in years. He hid it while Bertha was there, but he hated the fact that she was now in love with Bubba. He knew that it was Bubba she had fallen for because of rumors around the plantation.

Master Jackson remembered that when she was a girl, she hated to talk to or be around any boys, but now he had witnessed her defend the time she spent with one. He had known that the day would come when Bertha would fall in love, and it had finally arrived. It felt like his prized possession was being taken away from him right under his nose, and he didn't like it.

Master Jackson was married, but Bertha was attractive to him. In an odd way, he wanted to keep her to himself. It was a feeling that he had been in denial about, and now he had to face it. He knew that she was young and in love, but when he thought about it, a feeling of rage crept up in the pit of his stomach. He was so helpless at the sight of Bertha's almond-shaped eyes and beautiful smile and knew that he would never be able to stand up to her and tell her that she couldn't see Bubba. He had to think of something else to do that would stop this romance. As he thought of a plan, he put away the paperwork he had been working on and pulled out a bottle of whisky. He wallowed in his sorrows until he passed out on his desk.

The next day Bertha was swamped with work. Master Jackson requested that she clean out all of the storage areas in the house. When she finished, she found herself leaving the big house for home much later than usual. To her surprise, when she got outside, Bubba was there waiting.

"I thought you woulda left by now and headed home. I even worked later than I normally work when I work late."

"I been waitin' out here the whole time," Bubba said.

"That's mighty grand of you. I'm glad you did, because I really missed you today." She smiled, grabbed him, and gave him a tight hug from behind.

She was really excited to see him. Every time she let down her walls and showed him affection in public, it made his day. He just loved her touch. However, on this day, he didn't seem to be moved by it. Bertha didn't understand or put that much thought into his demeanor until he continued to be eerily silent during their walk home. Finally, she realized that it was something bothering him.

"Bubba, what's wrong?" she asked. "You don't seem like yo'self."

"I don't know," he said. "It's just a lot on my mind."

"Oh all right, how was it out there today? I miss the likes of you folks. I wanted to come out there, but Masta had me dustin' out all of the storage spaces and shelves in the house. I was lucky Miss

May helped me, because if she didn't, I might still be in there now."

"My day wasn't too good, but I don't wanna talk about it." His tone was somber, and it juxtaposed Bertha's excitement to be with him.

"Uh-oh," Bertha interjected. "Usually when folks say that they don't wanna talk about it that means it's a whole lotta stuff that needs to be talked about. Let's go to the pond and sit and talk for a while."

She grabbed his hand and dragged him in that direction. When they got to the pond, the sun had almost completely set and the moon was shining in the dusk.

"I figure we got just about a hour of light left, so let's talk about it." She tried to soothe him.

Bertha reached up to caress his head while they sat on the ground by the pond. Bubba hesitated to talk, because he was so infuriated by what he had seen that day. However, he knew that if it were anybody he could open up to about it, it was Bertha. He was deeply in love with her, and he knew that she loved him too.

He had been planning a secret escape to the North. Not even Bertha knew about it. The plan involved him and three other young men from the plantation, but when he met Bertha, not even freedom could keep him away from her, so he put the plan on hold. She made him hopeful that one day soon things would be better for all Negro slaves. He didn't want to believe it, but to justify him staying, he did. Bertha had been really convincing while telling him about people called abolitionists. She told him that they were good white folks, some of them rich, who believed in God and believed that slavery was wrong and a crime against Christ and God. He couldn't imagine it, but looking into her eyes, he would believe anything that came out of her mouth. Bertha had been taught those things early in her life by her former master's wife who was a schoolteacher and who also taught her to read children's books and write when she was a child.

When Bertha and Bubba found themselves back at the pond alone, he began to open up. "Now, Bertha, I love you, and you knows I do. I try to tell ya that every day, but I don't know how much more of this I can take."

"What you mean, Bubba?"

"Today we was lined up workin' down deep in the fields. We was in that thick stuff where if the sun don't get ya, them scrapes and pains will. Old Man Aims couldn't keep up with the rest of us. You know he sixty-five with a bad back? He walks with a stick."

Bubba became demonstrative and emphatic. The rage boiled up in his eyes, but he kept on with telling Bertha what had happened.

"We all asked for him to be released from the line, us young boys did, but Bob Jenkins was over the work today, and he wouldn't let him go. Bob kept gettin' in the old man's face, and he slapped him a few times for movin' too slow. Bob told old Aims that if he couldn't keep up, he would get three lashes."

Bubba stopped talking for a while as he was so overcome with anger that he had to pause so he could get his words to come out of his mouth. Bubba was a fighter and a protector. He believed that you should fight for those who can't fight for or protect themselves. However, that day he could not protect the old man, and Bertha knew that he wanted to.

"The old man tried and tried, but he couldn't keep up, so he just gave up and stepped out of line to get his lashes. That bastard Jenkins was more than happy to do it too. I wanted to smash his head in, but I couldn't, Bertha. I couldn't. Bertha, I love you, but I don't know if I can stay here."

"What do you mean?" Bertha asked. "I love you too, Bubba, and I know that it's tough out there, but you gotta hold on. Listen, just sleep on it and see if you don't feel better in the mornin'."

Hearing her words reassured him, and eventually, he was able to calm down. Just when Bertha saw that he was beginning to calm, she got up and did a little shuffle in front of him to temp him into a game of chase. This was a game that they always played. She would take off running, and he would eventually come after her. If she was lucky, he would give her just enough of a head start that she could find a place to hide before he would come search for her. He would always find her quickly, and when he did, he would grab her entire body and squeeze her so tight that she would claw at him. They would then fall on the ground and laugh. They would laugh and wrestle. That is exactly how their game played out that evening right before the sun was completely set. Visibility was slim with only the moon lighting their walk home from the pond.

Chapter 4

Bubba's Rude Awakening

Bubba was sleeping alone in his cabin like he normally did because he had no biological relatives living with him on Master Jackson's land. The other workers in the field had become his family. They watched out for him like he was one of their sons, and Bubba was such a likeable young man that people around the field adored and respected him. During the day, he was never lonely because of all of the love he received, but at night, Bubba slept alone. He had been sleeping in the cabin for about a year. As soon as more workers were assigned to the plantation, he would have to share the space with them, but until then, he stayed there alone many nights.

That night, after he walked Bertha home and made sure that she was safe, he went to his cabin and was soon off to sleep. He had been in a deep sleep for hours when all of a sudden he was viciously awakened by a punch to the gut. The blow immediately knocked the wind out of him so violently that all he could do was gasp for air without making much of a sound. Naturally, his body jerked up, and his hands grabbed at his stomach. Just as soon as he could get a second wind, someone quickly shoved a gag into his mouth to keep him as quiet as possible. His eyes bulged from their sockets out of terror and pain, and he grabbed at the gag and struggled with his assaulter.

Because of his youth and his extraordinary strength, he was almost able to overcome the person who was attacking him from behind until a second person punched him in the side, cracking one of his ribs on his shirtless upper body. He howled and doubled over in pain. At the age of twenty, he had never broken a bone, and the pain of having a rib broken shot through his body like a burning flame. One of the assailants shoved a brown potato sack over his head to blind him, and Bubba then felt a head blow from a blunt object. It hit him with such force that his consciousness faded away.

When he regained consciousness, Bubba found himself still in his undergarments and hanging from the rafters of a barn by his wrists, which were tied to a rope. He hang there as his body dangled beneath his arms. The potato sack had been removed from his head, and he was in a lot of pain. He had a broken rib. There was also a three-inch gash on the top of his head caused by the final blow that had knocked him out. Blood that had leaked from the gash had now dried on the side of his face. He woke up in that predicament with a violent cough and gasping for air. His vision was blurry, and one of his eyes was nearly swollen shut. There was almost complete darkness inside the barn except for a lantern that was lit in the back.

"Help! Where am I?!" Bubba cried desperately.

That's when two men stepped forward and came closer, close enough so he could see their faces through his obstructed vision. He looked down at them, and that's when he saw who they were and soon realized what this was all about. It was Master Jackson and Bob Jenkins, and Master Jackson was holding the paper that Bubba had used to draw out the rough copy of his escape route. There were no words; only shapes, lines, arrows, and symbols drawn by an illiterate field hand. However, it seemed to be well thought-out and intricate. Bubba had known previously that if it got into the wrong hands, there would be a lot of trouble to follow. He knew then that one of his counterparts in the plan must have sold him out. He had no idea who it was, but at that point, it didn't matter.

At that moment, he knew that his punishment would be severe. There had been threats that the next person who was caught in an attempt to escape to the free states would be legally punishable by death. This was a recent order that was temporarily put into place because of the volatile political times and a large increase in slaves who were successful at escaping to the North. Escaped slaves at that time posed a major economic problem for states in the slaveholding South, and government officials wanted to eradicate the problem. They thought that the penalty of death was a consequence that would greatly deter anyone from trying to escape. Bubba hung there all bloodied and in a great deal of pain with blurry vision and a swollen face.

Again, Master Jackson stepped forward. "Boy, I think you know what this is all about."

Bubba did not reply, and Bob Jenkins stepped from the depths of the dark barn and into the light. Both Master Jackson and Bob Jenkins were dressed in all black, like trained assassins stalking their prey. Bob was holding a rawhide whip. After continued silence from Bubba as he hung there in agony, Bob took the whip and cracked it across

Bubba's bare chest. He howled out in pain with the grunt of a stubborn mule. The blow left a diagonal cut across his chest, and blood soon began to flow from it. He still did not speak a word. Master Jackson pleaded with him.

"Bubba, tell me what this is all about." Master Jackson's eyes were burning red with fury as he looked at the helpless Bubba, who looked back at him with equal furry but stayed silent.

"I don't think the nigger is gonna talk to us, boss," Bob interjected.

Bob was waiting and all too happy at the chance to have another crack at Bubba with the whip. When Bubba still did not talk, Master Jackson gave Bob a quick nod. Just that fast, Bob cracked the whip against Bubba's chest again, creating a deeper cut parallel to the one created by the first blow. Bubba howled again and gasped for air, as the pain was so severe that he could barely breathe.

The two men let Bubba dangle there from the rafters awhile longer as he continued to bleed. He grunted and grimaced, and some tears got loose. A few of them fell down his face and became a victim of gravity, but he did not speak. Bob Jenkins pulled back the whip again to have yet another crack at Bubba, but Master Jackson stopped him.

"Cut him down," he said. "I want to reason with him a bit."

Master Jackson gave his orders to Bob, and Bob grabbed a wooden ladder, climbed to the top of it, and with a sharp knife that he pulled from his leather cowboy boots, he cut at the rope that kept Bubba suspended in the air until it severed. Bubba fell to the hard barn floor with a thump and another howl from the excruciating pain of his broken body landing with no cushion.

Master Jackson walked over to Bubba while he was curled up in the fetal position on the barn floor. He stood over him and turned him onto his back. Then he grabbed Bubba by the neck and yelled at him, waving the paper in his bloodied face. Bubba's ears rang because of the blow to his head. Although he could not hear or see Master Jackson clearly, he knew exactly what he was demanding. Bubba did not speak, so Master Jackson forcefully threw the map on the ground beside him, nearly hitting him with it. Then he quickly took a few frustrated steps away from. Master Jackson returned to Bob to talk things over with him. Bob was a few feet away waiting for orders.

"What are we gon' do wit' him, boss?"

Master Jackson ran his fingers through his hair and sighed out of the frustration of one of his slaves trying to escape. He took this personally, because he'd never had a slave escape from him before. He felt that he was good to his workers, and because of this, they should never double-cross him by running away. For most slave owners who had a slave run away, it was a business loss, but Master Jackson took that sort of thing as a stab in the back. He felt that he treated his workers better than any other slave owner in the area.

He was frustrated with Bubba for trying to escape, and even more so, he was frustrated with Bubba because Bertha loved him. The thought of Bertha and Bubba together kept running through Master Jackson's mind, and the rage that he had felt once before returned to the point that he had to get hold of himself. If he didn't, he would have tortured Bubba way more than he deserved or let an eager Bob Jenkins have his way with him. Master Jackson knew that this would not solve any of the problems at hand, so he paced back and forth in front of Bob until he got an idea.

He walked back over to Bubba who was slipping back into unconsciousness. He stepped over Bubba's battered body and slapped him across the face. "Wake up, boy."

Bubba grunted quietly in delirium.

"Get up onto your feet, boy!"

Bubba tried his best to stand up but soon fell back down onto his knees because the head wound had thrown off his equilibrium. Master Jackson kneeled down to get eye-level with Bubba.

"Look here, boy. I could kill you for this sort of thing. Now you about as stubborn as a mule, and they warned me about that when I got ya. I haven't had no trouble outta you since you been here, so I'll give you a break if you bargain with me."

Bob Jenkins stepped in and got into Master Jackson's face, interrupting him. "What ya mean you gonna bargain with this no-good nigger? He should be dead by now!"

Master Jackson became infuriated at Bob for his insubordination and had to address him. They stepped away from Bubba. Master Jackson grabbed Bob by his collar.

"Don't you ever question my decisions." He spoke through tightly clinched teeth. "I have some personal business to take care of with the boy, and if you ever challenge me like that again, I'll have you layin' over there in a worse predicament than he's in."

"Yes, sir!" Bob reluctantly answered, but he quickly got the message.

Master Jackson walked back over to Bubba and kneeled down again so that he could look at him face-to-face.

"Listen here, boy. I could easily have Bob over there kill you right now in the blink of an eye. I'm gonna give you an opportunity to get out of this li'l mess you got yourself into since you ain't been givin' me no trouble and I'm a just man. You been running around here getting friendly with Bertha. Everybody knows that she is very dear to me, boy, and I don't want to see her hurt. Since you are unlucky enough to find yourself in this situation, I'm going to give you an out. You leave her alone, and I'll spare your life. When everyone else sees the whipping we put on you, that will be enough to stop them from running. We don't even have to let the law know about our little situation here."

Master Jackson bargained with Bubba as he remained on his knees with his hands still tied together in front of him with a piece of the rope that he'd previously hung from. Bubba, in his weakened state, heard every word that Master Jackson said. When he heard Bertha's name and the request that Master Jackson made, he took a labored gulp of his own saliva and could taste blood in his mouth. He scowled back at Master Jackson, wanting with every ounce of his own broken body to get up and choke him until his eyes popped out of their sockets. Bubba's passion for Bertha was visible in his eyes, and it shot out like a laser burning a hole through Master Jackson's face. Then he spoke in his deep voice as the thought of Bertha gave him enough strength to talk.

"I love her."

He was defiant, and he did not add the title of master behind the statement like he had every time before when addressing Master Jackson, as a way to show respect and let him know that he accepted his subservient position in life. This time there was no salutation, and Master Jackson picked up on this subtle disrespect and became angrier.

"Are you crazy, boy?" Master Jackson yelled as he grabbed hold of Bubba and punched him in the face as hard as he could, nearly knocking him off of his knees and back onto the ground. He had not gotten the answer he wanted.

Bubba regained his balance somehow and again stared straight back into Master Jackson's face. At that moment, Bubba turned into the man he'd always wanted to be. He had drawn the line. He had nothing. He had been taken away from his family, his mother had gone missing when he was a young child, and he had no control over anything, not even his freedom. He was born an alpha male who was a natural leader and protector; however, his pride as a man was constantly being trampled on throughout his existence as a slave, and he had to put up with it day in and day out. Now he'd had enough and would never bow down again. He drew the line at the only woman he'd ever been in love with. He wouldn't negotiate with loving Bertha, and nothing could change that, not even the circumstance that he found himself in.

Master Jackson punched him, knocking him over again, and Bubba quickly got back to his knees, blood dripping from his mouth. On his knees, he stayed upright. His hands were still tied defenselessly in front of him, but he was upright and ready to take whatever was thrown at him.

Master Jackson bent down again to give him one last opportunity to concede. "Stay away from her."

Master Jackson had drawn his line too. His plantation was his kingdom, and he was the ruler. He would not be defied. With his speech a bit slurred from anger and intoxication, he got nose-to-nose with Bubba, who could now smell the alcohol on his breath.

That's when Bubba said the last words that he would ever say in his young life, and he would say them defiantly, slow and steady. "I will not. I'm in love with her. I love her."

Then Bubba spit right into Master Jackson's face. Blood and saliva splattered across his forehead, landing partially in both of his eyes. This blinded Master Jackson for a while, and he jumped back out of shock, wiping his face. Bob Jenkins ran over ready to pounce on Bubba.

Master Jackson took one long, deep breath and slowly and deliberately told Bob to take over. "He's done."

That's when Master Jackson left the darkened barn, leaving Bubba alone with Bob as he slammed the door behind him. Bob dropped the whip and walked over to a darkened corner of the barn where he was not visible to Bubba anymore.

Bubba stayed there on his knees silently with his chin high in the air and anger and fear emanating from his eyes simultaneously. Bob emerged from the darkness with a shotgun loaded and ready. He walked over to the lighted area where Bubba waited like a brave prisoner of war. He got within two feet of Bubba and pointed the barrel of the gun right at him.

Meanwhile, Master Jackson slowly stumbled and hobbled his way through the darkened wooded area right outside the barn. Branches smacked his face as he sped up and walked faster, fleeing the scene. He was only a couple of yards away from the barn when he heard the loud blast of the shotgun. With that sound, he knew that Bubba was no more.

Chapter 5

Master Jackson

Master Jackson wasn't always a drunken mad man in the night willing to order the execution of a young man. He had been nearly driven out of his wits by years of extraordinary stress. He had been dealing with his wife's illness for a long stretch of time. He had mounting financial issues and dwindling inheritance funds from his deceased parents, and he refused to swallow his pride and ask his brother for help. Although he was a bit arrogant, Master Jackson had been a good man relative to the time that he lived in. He treated his slaves better than most slave masters. He did not put pressure on them to keep up a high quota of work. He was very reasonable with his workers, and they found that bit of freedom refreshing and tended to work as hard for him as anybody else. Most of them respected him, and none ever tried to escape. Master Jackson had been bold enough to let young, dark-skin Bertha work in the house when she could not find a fit working out in the fields. This action became the talk of the town and around the plantation.

It was a hot summer day, nearly eight months ago, when Master Jackson sent Bob Jenkins to inform Bertha that she would be working inside of the house from then on. It had been an eventful week in the field. All month long Bertha and her complaining slowed down the work of the other slaves in the section of the field where she was working. Bertha had reached her limit of carrying large pails of water in the beaming sun in a relay-style manner, handing them to the next in line for the watering of the fields.

Every day around noon she would collapse and fall down in exhaustion while kicking and screaming like a child in the middle of a tantrum and refuse to go on doing the task that she was assigned. Bertha's limited stamina working in the fields was partially due to an injury she had suffered as a child when she fell off of a wagon, which collapsed one of her lungs. She had not been able to breathe the same since the accident and labored dearly when working under the shine of the sun. The other field women had had enough of her, and many of them complained to Master Jackson's field overseers to get her whipped. This had been the fifth task that Master Jackson had assigned to her, and he did not know what else he could do with her or where else to put her. Many other slave girls who acted the way Bertha did had their backs lashed four times or more with a whip.

Bertha was almost fifteen years old at the time she began working in the big house. Master Jackson had purchased her, her cousin Zeke, and her aunt Lola years earlier when Bertha was around the age of five. He had paid a stiff price for the three of them, because the previous owner, Mr. Bates, did not want to part with Zeke because of his large stature. Zeke was a one-year-old at the time of the purchase, but he was the size of a two-year-old. Mr. Bates did not want to part with Bertha because she and Mrs. Bates, the school teacher, had developed a strong bond. However, in the middle of negotiations between

Mr. Bates and Master Jackson, they decided that in order for Mr. Bates to get the price that he wanted for Zeke, he had to include one female Negro from the same family in the deal, and this female Negro was Bertha. Mr. Bates did not want the grief-stricken Lola, who was beginning to become too depressed to function as a person let alone a working slave, so he convinced Master Jackson to take her too despite the fact that she was nearly worthless to him.

"A boy gotta have his momma," Mr. Bates told Master Jackson in order to get Lola off of his hands.

When Bertha turned thirteen, Master Jackson became very fond of her. He would take her and Zeke horseback riding, and Bertha learned to ride fairly quickly. Zeke, on the other hand, with his oversized body, did not learn as fast. Soon they began leaving him behind to go off riding, just the two of them. Thirteen-year-old Bertha loved to ride and developed a trust of Master Jackson because he was always so nice to her. Sometimes he would bring along iced treats for the both of them on the hot summer days, and Bertha loved that the most. He would tell young Bertha about his childhood and stories about things that she couldn't imagine, having never been outside of the State of Mississippi. He told her about sailing on the open sea and traveling to places such as Paris and other faraway lands he had visited before.

Master Jackson was nearly fifty years old and had become very wealthy upon receiving his portion of inheritance money when his parents died. He was tall and very handsome with blue eyes and a head of thick dark-brown hair. He had a trusting face and a smile that many women fell in love with. He was known to be a lady's man, despite the fact that he had been married to Mrs. Jackson since he was nineteen. He would reel the women in with his looks and incapacitate them with romance and a great sense of humor. He was a smooth talker and a very gentle man. He was a man who was used to getting whatever he wanted in life, from material things to women. If he couldn't have what he wanted, he did not know how to handle the disappointment. Many times, he did not have to deal with disappointment because he had enough financial resources to afford anything. Although he was married, women jumped in bed with him easily. Around the time that he assigned Bertha to house duties when she was almost fifteen years old, he was going through a midlife crisis and began to feel uninspired in life, as if he had done all that there was to do. He turned to liquor to ease his depression.

Before the liquor addiction, many times on his horseback riding trips with Bertha, when she was thirteen, he would bring Sage along. Sage was two years younger than Bertha. It would be the three of them riding along the countryside in the open air. Sage was a very clumsy and goofy child who acted much younger than her own age of eleven. She was five feet, five inches tall with long brown hair that looked so pretty when she brushed it. She had chubby jaws and beautiful blue eyes like her father. She admired Bertha, and Bertha would often encourage her and instill in her a lot more confidence than her less patient dad could. Sage was always falling off of her horse, and they would frequently have to stop riding and wait for her to climb back on the saddle to resume riding. This drove Master Jackson crazy.

He would always yell at Sage in his frustration. "C'mon, honey, can't you learn to stay on your horse?"

This would embarrass her, but that was usually when she would hear Bertha's voice. "Come on, Sage. Get back on. You can do it; just hang on a li'l tighter!"

Bertha was a natural motivator, and this encouragement always inspired Sage to get back on the horse with pride. Seeing Bertha encourage and inspire his daughter gave Master Jackson a warm feeling. This was one of the reasons he had grown very fond of her. He would often bring Bertha and her family food in the middle of the night, which made all of the other slaves in the field envious when they found out. Bertha did not care about how the other slaves felt. Going on riding trips with Master Jackson was fun and an escape from the everyday grind of working in the field.

What Bertha loved most about spending time with Master Jackson was the time by the pond that the three of them spent together. The pond was calm and serene, and Bertha loved the water. Soon, it would become a regular place for the field slaves to hang out, and Master Jackson allowed them to do this as a gift from him. The pond was usually good for fishing, and Bertha even caught a fish there once. It was a special place for the three of them, and soon Master Jackson began brining Bertha there alone to relax with him. Bertha would often ask about Sage's whereabouts when she didn't come along, but Master Jackson would always tell her that Sage was busy with schoolwork or that she had family or friends over visiting.

One day at the pond Bertha began to feel strange about spending time alone there with Master Jackson because he would look at her in a way that made her feel a little bit uncomfortable as a young lady. He would always tell Bertha how beautiful she was becoming as she got older. Soon those trips to the pond would not continue, as Master Jackson started to find more joy in consuming alcohol. Bertha would soon avoid him when he would try to get her to come along to the pond while he was intoxicated.

Chapter 6

The Girls

A couple years later, when Bertha began working in the big house, there were nine other girls residing there. Mattie was in charge of them all. Miss May was the second in charge of all of the girls. Miss May had been working in the big house longer than Mattie. She had grown old and fragile at the age of sixty-three and no longer had the energy to keep up with most of her work, let alone manage a house full of young women, so she let Mattie handle managing the bunch. She was the sweetest little lady with the most caring of hearts. She never had children of her own, so she saw the girls in the house as her grandchildren and Mattie was like a daughter to her. The young women in the house were Myrtle, Bernadette, Pearly-Maxille, Agnes, Isabelle, Beatrice, Bernice, Lucille, and Sue, who was the oldest.

Myrtle was fifteen. She usually stayed neutral whenever there was a disagreement between any of the girls. She desperately wanted to be a part of the group and found that neutrality was the best way to see to it that she did. She fit in by always keeping the group laughing, and this came in handy when things would get tense and uncomfortable inside the house because of an argument or a poorly handled situation. She liked Bertha, but because she had to go along with the group, she initially treated Bertha very badly. She had long black, shiny hair and high cheekbones.

Beatrice and Bernice were sisters, so they had a natural alliance. They were very tall for young women and overweight. They were the leaders of the gang at seventeen and eighteen. The other girls followed their commands almost more than they did Mattie's. Bertha thought that they were masterminds with a plan to further their own interests no matter what, which was why they were so fat. They would con and bully the girls into stealing food and other things from the kitchen while Mattie wasn't looking. They would secretly carry their food down to their bunks, and they could be heard giggling and chomping away at their stolen goods in the middle of the night like little mice. They bullied Isabelle mercilessly.

Bernadette was the most talkative of them all. She always had the latest gossip on everything that was going on around the plantation. Beatrice and Bernice never picked on her, because if they ever needed information on anything, they went to her first. She was seventeen.

Pearly-Maxille, most people called her Pearly, was shipped to Master Jackson's plantation when her parents were killed attempting to escape to the North. They left the children behind with other members of the family, but Pearly-Maxille was soon bought by Master Jackson who knew that she would have a better life working in the house on his plantation. Pearly was fourteen. She was adventurous and had a wild imagination. A g n e s was the troublemaker of the crew at seventeen years old. She had a unique look and this made her feel ashamed. The other girls would tease her when she wasn't around and sometimes to her face. They would call her Ug-ness because they said that she was ugly. She never let the teasing get to her, and if she did let it get to her, she never let it show.

Isabelle was fourteen and very timid. She was always pushed around by the girls, and before Bertha became a part of the big house crew, she was the one taking all of the flak from the other girls. She was so glad when she heard that a dark-skin girl named Bertha was coming to work inside the big house, because she knew Bertha would be the new target.

Lucille was sixteen, and she was tall and thin. She had blue eyes because she was half white. She was very smart and used her wits to keep herself out of any trouble that Beatrice and Bernice would try to pull her into. She would grow to love and admire Bertha because they had a lot in common. She and Bertha both had great physiques and nicely shaped arms and shared a similar sense of humor.

Sue, the oldest of all of the girls, was very pretty and never got wrapped up into any of Beatrice and Bernice's mess. Before Bertha got there, she was the only one in the house who wasn't afraid of the two sisters. Bertha noticed that Beatrice and Bernice seemed to respect Sue more than any of the other girls in the house. Although Bertha knew that the two sisters were not afraid of Sue, she observed how they took a different approach when communicating with her. Beatrice and Bernice approached all of the other girls as inferiors. This was not the case with Sue. Bertha could not understand why they respected Sue more but she figured that it was probably because Sue was the oldest at twenty-one.

When fifteen-year-old Bertha arrived to work in the house, she couldn't care less if she fit in with the girls because, unlike them, she had family living on the plantation, and she did not reside where they resided. She would finish her house duties and head back to the small cabin in the separate living quarters where the field workers lived. The other girls in the house were all bought from other slave masters without any family except for Beatrice and Bernice, who were bought together in a special deal. Master Jackson intentionally set up the dynamics of his in-house workers this way. With no outside influence from mothers or fathers and other family members, he would have complete reign over his house workers.

The girls who worked in the house were kept in better conditions than the other slaves. They slept in bunks in the cellar of the Victorian home that had a total of ten bedrooms. This cellar was specially built near the back of the house and had an indoor tub for bathing with water brought in from the nearest well. Although it was a far cry from the washing facilities located in the master's living space, it was warm and somewhat cozy even though it smelled of cement floors and wet clay and had little sunlight shining through the small windows.

Mattie had a separate room located in the same area, and Miss May had a room located right off of the kitchen, which Master Jackson had given to her for her long years of service. Miss May had been born on that plantation and worked under the previous owner, Master Jones, who died of whooping cough before Master Jackson purchased the plantation twenty years prior.

The in-house workers managed by Mattie and Miss May ate much better food than the field workers. They ate the leftovers of the day's meal as well as fresh bread and milk. The field workers were left to eat vegetables from their poorly maintained gardens or bowls of slop with mixtures of animal feed, oatmeal, cornmeal, and whatever else they could get their hands on. The pond on Master Jackson's land, if the field slaves were lucky, would provide them with fish, but it was small and catching a fish there became difficult because of the old and unreliable fishing lines that were available for them to use.

Bertha's first day working in the big house was like none other. She was hopeful even though she knew that being the girl with the darkest skin pigmentation working in the house would make it hard for her to fit in with the lighter girls. However, she was not worried and did not care. She knew that Master Jackson and his daughter, Sage, were very fond of her, and she would use that to her advantage if she ever got into a sticky situation.

Bertha was known for not taking any mess from anybody. This usually got her through controversial moments in her life, but inside the big house, she was outnumbered. She entered the house on her first day as if she were God's gift to house Negros. She had always been savvy at house duties even though she hated working in the garden, which was a part of house duties. She was really confident in her abilities. She was also excited to be removed from the fields, because now she could finally do work that she thought really mattered. She wore a large woven handbag that was given to her by Aunt Lola and had previously belonged to her mother who, as far as she knew, still worked on Master Bates's plantation. The bag was very dear to her, and she wore it everywhere she went.

In the kitchen on the day before Bertha arrived, most of the girls were lollygagging and joking around while they prepared food. Beatrice and Bernice, the two sisters and ringleaders of the bunch, were always the first to start insulting the other girls, and they were seldom met with insults in return, especially when they picked on Isabelle who was quiet and nearly afraid of her own shadow.

Chapter 7

The Girls (Part 2)

"**H**ey, Agnes, you gon' help clean these greens, or you just gonna stand there looking ugly, wit' yo ugly self," Beatrice yelled at Agnes.

Agnes was standing in the kitchen leaning up against a wall while the other girls worked. "I ain't ugly," she retorted. "I was born on a full moon, and that means that my face was kissed by God. That's why I look a little different."

Agnes had many superstitions that she had been taught as a child. The girls wondered where she got some of them from and who told her such ridiculous things. Some of the girls began to think that she made them up as she went along. They couldn't understand what being ugly had to do with a full moon, but they eventually stopped asking her about her way of thinking.

"You shouldn't be the one to comment on another's looks, you fat pig. And I don't know how you get so fat because you eat the same portions as we do," Agnes shouted at Beatrice.

"Well everybody knows that I got big bones, but I carry my weight good, Ug-nes. And what in the world do the moon got to do with yo' looks anyway? Don't blame that ugly on the moon or on God," Beatrice shot another quick-witted insult at Agnes.

"Shut up, fat pig!" Agnes yelled back because she couldn't think of anything else to say.

"Don't call my sister no pig, monkey face," Bernice chimed in, defending her sister.

"Well don't call Ug-nes monkey face, Bernice, because we all know you got dog breath." Pearly-Maxille inserted herself into the argument in defense of Agnes.

While the four of them argued, Isabelle stood quietly in the corner and listened to the insults while trying not to break out into hysterical laughter as not to offend any of the girls on either side of the argument. Isabelle was always secretly happy when the girls would go at each other, because this meant that the focus was off of her for once and the insults weren't coming her way. During all of the commotion, she stood there quietly and was thoroughly entertained as Bernadette and Myrtle laughed loudly, egging on the confrontation.

"Oh Lawd," Myrtle instigated. "She done called Ug-nes monkey face!"

"Yeah, and she said you was fat as a hog, Beatrice." Bernadette added her input as they both laughed at the insults that the girls spewed.

"You is kinda ugly," noted Bernadette, pointing at Agnes and busting a gut laughing while bent over holding her stomach.

"And you is fat as a filthy pig." Myrtle laughed the same way as Bernadette as tears began making her eyes misty.

In the middle of the hurrah, Mattie walked through the kitchen door, and the girls immediately became quiet. "What in the world is goin' on in this here kitchen?"

Mattie was very annoyed as she burst through the door. "It don't sound like nobody gettin' no work done. Now I'm gonna need y'all to shut up and listen here. I have somethin' to say."

The girls held their laughter in and quieted down. The ones involved in the argument tried to reel in their anger. Mattie did not allow any nonsense in her kitchen, and all of the girls feared and respected her so they never disobeyed. Mattie ruled her kitchen with an iron fist, and she never let the girls get out of control. As she started to make her announcement, they all listened.

"Tomorrow we gonna be addin' another girl to our kitchen, and she ain't the usual type of light-skin nigga that's allowed to work inside the house. Now she a bit on the dark side."

The girls all gasped. Confusion was rampant. They knew that this had not happened before where they lived. It was common practice at the time to only let Negroes with the lightest of skin work inside. Mattie sensed the confusion and outrage that the girls were feeling. They all looked around at each other and whispered quietly among themselves, so she reeled them back in and regained control of the room.

"Now hold on!" she announced. "I know, I know! This ain't normal, and I feel like it might cause mo' problems than it will help, but this is Massa's choice and he got the last say in the matter. If you got a problem with it, then you gonna have to speak it to Massa, and I know ain't none of y'all gonna to do that so you gonna have to live with it. Now she gonna be here tomorrow mornin' and ain't a thang anybody can do about it. That's all I wanna say. Now all y'all get back to work. Me and Miss May will finish up linens."

The girls always complained when Mattie said that she and Miss May were washing linens, because this usually meant that the laundry was already done and the two of them were going to sit out back and sip lemonade while they relaxed, waiting for the linens to dry on the clotheslines while all the girls sweated it out in the hot kitchen. However, on this occasion, they were so enveloped in the news that they forgot to complain. When Mattie left the kitchen, the girls spoke their minds.

"I don't know why we gotta let a darkie inside the house to work with us. What a field nigga know about doin' housework? I bet that she can't even get the fire on the stove started." Bernice talked in a low voice so Mattie wouldn't hear her complaining.

"Now I never thought I would agree with ya, but you is right," Agnes told Bernice.

"This ain't neva been done before. Why he doin' it now? This gonna mess up the flow of things around here. We already have a hard enough time gettin' along between us we already got in here and now you go and throw a dark-skin in here. It's gonna be nothin' but trouble I tell ya." Agnes folded her arms and pouted.

"I'm tellin' you, I don't know what she comin' in here for either. What, she couldn't make it out there in the fields? How she expect to make it in here around us folk?" Bernadette cried out in objection.

"Now listen to you fools," Myrtle told the group.

"You's ain't got the sense God gave a mule. We's all light-skin niggas and that's true, but we still all niggas. So what do it matter how dark she is? It shouldn't matter, because it don't matter to them white folk if yo' skin is light or dark when you's out there hangin' on that whipping post or when you's hangin' from a tree." Myrtle spoke passionately as her eyes scanned the room looking into each of the girls' faces.

"Yeah, you is right!" Isabelle nearly shouted.

She took a step forward and awkwardly broke her silence. The girls in the kitchen all stopped talking and turned and looked at her with annoyed glowers that sent the message for her to shut up because she wasn't allowed into the conversation. She quickly took heed and put her head down as she stepped back and continued her silence. Isabelle began to think about how having a dark-skin girl in the kitchen could benefit her. She realized that she might have a companion against the other girls' treachery, because they were sure to torture the dark-skin girl when she started working in the house. At the least, Isabelle thought that she wouldn't have to absorb all of their duplicity by herself every day. She continued her silence as the other girls debated and protested about Master's decision.

"Now this ... thing. This girl—I guess you would call her a girl—but she ain't one of us." Bernice was condescending. She had already decided that Bertha was less than a person and certainly less than those of them who worked in the house, and she had yet to meet Bertha.

"Who is she, what's her name, how old is she, what she look like, what she smell like?" Bernice rattled off.

"What in the world do you mean what she smell like?" Myrtle was bewildered by Bernice's line of questions about the new girl as the other girls burst out into laughter.

"I knew it was somethin' strange about you, and I'm not gonna get undressed around you no more." Myrtle continued.

Myrtle wore a disgusted expression as Sue walked through the door of the kitchen with a basket of laundry. As she entered, she heard the laughter and a bunch of commotion.

"What is goin' on in here?" Sue asked.

"Sue, you missed it. Where were you?" Beatrice was chomping at the bit to break the news to Sue.

"I was in the cellar scrubbin' the floor and helpin' Miss May put away linens. So, what's goin' on?"

"We havin' a dark-skin girl come work in the kitchen," Isabelle blurted.

Again, the girls looked at her in order to intimidate her and let her know that she still didn't have permission to talk.

"What?! You got to be pullin' my leg. Who said it?" Sue demanded.

"Mattie just came in here and told all of us. She startin' tomorrow," Bernadette informed Sue.

"Oh goodness, this should be somethin' to see," Sue sighed.

The girls quickly dropped the subject and got back to work.

The next day Bertha woke up at the crack of dawn, packed up her bag, and headed for the big house. She had her head held high and her chest poked out with pride. Aunt Lola and Zeke were already attending to their normal field duties by the time she headed out. She arrived at the house and entered through a back door that was slightly ajar. She slowly pushed it open and knocked.

"Hello! Where y'all at?" she called out.

Bertha walked through the dark hallway and could hear nothing. There was little natural light in the hall, but she could see some light in the kitchen, so she slowly made her way toward it.

Chapter 6

Bertha's First Day

Bertha had no idea what to expect working inside of the house, but she knew that it could not be any worse than working out in the field. When she found her way into the kitchen, she found the other girls all huddled up around Mattie, who was quietly giving them their daily assignments. When Bertha walked through the door, everyone stopped and looked back at her.

"Hello, everybody, I'm Bertha Oliver. I'm supposed to be startin' today in this here kitchen with Miss Mattie."

Mattie stopped talking and looked up at Bertha. She then waved her hand to signal for her to come over to the group. As Bertha nervously walked over, all of the girls standing around Mattie huddled tighter together to obstruct her path.

"All right, girls, let her through," Mattie directed. "Come on over here. And you can call me Mattie. Ain't no need to make me sound older than I am."

Bertha tried to make her way through the huddled up girls, but as she moved past them, she felt a slight elbow to her stomach. She turned around to confront the culprit, but all of the girls stood up straight and looked ahead. She could not figure out who had done it, so she continued walking toward Mattie. When she reached Mattie, she was given her assignment.

"You right on time. That's good. I was just givin'

the girls their duties for today. I think I'm gonna have you work with Isabelle. She will show you what to do, so don't worry about much."

"Oh, okay. Will I be cookin'?"

Bertha was excited about learning to cook, and she flashed a smile with a happy glimmer in her eye. Her eyes twinkled like a child who was expecting a day of fun. The girls all giggled quietly because they knew that she was already in over her head. They knew she didn't realize her subservient place in the house that her darker skin afforded her, and they also knew that cooking in Mattie's kitchen was a privilege that had to be earned. This was how Mattie kept the quality of the girls' work up. She made them feel important for being assigned certain duties, and this, in turn, influenced them all to take pride in their work, especially when it came to cooking.

Newcomers were always surprised when they were not allowed to cook until they had been working for Mattie for almost a year. They would start off cleaning, then they would have to work their way up to gardening, next they were allowed to prepare the vegetables for cooking, and if they succeeded in those tasks, they were allowed to cook. Bertha had no idea about any of this.

Soon the girls all dispersed with their daily assignments. Bertha and Isabelle spent the day dusting throughout the house and washing walls. Bertha found those tasks mundane and boring, and she complained nearly the whole day. Because of Bertha's complaining, Isabelle immediately thought that Bertha's stay in the house would be short-lived. Isabelle knew that all of the tasks that they were doing were easy first-day tasks. However, Bertha still found reasons to complain. She had many issues with the jobs they were assigned.

"Why do we have to do this all day? When do we get a chance to eat? Why don't we have two buckets? Why do I have to do it this way? I don't like this." Bertha's questions and complaints were a steady stream of whining throughout the day for Isabelle to soak up. The two of them were in the living room stooped down on their knees washing the wall behind the couch when Bertha's complaining took its toll on Isabelle.

"Do you know how lucky you is to be doin' this on ya first day? Do you know that I had to spend the whole day cleanin' up horse crap on my first day? If I hear one more complaint from you, I'm surely gonna scream."

Isabelle was frustrated with Bertha's antics, and her frustrations became plainly obvious to Bertha so she took heed of the warning and decided to shut up.

"Look, Bertha, you have a lot to learn about workin' inside of this house, and the first thing I think you should learn is how to shut yo' mouth. Now I gets picked on a lot around here, and I suggest that you prepare yo'self for what you gon' have to face workin' inside this house, especially with that dark skin of yours."

Isabelle looked around to make sure that they were still the only two in the room and then began to quietly give Bertha a quick rundown about life in the house.

"Now, Bertha, most of the girls in the house don't like the fact that you's workin' in here with us lighter skin folk," Isabelle began. "We ain't got much to be proud about as Negroes workin' on a plantation. Workin' inside is the only thing some of them girls have to make them feel important. Now me, I really don't care about how dark you is, because all of us was in the same boat no matter how dark or light our skin was. But the other girls see you as somebody who takin' away the one thing they have to be proud of."

"Workin' in the house is that important to them?"

Bertha's eyes went side to side in confusion, and her forehead wrinkled, creating frown lines across the bridge of her nose. She could not understand how a slave could feel privileged no matter what area of the plantation they worked in. Even with the very small amount of perks that the house slaves had, they were still slaves. Even though she didn't understand, she knew that Isabelle was speaking the truth and telling her what turned out to be useful information to Bertha's survival in the house around the other girls who hated her. She knew it made sense because of the looks on the girls' faces when she walked through the door and the blow to the stomach she'd received when she tried to walk through the crowd of girls earlier. That's when it dawned on Bertha that working in the house would not be what she expected, but somewhere deep inside, she knew that she belonged there and that anything would fit her better than working out in the field for the rest of her life.

"Yes, Bertha! Workin' in the house is somethin' that makes them feel special, and it's the only thing that they have."

"Why they pick on you so much?"

"I don't know," Isabelle admitted. "I guess it's

because I don't think like they do, and I don't acts like them either. Some of them act like a bunch of vicious animals scratchin' and clawin' at one another just to get ahead or a bit of notice from Mattie when none of us really gettin' ahead, not even Mattie. We's stuck in the same spot year after year. Not even Masta Jackson is doin' all that good nowadays. What's the sense in bein' at each other's throat every day?"

"Isabelle, you seem like a good girl, and you shouldn't let them treat you bad. You shouldn't take that. If you can stand up to me and my whining, you can stand up to them. You have to defend yo'self. And what do you mean Masta ain't doin' well? He own this plantation, don't he?"

"Yeah, he's not poor by no means, but he runnin' through the money his folks left him when they died and he ain't been too keen on his finances like he should be. He been drinkin' more, and pretty soon, Sage will be old enough to go off to school and that's gonna cost a lot more of his money. Ever since Margaret been ill, he been slowly fallin' apart. Hopefully, he will remarry a good woman who will get him back on track if she passes away. If he don't, this place could wind up bein' sold, and we all could be sold with it. Who knows what the next masta would be like."

"How you know all this?" Bertha asked. "I know how white folk be hushed when it come to they money."

"Bertha, you could learn many things if you just paid attention."

Chapter 9

The Torture Begins

"Now, Bertha we almost done here," Isabelle noted. "It's almost time for us to eat." She got up from her crouched position behind the couch.

"Where we supposed to eat at?"

"We eat every day at eleven o'clock. This give us time to fill our gut right before we serve Masta at twelve o'clock on the days when he here. Today he off into town, so we don't have to worry about that, but when he ain't here, that means we have to do a few extra chores around the house to fill the time."

"We eats out back every day on the tables in the yard. When the weather don't agree with that, we eats by our cots. You know Masta good about feedin' us. He said the better we eats, the better his eatin' will be."

Bertha's focus was locked in on Isabelle. She listened to every word. Then she stood up and brushed herself off. "I'm glad it's around that time, because I sho' is ready to eat. That's music to my ears, Isabelle."

"Good. Now, Bertha, I'm gonna try to help you as much as I can. You seem like the type that needs a little help every now and then, but don't get me wrong; this is my life, and I have to be here each and every day with these girls. It's best that I keep quiet and stay out of trouble. So if anything ever goes downhill, I will not be ashamed to throw you to the wolves. Don't ya understand that, Bertha?"

"Yes, I think I do. Nobody's ever done nothin' for me, and I wouldn't expect anything more."

Bertha's sly smile appeared as she stood up straight. Right as the two of them were packing up their cleaning supplies and getting ready for lunch, Beatrice and Bernice scudded around the corner with intent to destroy in their eyes. Mattie and Miss May were out back hanging laundry, and the two sisters found an opportune time to strike. Bernice carried a bucket of dirty, soapy water, and Beatrice had a bottle of mustard in her hands.

"Hey, you li'l dark monkey!" Beatrice yelled as she and her sister quickly approached Isabelle and Bertha. "You think you can work in the house with us like you good as us or better than us? You ain't no better than any of them other crispy coons workin' out there in that field."

Just then, Isabelle knew that things were not looking good, and she moved as far away from Bertha as the limited space in the room would allow and cowered in a far corner. Bertha just stood there stunned but ready to physically defend herself.

"What you say to me, you fool?" Bertha asked. As she spoke, she stepped toward Bernice, ready to strike her.

With that provocation, Beatrice took a few quick steps toward Bertha and pushed her to the floor. As Bertha quickly tried to get up to strike back, Bernice dumped the soapy water on her head, and Beatrice grabbed a handful of yellow mustard and slung it across the wall that Isabelle and Bertha had just cleaned. Then the two sisters tried to run away from the ruckus they had just caused.

Bertha sprang to her feet as fast as she could and sprinted toward the two girls before they were out of sight. Before they could get away, Bertha reached out and grabbed the youngest sister, Beatrice, by the back of her collar and threw her to the floor. Before they knew it, the two girls were wrestling wildly on the floor. The oldest sister stood and watched in shock, because she wasn't expecting Bertha to take the altercation that far. When she saw that her sister was being physically overpowered by Bertha, she jumped on the top of the two of them as they rolled around on the floor. Isabelle was watching the whole thing from her safe spot in the corner until she looked up, and her eyes widened.

Miss May was making her way to the fighting girls as fast as she could, wearing the most displeased look that Isabelle had ever seen her wear. Even though the old woman moved as fast as she could, it was still relatively slow compared to how quickly Bertha had just sprang from the floor and grabbed Beatrice around the collar. This is what crossed Isabelle's mind at that moment as she continued to watch in horror. Isabelle knew that some sort of punishment loomed afterward.

Before the girls involved in the fight knew that they had been caught, Bernice was pulled from the top of the pile and shoved away by Miss May. Quickly, Miss May had Bertha and Beatrice by the collars as she pulled them from the floor and separated them with each of her hands. The old woman had incredible strength in her old age, and

Isabelle watched the swift way that she broke up the fight in amazement.

"What in the world is goin' on in here? And what in the world is this empty bottle of mustard doin' on the floor?"

Miss May still held each of the girls' collars tight and was looking them each in the face as they scowled at each other. That's when she looked up and saw the mustard splattered across the white wall, and she nearly fainted from the spike in her blood pressure caused by the stress.

"Oh my sweet Jesus!" she gasped. "Who threw mustard all over this wall?"

By then, the old woman was in a frantic panic, knowing that there would be a huge problem if Master Jackson walked in and saw the mess. The girls said nothing, and Miss May quickly became more hostile.

"Who in the world threw mustard all over the wall?" She spoke as loud and as authoritatively as her old lungs would allow, but still none of the girls answered. That's when she decided to take charge.

"Beatrice and Bernice, get yo' tails down to the bunks. No lunch for y'all today. Bertha and Isabelle, get this mess cleaned up quick and get out to the tables when you done."

The two sisters stomped away furious because lunch was their favorite part of the day. They were even more furious at Bertha, because she got the best of them in the fight and ended up causing them to get in trouble in the end. They were not expecting that. In the years that the two sisters had worked inside of the house at Master Jackson's plantation, nobody they picked on had ever fought back. Everyone else was afraid, but not Bertha. They pouted all the way downstairs where they had to stay for the rest of the day. They sat thinking of a way to get back at Bertha and to continue the war with her that they had started, a war that would end in a huge brawl that sent them all tumbling down the staircase leading to the girls' cots.

Chapter 10

Bertha Perseveres

After tumbling down the stairs during the brawl that day, Bertha and the two sisters, Beatrice and Bernice, were worn out from the fight that was the climax of an ongoing and volatile battle. During the past weeks, they had attacked Bertha while Mattie wasn't looking. They had tripped her while she carried bundles of food in her hands, they had intentionally spilled things on her clothes, and they had constantly made fun of her. They talked about her ragged clothes, they talked about her hair, and they even made fun of how she looked, even though she was very pretty.

Bertha did not take the harassment silently. She got a bit of revenge on them whenever she saw the opportunity. She made fun of them; she hit them back whenever she could. One time she even landed a punch on the shoulder of Beatrice so vicious that it left a bruise that stayed for three days. The battle between the girls was out of control, and Bertha was too stubborn to back down. She knew that she had just as much right to work in the house as they did, and she did not accept the harassment. The battle culminated with a brawl of wrestling and throwing punches that sent the three girls tumbling down the stairs leading to the girls' sleeping area. Mattie and Miss May were out of sight, so the other girls all watched and laughed at the ruckus.

Bertha, Beatrice, and Bernice were all battered

and bruised as they sat there at the bottom of the steps, exhausted and too tired to fight any longer. Each girl was winded. Bertha was smart enough to know that the battle had gotten out of hand, and she decided to be the first one to speak up.

"I don't know about y'all, but I'm tired of all this fightin'. I really don't mean no harm to either of you. I have about as much say over bein' here or not bein' here as the both of you. Workin' here ain't nothin' special for me. I just wanna know why y'all hate me so much."

The sisters were sitting on the cement floor across from Bertha. They lifted their heads, and then looked at one another to find an answer while they clutched their wounds. The truth was they didn't know or didn't remember why they had so much disdain for Bertha.

"We hate you because that's what we do," Bernice announced, and she was not in the mood for chumminess.

"Aside from Mattie, we rule in this house. That's how it's been, and that's how we likes to keep it."

"You rule in the house?" Bertha questioned.

"Yeah, we like to think that it's the only power that we got." Beatrice spoke up from her silence.

"We can't have no field nigga comin' in here takin' away the only thing we have and what we worked hard to get. We had to show each and every one of them girls in this house that we don't take no mess, and if they don't go along with what we say, then we will beat them in the top of they head." Beatrice pounded her fist in her hand as a demonstration of her physical force.

"I think I understand that, but it still is the

same," Bertha said. "This fightin' between us can't go on no more, or else we'll kill each other!" Bertha looked at each of the girls, desperately hoping they would agree. They didn't reply. They all sat there in silence for a while, still exhausted. Then Bertha got an idea.

"Hey, there is a candy jar that Masta keeps. I know where it is. If you want, I can get him to give me candy, and I'll save all of what he give me and give it to you if you leave me alone."

Beatrice looked at Bertha like she was from another planet. "Look, child, we know all about that candy jar. We been stealin' out of it for a long time now. You gotta do better than that if you wanna keep us up off ya."

"All right, all right, let me think."

"You better think and think fast, because I think that my eye is gonna be blackened," Beatrice said," and you about seconds away from me catchin' my breath and smashin' yo' head into this floor."

"All right, all right!"

Bertha was searching for a form of payment to offer the girls to keep them from harassing her.

"You both like to eat, right?"

"Yes we do," they both answered simultaneously.

"All right, when you get in trouble with Mattie, she usually keep y'all from eatin' right?"

"Yes." The sisters spoke in a synchronized language.

"Then the next few times y'all gets in trouble, I'll take the heat," Bertha offered.

"Hmm. That sounds like it might work. What you think, Bernice?"

"No, we still ain't lettin' her off that easy."

Bernice got up off of the floor, walked over to Bertha, and then bent down and grabbed her by her collar. Bertha became terrified and began to brace herself for a blow.

"Listen, black monkey. If you take our punishment every time for the next few years, you got a deal. Master Jackson ain't gonna let nothin' happen to his little pet anyway. Right, Beatrice?"

"Right."

Bertha was happy that the girls had been willing to negotiate the terms of leaving her alone. It was a shot in the dark, and Bertha never thought that they would reason with her because of the hate that they seemed to carry for her, so she quickly accepted their conditions. From that moment on, there was no more war between Bertha and the two sisters. When the other girls in the house saw that Beatrice and Bernice were not picking on Bertha anymore, they eased up on her too.

Chapter 11

Julia's Arrival

Julia Jackson came to Master Jackson's plantation riding in a fancy carriage. The day was cloudy and slightly muggy, the wind was gusty, but the temperature was near eighty degrees. Julia, who was the niece of Master Jackson, was donning the finest silk and satin dress that shimmered even in the cloudiness of the day. She was wearing a large hat to accessorize her beautiful dress—a hat that she had to hold on to with one hand in an effort to keep the wind from taking it.

She had a petulant and almost arrogant demeanor to match her opulent wear, and she was stunningly beautiful. Her face glowed of beautiful, soft skin. Her cheekbones were high and welcoming with every smile. Her teeth were perfect and of a florescent white color. Her blondish tresses flowed effortlessly from her head and came to a stop at perfectly trimmed ends. Her hair blew in the wind, giving her a romantic and glamorous appearance as she rode in on the carriage. Her eyes were the center of attraction. They were inviting and hypnotizing. They were the color of soft sand on a tropical beach, and men found it hard to look into them without falling in love. They were her means of getting whatever she wanted, and she used the tools swiftly and as often as she could.

She was the niece of Master Jackson by way of her father, Rufus, who was the older brother and only sibling of Master Jackson. Master Jackson became a fairly successful man in his forty-odd years of life, but his older brother, Rufus, was wildly successful and owned a plantation about three towns over that was twice the size of Master Jackson's. Rufus held a special seat in the government. Along with his money, he had a lot of political power. Rufus raised his four children fully aware of their prestige and place in society, and they acted accordingly. The upbringing of Rufus's four children was the most obvious in Julia, who was the youngest of the family. She was a young woman who had never heard the word *no*. She was the epitome of a spoiled, rich brat. She was sheltered and thought that the world revolved around her. She was a handful to deal with when she got into one of her pouty moods, and she always got her way. She had a high-pitched voiced that managed to go octaves higher when she was upset.

As irony would have it, the spoiled, self-centered brat developed a passion for caring for others and decided to be a caregiver at a young age. She felt that caring for the sick was her calling in life, and she was really good at it. She had attended the best schools in the South and excelled as one of the best in all of her classes during her senior year in high school, at the age of sixteen. She worked harder and longer than any of the other students in her class. Part of the reason for her complete focus on her schoolwork was her attitude. Even the other rich, spoiled brats found her annoying and hard to deal with most of the time.

Her attitude was the reason she had few friends. While the other students were out celebrating and living the boarding school life of the young and privileged, Julia was all alone in her room studying and preparing to ace the next exam, and the next, and she always did. She dreamed of becoming a doctor, but as her luck would have it, there were no women being admitted into Southern medical schools at the time. Being young and ambitious, she dreamed that she could be the one to change this, but that was not the case. The first woman wasn't admitted into medical school in that area of the South until Julia was long retired from working as a nurse. However, not being able to live her childhood dream of becoming a doctor because of her sex would only be the second biggest disappointment in the life of a kindred and ambitious spirit seemingly born at the wrong time in history.

Julia's carriage stopped in the front of Uncle Jackson's big white house with black shutters, freshly painted by some of the male workers. It was the first of July 1858, and Julia had come ahead of the rest of her family who were preparing to visit in celebration of the upcoming American Independence holiday. Her family's home was located three towns over, but the boarding school that she attended was just one town over. All of the students there had been released early so they could travel back home for the holiday. Julia decided to get a head start to her uncle's home because she loved spending time there with him and her cousin, Sage. She would always get Sage into trouble because Sage was goofy and very gullible. She got a kick out of manipulating Sage into doing things, and Sage would later kick herself after realizing that she had again fallen for another of Julia's tricks. On one occasion, Julia got Sage to walk through the kitchen door in the big house as a bucket of yellow paint, which Julia had rigged up, fell from the door ledge and dumped its contents all over Sage's long locks. The paint leaked all over Sage's sundress, which then became completely unsalvageable.

Sage and Julia shared a sisterly bond. Sage was very easygoing and did not mind letting Julia have her way, and she was usually a good sport about Julia's trickery. In fact, she liked Julia better when she was up to her tricks as opposed to when she was in one of her tantrum-throwing moods. Sage was a few years younger than Julia, and she admired Julia, but she was also somewhat envious of her. Julia's parents were always raving about her achievements in school and all of the awards that she had earned because of her perfect grades. Sage was an average student who loved painting and the outdoors much more than being cooped up in her room doing homework or studying. Julia was secretly envious of Sage too. Sage had a way of getting along with everyone, which was something that she was not able to do.

When the door on the carriage was loudly slammed shut by the hired driver, Julia was already planning her next prank for Sage. One of the hired workers helped Julia carry her ample amount of luggage across the long walkway leading up to the large, dark-red front door of Master Jackson's home that opened to a gorgeous foyer. The other worker waited in the carriage. Julia and the worker who helped her carry her bags up to the door stood on the front porch for a while and rang the doorbell, waiting for someone to answer before they could enter the home.

Sage was in her room reading a famous play by William Shakespeare for her summer literature class. She was surprised by the bell, because she and her father had not been expecting any company for a couple of days. Sage glanced out of the window from the comfortable window seat in her room and saw the carriage parked out front. When she was able to get a better look from her second-floor window, which was located in the front of the house right above the front door, all that she could see was many bags of luggage stacked at the door. Immediately, she got excited, because she knew who was standing in the midst of all of that luggage. Sage knew that it had to be her cousin Julia, because she was the only one who brought at least twice as much luggage on each visit than she would ever need.

"Daddy, Daddy, Julia is here!" Sage yelled from her room very happy to find out that her cousin, who she hadn't seen since last Christmas, was standing outside waiting to be let in.

Sage threw her book down, rushed out of her room, and quickly sprinted down the spiral staircase leading to the hall across from the foyer. Master Jackson was across the hall from Sage's room attending to Mrs. Jackson, who was ailing in bed. Margaret was too weak to talk as she lay in bed with a slight fever and stared blankly at the ceiling. Every few minutes she would cough and then labor from the pain in her chest.

"Do you want me to get you any water, honey?" Master Jackson spoke to his wife in a voice that was soft and just audible enough for her sensitive ears to absorb. Mrs. Jackson lay there in utter despair and did not respond. Master Jackson had the lights dim and the curtains pulled shut. He was there the whole day to care for his wife and to soothe her suffering as much as he could. He heard Sage announce that Julia had arrived, so he decided to quietly leave the room.

"I'm going to attend to Sage. I think she just told me that Julia is here. That's good news, right?"

Margaret continued to lay silent. In her healthier days, she loved to spend time with Julia and Sage, because they reminded her so much of her and her younger sister when the two of them were children. However, due to her chronic illness, she was left bedridden for a lengthy time, and the illness was starting to take a toll on her physical and mental well-being.

Master Jackson stared at his sick wife momentarily, hoping to get a response, which would give him a ray of hope about her condition. Margaret said nothing, so he hung his head and silently left the room, closing the door behind him and leaving her in the bedroom alone, still staring at the ceiling.

He left somberly, but as he slowly made his way down the stairs to greet Julia and help her with her bags, he made a strong effort to change his expression to hide his grief from the girls. Sage made it down the stairs before her dad, but even before she could reach the door, Miss May, in her old age, was there to greet Julia and welcome her into the home.

Miss May had been in the kitchen helping Bertha, Mattie, and Isabelle start the evening's dinner. The other girls were assigned to special cleaning duties to help prepare the home for holiday company, which was an easy task, because the house always stayed spotless. The crew of Isabelle, Bertha, Mattie, and Miss May had all been in the kitchen snapping green beans and chopping tomatoes when they heard a knock at the door.

Miss May always felt insecure about her old age, so she made a point of proving to all the other house workers that she could keep up with them in every task. She had to be the one to pick the most vegetables in the garden or be the first to finish chopping onions, and of course, when an eager Julia banged on the door, Miss May had to prove that she could quickly answer it and greet the guest. She tossed her apron to the side after wiping her hands on it and made it out of the kitchen and to the door by the time an impatient Julia could bang on the door again.

Miss May opened the door in the middle of the second knock. She was surprised to find Julia standing there, because they weren't expecting her or the rest of the family until Sunday and it was only Friday. Although surprised, she was happy to see Julia. Julia was always nice to Miss May in her own way. Julia always asked for seconds when eating dinner that Miss May prepared, because she loved Miss May's cooking. When she was all done eating, she would stubbornly compliment Miss May by saying, "Well, I suppose dinner was satisfactory. Now tidy up quickly." This would irk the rest of the house workers to the bone, but Miss May understood that this was Julia's way of saying thank you. *Thank you* were two words that would hardly ever be heard coming out of Julia's mouth back then.

Julia was far too stubborn to show appreciation even when she wanted to. Miss May was the only one who understood this, and because of this understanding, Julia took a liking to her. She never felt as judged around Miss May. Of course, she was too proud to express that she liked the lowly slave servant, so she would show her affection by not being as rude to Miss May. Miss May knew that beneath the façade of stubbornness and rudeness there was a kindhearted person who was gentle and caring.

Miss May could find a reason to love anyone, and Mattie always joked about it. Mattie would say, "You know what, Miss May? God must have gave you special eyes to see good in anybody, because you see good in that Julia that everybody else just ain't seein'."

"Well hello, Jewels," Miss May said standing near the threshold of the door after she opened it. The luggage carrier that Julia was accompanied by stood there silently, waiting on his next orders. He looked extremely exhausted, either from carrying all of Julia's baggage or from having his patients worn out from putting up with her demands for the long ride over.

"Hello, Miss May," Julia answered in her snobbery, not making eye contact with her and quickly brushing past while making her way over to her cousin who was walking toward the door.

Before she could reach Sage to embrace her, Miss May would not be ignored.

"Well ain't you glad to see me, Jewels?"

Jewels was the nickname that Miss May had given Julia when she was a child, because she thought that Julia's eyes shimmered like polished jewels. Julia loved the nickname but never acknowledged the fact that she did. The only person who she would allow to call her Jewels was Miss May. Whenever anyone else called her Jewels, it annoyed her.

Julia responded to Miss May's question by looking at her and giving her an awkward smile as she continued to make her way into the home and toward her cousin standing a few steps away. When she reached Sage, she dropped the one bag that she was carrying and gave her a big hug as they both greeted.

"What are you doing here so early, Julia?" Sage asked. "We weren't expecting you today."

"Yes, I know, but I was released from school early for the holiday and decided to come ahead of everyone else to get the first pick of the guest rooms. I've always loved the one next door to Uncle's room with the big window. You can see the pond from there."

"Yeah, sure, you came early because you have nothing better to do."

"Well, you're surely happy that I did come early, because you're clearly blushing," Julia fired back. "Plus, I needed a break from burying my head in the books. I hope I'm not too much of a burden." Julia was dramatically sympathetic with her lips poked out.

"Not at all." Master Jackson interrupted them. He had made his way down the steps and over to the girls. "We are more than pleased to have you here."

He opened his arms to embrace Julia with a hug and a kiss on the cheek. Julia hugged her uncle and then turned her head toward the kitchen.

"Wonderful smell coming from the kitchen, Uncle."

"Yes it is."

"Well, I must have come at the right time after all." Julia began anticipating another one of Miss May's and the girls' delicious dinner meals. "I hope there is enough for an extra guest."

"Well of course there is, sweetie," Master Jackson looked over to Miss May who was still standing in the doorway with the door propped open.

"Miss May honey, will you hurry off to the kitchen and tell the girls to prepare enough for an extra guest."

"Yes, right away, Massa." Miss May smiled as she hurried off to the kitchen with a slight limp from arthritis.

Master Jackson looked at Julia. "All right, while the girls are preparing dinner, we'll help you get the rest of your things into the bedroom. Did you bring a whole house with you this time?"

Master Jackson walked to the door and addressed the worker who was still there standing in the midst of the luggage and still hanging on to three large bags that were weighing him down.

"Is this everything, sir?" Master Jackson witnessed a slouched over worker who was standing alongside a mound of luggage.

"No, sir," he replied. "There are a few more bags in the carriage."

"Well, bring the rest of her things to the door, and I'll take it from here."

The worker nodded his head and hurried off to grab the rest of the bags. He was excited that his assignment with Julia was almost over, and now he could hurry back and collect his payment from Julia's father who had hired him and the driver. The worker grabbed the remaining four bags from the carriage and dropped them off on the doorstep. He then said good-bye to Master Jackson and hurried back to the carriage so that he and the driver could begin their trip back. Before Master Jackson could thank the two men or give them a tip, they were already speeding off down the country road in the carriage.

Master Jackson noticed the two men's haste exit and turned and looked at Julia. "What'd you do to those fellers to make them so quick to scat?"

"Oh, they're just lazy," Julia announced, absolving herself from any wrongdoing.

"I see that you're the same old brat that you've always been, Jewels," Sage said, mocking her cousin's nickname and history of behavior. "You must've worried the poor guys to death."

"Oh enough, Sage, and don't call me that name." Julia pointed her finger at Sage as a warning for her to shut up.

With that, they all carried the luggage upstairs and into the guest room that Julia had picked out, right next to Master Jackson's room.

Chapter 12

Chicken Dinner

By the time Master Jackson, Julia, and Sage were finished getting all of Julia's bags into her room, Miss May and the girls in the kitchen had dinner just about ready. When Sage was out of earshot, Julia pulled her uncle to the side and asked about Margaret's health. The whole family knew that Margaret had been ill for a long time, and Julia was concerned if Margaret had shown any sign of improvement.

"So," Julia folded her arms and hesitated to ask him about Margaret. They were standing in the hallway near the top of the stairs right across from Master Jackson and Margaret's bedroom. "How is she?"

"Well, she's not doing very well."

Julia paused to gather her thoughts. The childhood slumber parties that she'd shared roasting marshmallows at the fireplace with Sage and Margaret quickly flashed through her mind. She thought about all of the fun that the three of them had when Margaret would teach them both new games to play and tell scary stories that would frighten her and Sage to the point where they couldn't sleep at night. Julia loved to visit her favorite uncle's house. Aside from Sage and her uncle, Margaret was a big reason why. Margaret would make treats for the girls and let them have as many as they would like to eat. This was something that Julia's very strict mom did not allow her to do. When Julia got the news about Margaret, she began to hold back tears. Master Jackson noticed the emotion building up that she was bravely trying to disguise, and he quickly tried to comfort her.

"Look, honey, don't burden yourself with this now. This is going to be a fun holiday. Plus, we have dinner waiting for us downstairs, and if we don't get down there soon, it will get cold. I think Miss May is making all of your favorites; we got collard greens, yams, and fried chicken. Now let's get downstairs, honey."

"All right, but first I'd like to see her."

Julia took a half step toward the bedroom where Margaret was, but Master Jackson stepped in front of her to block her path. Then he gently placed his hands on each of Julia's shoulders and turned her in the opposite direction.

"There will be plenty of time for you to visit with her, but right now it's time for dinner."

"All right, you're right."

He was the only person who could get through to her when she had her mind set on something that she wanted to do. If it had been anyone else telling her that she shouldn't go into the room at that particular time, she wouldn't have listened. She would have just barged right in. Instead, she listened to her uncle and headed downstairs for dinner, where Sage had taken a place at the table and was enjoying the company of Bertha and the other servants, who worked in the kitchen.

The table was nearly done being set by Bertha. Sage and the girls were loudly laughing at something that had been said before Julia walked through the swinging doors in the dining room. Julia was curious to know what was so darn funny. She squinted her eyes and became annoyed because there was fun being had, and she was just a moment too late and missed out on it. Whenever there was laughter around and Julia was not included in it, she would feel left out and would quickly interject herself into the moment. This time would be no different.

Julia stared Sage down, and her gaze was overflowing with envy. She looked as if she was trying to read Sage's mind to figure out what they were all laughing so jolly about. Sage's laugh began to die down to a small giggle as she picked up on her cousin's expression. The others all stopped laughing completely and got right back to work when they noticed Julia's demeanor. Beatrice and Bernice quickly shuffled back to the kitchen, out of sight. Bertha grabbed two plates from the cabinet and continued to finish setting the table, while Miss May went into the kitchen to take the hot chicken from the cooking oil. Mattie shuffled back to the pantry to grab some seasoning. Before Julia could walk over to her seat across the table from Sage, she spoke up in her high-pitched voice that gave away how annoyed she was. The angrier she got, the higher it went.

"Well what is so darn funny in here that you were all cackling like a bunch of crazy hens?"

Her face wrinkled as if she had been sucking on a lemon, and Sage looked back at her cousin with a crooked smile.

"Oh, Jewels, you wouldn't understand even if I explained it."

Julia became more annoyed and insisted that

Sage let her in on the joke. "Oh of course I would understand. Just tell me."

"Oh never mind it, Julia. I'm not the best at telling the story anyway," she said as she looked over at Bertha with a smirk. Just forget about it. It's really not that important." Sage protested.

Julia became more annoyed and folded her arms and then shot her cousin another intimidating scowl. "Well all right then, I'll just forget about it. Just forget that I asked, but leaving someone in the dark on a good laugh is no way to treat a guest."

"Oh come on, Julia. Really, it's not important. There's no need to make a fuss." Sage picked up on Julia's obvious discontent and tried to calm her.

"I'm not making a fuss."

Julia was snappy and pulled her chair out from the dining room table and quickly flopped down, making a small thud when her bottom hit the seat.

"Oh, here she goes again." Sage had a pinch of disdain in her tone, and in an act of abjection, she flailed one arm in the air. She was already fed up with Julia's attitude.

Bertha was standing and watching the exchange of words between Sage and the new guest, whom she hadn't met yet, and noticed the tension in the exchange. To smooth things over, she chimed in on the conversation uninvited to rescue Sage.

"Excuse me, miss, but we was talkin' about how bad of a rider Sage was when she was a li'l younger. She had problems fallin' off. She never could learn to stay on the horse. I would go along with her and Masta Jackson to help Masta see about her. One time me and Masta was so off into our ridin' that we didn't notice we left Sage some yards behind us.

Lo and behold, she'd fell off her horse again, and when we got back to her, she was stuck flat-faced in the ground with her face buried in a pile of mud and horse crap. It took the two of us to pull her from that mess. When we finally got her out, she started screamin' and cryin' from embarrassment, even though it was just me and Masta around, and nobody else could see. It was tears full of crap and mud comin' down her face, and she was still screamin', 'Help me, help me!' I guess that was because of the upset of the moment." Bertha filled Julia in on the story, holding back laughter.

Julia listened but stubbornly, and for the mere sake of being upset, she refused to engage in the comedic moment. Bertha continued anyway.

"So she left a nice big print of her face in that crud. It was a sad sight. So that was the end of our day ridin'. We took her back home, and it took Mrs. Margaret about two days to wash all of the junk out of her hair and ears. Yep, it was a sad, sad sight, but it's funny lookin' back."

The girls all started laughing again, but Julia turned away from Bertha and looked at Sage as Sage began to add to the story.

"Yeah, but I was only screaming help because I couldn't do it while my face was stuck in the crap. I was too afraid to open my mouth. I didn't want to get God knows what in it. That would have made it worse! Yeah, it was a very pathetic day for me," Sage laughed.

"Oh I see." Julia cracked a slight smile and then turned back to Bertha as her expression quickly changed. She looked at Bertha, and her disapproval mounted.

"And just who are you?" Julia sized up Bertha.

The mood of the room quickly went from lighthearted to tense again as most of them all stopped laughing. However, Beatrice and Bernice, who had made their way from the kitchen, quietly snickered in the background at the look of embarrassment on Bertha's face.

"I-I'm Bertha Oliver. I'm sixteen, and I been workin' inside for about a year now," Bertha nervously replied with a stutter.

"Well what are you doing inside my uncle's kitchen? You're a bit dark to be working inside, don't you think? Shouldn't you be outside in the field with all of the other darkies?"

Julia verbally annihilated Bertha in a blatant effort to embarrass her. Bertha's face dropped like a little kid who had just had a piece of candy snatched away. She stiffened and straightened up her body, puckered her brows, and placed one hand on her hip. If Bertha had been Caucasian, her face would have been beet red with anger. Right as she was about to give Julia a piece of her mind, Mattie grabbed her around the mouth and gently shuffled her back to the kitchen. When Bertha and Mattie were out of sight, Sage gave Julia a piece of her mind.

"You see, Julia, that's the problem with you. Why'd you have to go and spoil the mood?"

Sage scolded her cousin in a lowered voice because the other women were still present in the kitchen and could easily hear.

"Oh, what's wrong, Sage? Becoming too friendly with the help?" Julia's eyes dimmed and her mouth became tightened as she squeezed her words through her lips, but did not lower her voice, in an effort to cause a scene.

"Well I'll have you know, Jewels, Bertha is one of daddy's favorites, and that's why she's working inside. She's a good worker, and she's smart."

"Oh, she's smart you say? If that's even possible! Well aren't you just in love with her?"

"Now don't be ridiculous, Julia. You're a sick and twisted person. Do you know that?"

Julia rolled her eyes, and they both placed napkins over their laps and prepared to eat dinner as Master Jackson walked into the kitchen and took his seat. While Julia and Sage engaged in their argument, Mattie was busy calming Bertha down in the back.

"Well they're taking all night to prepare this dinner, aren't they?" Julie said.

"We're about to start serving the food now, Ms. Jewels." Miss May politely reassured her in an effort to suffice Julia's whining.

Back in the kitchen, Mattie and Bertha continued to talk a bit more about Bertha's reaction.

"Look here, Bertha, I knows that you one of Massa's favorite workers and that's why he got you in here, but you have to respect Ms. Julia. I know she can be a tough one to deal with. Lord knows I had my share of run-ins with that child."

"I can't deal with the way she talkin' to me, Mattie. I'd rather work the field than to deal with that."

"Girl, you better get yo' head together," Mattie shot back. "The way she talkin' to you ain't nothin'. Would you rather be hangin' from a tree? You been spoiled all yo' life by Massa and his treatment of you, but she's Massa's family and that's that. I seen way worse than what she doin' to you in my day. If she wanted to get up and slap you in the face, she could do it and it wouldn't be nothin' you can do about it. Now I will say this, no matter how sharp she can be with her tongue, I never seen her lay a finger on anybody or have anybody put on the post. She could do it if she wanted, so just remember that. You just gonna have to learn to bite yo' tongue around her. Bertha, you have to respect her no matter what. You hear me? Now is you about ready to get back to work?"

"Yes, ma'am." Bertha agreed. She had stood silently as she was scolded by Mattie.

After their discussion, they both returned to the dining room to continue to serve dinner. Master Jackson had arrived shortly after the commotion. He felt the tension in the room, but decided to ignore it.

"Well, are we all swell tonight?"

"Hardly," Sage answered her father while spitefully staring Julia down.

"Well I sure am ready to eat," Master Jackson said, changing the subject. He was not one to get involved in spats between women or girls in the family.

Bertha grabbed a bowl of corn and began to serve. She gave Master Jackson a scoop, and he thanked her. Then she served a scoop to Sage. After that, she made her way over to Julia and reached down to scoop out a portion for her, but she protested.

"I don't want her serving my food."

"What do you mean, Jewels?" Miss May spoke up.

She was standing next to Bertha with a serving bowl and a large spoon.

"I don't want her scruffy looking man hands serving my food," Julia elaborated.

Everyone in the kitchen paused because they had been encapsulated in awkward tension. By that point, Bertha had had enough of Julia's attitude. She placed the bowl on the table, nearly slamming it down, and then walked out of the dining room. Again, it was silent except for the quiet snickers of laughter from Beatrice and Bernice. Mattie gave them a quick eye of disapproval, and they swiftly became silent. She went after Bertha for the second time and found her standing in the back hallway leaning up against a wall with her arms folded.

"Look, child, you better get your head together. You can't just walk out like that every time somebody say somethin' to you that you don't agree with."

"I know, Mattie, but I told you that I can't take her treatin' me like that. How would her hands look if she had to work out in the fields her whole life?"

"I know, I know, but you gonna have to get used to folk talkin' to you like that, or else you gonna end up dead. How about you get back to yo' folks early tonight. Me and the other girls will finish up dinner, but be back here early in the mornin', because I got a special job for ya. Take this bird and pie with you, but don't let other folks know what I've given you. We ain't supposed to have pie. Let's keep this between me and you." Mattie handed Bertha a brown paper bag with the food in it.

"All right, Mattie," Bertha said. "Thank you so much."

Bertha grabbed the bag and headed for the door, but Mattie called out to her.

"Oh ... and, Bertha, child, put some grease on them hands please."

"All right, Mattie, I will."

Bertha smiled and then left the big house for the day and headed back to the family's cabin right as the sun was beginning to set on the plantation.

Chapter 13

Back at Home

When Bertha arrived at home that evening, Zeke and Lola were not home yet. She was exhausted so she tossed her bag to the floor and kicked off her shoes. Her feet were sore, and she desperately needed to sit down and rest after such a rough day. With her bare feet, she walked a few yards to the water well to grab a pail of drinking water. She filled the pail and headed back to the cabin. As she walked back, she saw Aunt Lola and Zeke in the distance. She started to wave at them to get their attention. When twelve-year-old Zeke saw her, he took off running in her direction, leaving Lola lagging behind slowly. At twelve, just as the doctor had predicted years earlier, Zeke was unusually tall for his age. He already stood five feet, ten inches tall, a whole four inches taller than Bertha, who was five feet, six inches. As he ran, he was able to gain ground with each long stride that he took and reached Bertha quickly, even though she was quite a distance away from his starting point.

"Bertha, Bertha. Look what I got!" Zeke yelled, jumping up and down and waving a jar in Bertha's face.

He was carrying a round jar that had initially been used for storing honey. There was no honey inside of the glass bottle, which was now enclosed with a metal twist cap. Instead, there was a bunch of thick green grass and a bit of dirt. Bertha looked at the jar but could not make out what was inside of it that Zeke was so excited about.

"What in the world is that?" she asked.

"Don't ya see? Look closer!"

"Well how am I supposed to look at it when you won't hold the darn thing still for me to get a good look? Stop jumpin' up and down, will ya?"

"All right. Now look," Zeke directed.

He stood still and held the bottle to Bertha's face. When she took a closer examination, she saw something move. It was green, and it had blended in with the grass inside of the bottle.

"Oh my goodness! Is that a grasshopper? Get that thing away from me!" Bertha quickly shoved the bottle away from her face. She hated insects, and she was not amused by the grasshopper that he had caught. Zeke started laughing at Bertha because of the disgusted outcry.

"Yep, took me about two hours to find this sucka and catch him. He gonna be my new friend."

"How you know that it's a boy?" Bertha asked. "It could be a girl, couldn't it?"

"It's a boy because I say it's a boy," Zeke answered. "What would I want to catch a girl for? I'm too tough for that."

Zeke flexed his muscles to demonstrate his manliness and poked his chest out because he was proud of his capture.

"Oh yeah? Well you just make sure that you keep that thing in the bottle and away from me."

"What, you a big baby? I might just put him in yo' hair whiles you sleepin'."

Zeke shoved the bottle back into Bertha's face, and she screamed at the thought of having it in her hair. Out of spite for the teasing, she knocked it out of his hand and smacked him on the head then took off running with the pail of water in her hand, nearly spilling all of it. The soft dirt and grass on the ground cushioned the glass bottle's fall and kept it from shattering. Zeke laughed and bent down quickly to pick it up and chase after Bertha, who had gotten a head start to get away from any retaliation that he could offer. He quickly caught up to her, but she ran faster and made it into the house. She felt Zeke right on her heels and dropped the bucket, spilling the rest of the water in it on the floor. She jumped onto her cot and covered her head with a blanket before Zeke could get to her. She was laughing the whole time, and so was he. Zeke jumped right on top of her, still holding the bottle, and pulled the cover back and shoved the bottle into her face again. She screamed loud enough to be heard yards away. Aunt Lola walked in and saw the two of them roughhousing. Lola looked down and saw the small puddle of water spilled on the floor with the metal pail laying on its side next to the spill.

"What y'all up to now? You chaps cut it out now, and somebody please get this mess cleaned up."

Aunt Lola was exhausted and had no energy for their foolery. She gave her orders and immediately went to her rocking chair and flopped down to kick her feet up. Both Bertha and Zeke immediately obeyed and stopped wrestling.

"All right, Zeke, I'll clean the water off the floor, but you have to go back and get more."

"Uh-uh." Zeke shook his head.

"Come on, you gotta go." Bertha insisted as she

picked up the pail from the floor and shoved it into his chest. "Besides, you way faster than me, so you can go faster." She massaged his ego a bit with her words.

"Well, you right about that." Zeke grabbed hold of it and took off running as fast as he could to the water well.

"Well that was easy," Bertha told Aunt Lola as Lola still sat in her chair with her head laid back.

"I tell you, men all the same. If you want them to do what you wants, you gotta swell up they big head," Aunt Lola said to Bertha, and they laughed together.

Zeke quickly came back with the water, and the three of them drank and ate the food that Mattie had given to Bertha. Soon it was time for them to go to sleep and start the day over again. Every night before they would go to bed, Bertha would read to Zeke. He loved to hear the stories that she read, and sometimes she would try to teach him new words. He was not good at remembering the words or how to spell them, and this would sometimes lead to an argument between the two of them. However, for some reason, Bertha was up to the challenge of teaching this time. She knew how important it would be for Zeke to learn to read. Even though this was not allowed and they could get in a lot of trouble, Bertha thought that teaching him was worth the risk.

That night the word for Zeke to learn after Bertha had read a story was *banana*. In the story, there was a little boy who loved to eat bananas, so Bertha felt that the word related and would be easy for Zeke to learn. Mrs. Bates, had given Bertha a stack of children's books to take with her as a gift when she found out that Bertha would no longer be living on her and her husband's plantation. She taught her a lot, and Bertha learned quickly. She had secretly kept the children's books since she was five. She had no further reading instruction, and she had to advance the rest of her skills on her own. She was somewhat literate but did not have the most sophisticated reading skills; however, she knew enough to pass down what she had learned to Zeke. She kept the books in a secret stash and read them over and over. When Zeke was old enough, she began to teach him what she knew. Bertha finished reading the last page of the story about the banana-eating boy and shut the book.

"Did you like that story, Zeke?"

"Yeah, I did."

"Do you want to know how to spell banana now?"

Hesitantly, he said yes because he wanted to learn, but he knew that learning to spell with Bertha teaching him always turned into a fight between the two of them.

"All right, this should be easy. *Banana*," Bertha said, enunciating the word as she wrote it down on a piece of paper, slowly spelling it out so that he could see. She gave him a few minutes to study the word, and then she took the paper away from him to quiz him.

"All right, spell it!"

She was excited that he would get the word right on the first try.

"Okay, *banana*," he repeated, and then he attempted to spell the word. "B-a-n-n-a!"

His eyes were closed tightly as he tried to picture the word in his head.

"No, that ain't it, Zeke. Try it again," Bertha said. "Here, have another look."

He grabbed the paper and studied the word for a while longer before giving it back to Bertha.

"B-a-n-n-a-n-a," he shouted, convinced that he was correct.

Bertha sighed. "That's close but still not right. Try again."

"B-a-n-n-a-n-a!"

"Zeke, that's the same thing that you just said, and I already told you that it wasn't right." She berated him. Her patients were gone.

Bertha's frustration was starting to build. This was obvious and did not help to ease Zeke's mind so that he could focus and get the word right. It only made him more nervous.

"I'm gonna try it one last time, and if I don't get it, I don't care and I'm goin' to bed."

"All right." Bertha agreed. "But here, have one more look at it. I think you'll get it this time."

After he surveyed the word for a few more seconds, his patients were gone too, and he was ready to take one last attempt.

"*Banana*," he repeated, and then he started to spell it aloud again. "B-a-n,"—he stopped a bit, hesitating to get the word correct—"n-a-n-a!" he shouted, sure that this time he was correct.

Bertha looked at him with a deflated stare. "Oh my goodness, you just said the same wrong spellin' three times in a row! I told you twice that it wasn't spelled that way!"

At this point, Bertha had lost all of her patients

and was shouting at him. "It takes less energy to teach that clumsy old Sage to stay on her horse!"

"I don't care! Leave me be. I'm goin' to bed. I don't need to know this crap anyway!" He stormed off, moving quickly to his cot that was across the room.

"Well fine, you moron!"

Bertha threw the paper in his direction but missed him as it drifted to the floor, not making it very far across the room.

"Fine!" he yelled back. "I don't even know what a moron is!"

He squealed like the young child that he was, and the commotion awakened Aunt Lola, who had fallen asleep in her rocking chair. She made them both quiet down and go to bed, and she did the same.

Before Bertha fell asleep that night, she was irate. She woke up in the middle of the night to the faint sound of buzzing. She had no idea where the sound was coming from, so she got off of her cot and started to search the dark room. She realized that the noise was coming from Zeke's jar with the insect in it. She thought about tossing the whole thing out the door because of the annoying sound. However, she could not bring herself to do that. She knew that Zeke would be upset if she tossed it out, and she remembered how excited he was when he caught it. She faced her fears and bravely picked up the jar and held it in her hand while she decided what to do. She eyed the bottle several times. After a while, she finally decided that she would just put up with the noise, but then she realized that the tin bottle cap had no air holes poked in it. She thought that the stupid grasshopper must be suffocating in the bottle, and for some reason, she could not allow that to happen. She quickly fumbled around in the dark and found a metal object sharp enough to poke a few holes in the cap. She poked about four holes and placed it back on the floor where Zeke had left it. Then she lay back down to rest. Soon, the buzzing noise stopped, and she was back off to sleep.

Chapter 14

The Rivalry

Bertha woke up bright and early right as the sun was rising, just as Mattie had asked her to. It was a dry sunny day right before the celebration of American independence. Bertha took her normal fifteen-minute walk to the big house. She strolled past the workers who were already busy working in the fields and passed the garden of brightly colored plants and vegetables. She also passed the shed near the garden, where she first met Bubba. It had been about six months since she last saw him. She did not know for sure what had happened to him, but she had heard rumors that he had been sold to another plantation owner. She thought that was a possibility, albeit strange because of the abrupt nature of the sale. Every day on her walk to the big house she was reminded of Bubba when she passed it. It still stood there, getting more and more weathered with each season, and its entrance door was as squeaky as it has ever been. Her memory of Bubba was all that she had left of him, and she hung on to it endearingly as she proceeded to make her way to the big house in the rising sun that was sure to make the outdoors scorching.

When she reached the house, she went to the back entrance where Beatrice and Bernice were busy hanging laundry. They looked up from what they were doing and saw Bertha approaching.

"Hey, darkie man hands. You black already? I mean, you back already?" shouted Bernice as she laughed.

"Yeah, what you doin' back here?" Beatrice shouted out.

"I thought Miss Julia had scared the pants off ya. We just knew you wasn't comin' back."

Bertha walked past them as if she didn't hear their teasing and then entered the home. When she was inside, she saw that Myrtle and Bernadette were cleaning the girls' sleeping area in the basement and Isabelle was helping Miss May and Mattie in the kitchen.

"Hello," Bertha said. "Good mornin', Mattie. I'm here early just like you asked me."

"Oh, good thing, child." Mattie barely looked up as she responded to Bertha. She was down on her knees busy pulling out pots and pans from the lower cabinet in an effort to reorganize them. "Today is the last day for preparin' the house." Mattie got up and wiped her hands on her apron, looking directly at Bertha.

"I have a special duty for you, and you knows how I trust you with all of the special duties around here," Mattie said. "I am puttin' you on step duty. I'll need you to take the scrub brush over there and get busy on those steps, ya hear?"

"But, Mattie, you know that scrub brush is old. It don't even scrub no more." Bertha protested.

"Look, that's all the scrub brush we have to work with. Now you gonna use it, and you gonna like it, and I don't wanna hear no lip outta ya."

Bertha knew better than to refuse her assigned task, so she walked over to the counter a few steps away and grabbed the shabby scrub brush. Then she went to the kitchen cabinet and grabbed the bucket of harsh, fuming cleaning solutions. When she had the cleaning supplies that she needed and was about to make her way to the stairs to begin working on her assigned task, Mattie yelled out to her.

"Oh, and Bertha honey, you also have to clean Mrs. Jackson's bedroom, so don't take all day on those steps, ya hear? And don't disturb Mrs. Margaret."

"Y-yes, ma'am." Bertha answered with her back to Mattie as she looked down at the floor in an effort to hide her displeasure of having more work added to her load. When she was on step duty, she knew that it would take a lengthy amount of time because she had to scrub the wooden steps and then wipe them down by hand just the way Mattie liked it. If the job wasn't up to Mattie's standard, she would have to start all over. Bertha also hated cleaning Mrs. Margaret's room. She was afraid to go inside, because she always feared that she would catch Mrs. Jackson's sickness she'd been told about. However, she never did get sick because of cleaning the bedroom.

When Bertha got to the staircase that led from the hallway near the foyer up to the hallway upstairs that led to the bedrooms, she found the steps in poor condition. They were dirty and tracked with dried mud from the first step to the last step at the top. She pulled the broom from out of the closet near the bottom step and made her way up to the top step where she began to sweep the dried chunks of mud down from step to step. This took about thirty-five minutes, and Bertha had to pluck some chunks of mud out of the corner cracks on nearly each step. When she was done sweeping, she was ready to start scrubbing the steps with soap and water. She removed the bottled cleaning products from the bucket so that she could fill it with water. The crew who worked in the house always kept a barrel of water for cleaning in a tightly enclosed closet upstairs. To retrieve the water, she had to make her way back up the steps and over to the closet.

When she began to make her way down the hall with the red bucket and bottled cleaning soap in each hand, she could see Julia, who was wearing a robe, coming from the opposite side of the hall. They were both headed the same direction—right toward the closet where the water was kept. Julia was barely awake and moving very slowly, but when she looked up and saw Bertha, she quickened her walk in an effort to beat her to the closet door. She and Bertha reached the door at the same time. Bertha stopped to let Julia pass and enter first. There was only room for one person in the closet and surely not enough room for Bertha to pull the barrel out and retrieve her water with both her and Julia inside. At the last moment, Julia decided that she wasn't going to go inside and walked away. Bertha decided to enter the closet alone.

Bertha grabbed the doorknob slowly and turned it then she pulled the door open wide enough to enter. She placed one foot inside, but before she landed her foot on the floor, she felt something pushing her out of the way. It was Julia who had doubled back and decided that she wanted to enter the closet to retrieve an item. Bertha felt a stiff shove, and the next thing she heard was the door being slammed in her face. She was startled and confused. When she realized it was Julia, whom she had previously stopped for in the hallway as a courtesy to let her enter first, who had just pushed her out of the doorway, she became furious. In a moment of quick reaction, she made a fist and held it up to the door so that she could pound on it as loudly as possible to get Julia's attention.

Before her fist could meet the door, she remembered what Mattie had told her in the kitchen the night before. She knew Julia was notorious for getting under people's skin, and she could not let her anger get the best of her because she was a servant and Julia was part of Master Jackson's family.

Bertha gathered herself and took a deep breath to calm down. When she was calm, she gently knocked on the door three times. There was no answer, so she knocked again softly, three times. During the second time knocking, Julia cracked open the door and stuck her head out, just enough to speak with Bertha, who was still holding the cleaning bucket in one hand. The expression on Julia's face was inquiring in a manner that seemed to display that she had done nothing wrong. It was as if she hadn't remembered pushing Bertha out of the way and was politely answering the knock on the closet door to find out what Bertha needed.

"Hello, can I help you?" Julia asked with the most innocence.

"Well," Bertha gathered herself, trying to reciprocate the politeness. "I was told to clean the steps today, and I was wonderin' if I could fill my bucket with water from that barrel so that I can start my job."

"Sure, I'll be coming out shortly," Julia responded before slamming the closet door in Bertha's face again. The sound echoed. On the other side of the door, Julia laughed quietly and stood there waiting for Bertha to grow impatient again.

Bertha waited for five minutes. When Julia didn't emerge from the closet, she went to the top step and sat waiting. Another five minutes went by, and Julia still had not come out. Bertha decided to return to the door and knock again. When she reached the door, she knocked softly. Bertha waited for five more minutes after knocking for the third time, and then suddenly Julia opened the door and came out and walked right past Bertha without acknowledging her. Bertha paused, immersed in perplexity, but after a short moment, she entered the closet and filled her bucket as Julia walked down the hall, back to her bedroom.

Once back in the bedroom, she couldn't get back to sleep. It was around six thirty in the morning, but the sun was shining bright so she did not want to return to bed. She proceeded to get dressed. When she was all dressed, she knew that she was the only one in the house awake besides the servants, and she began to grow bored sitting there alone. Meanwhile, Bertha was on her hands and knees scrubbing dirt off of the wooden steps.

Julia was all dressed and had nothing to do. She cracked open her bedroom door and poked her head out. When she did this, she managed to get a glimpse of Bertha hard at work scrubbing away at the steps. She could see that Bertha was stooped over with her hair messy and her dress riding up her legs as she worked. Bertha did not look too pleased to be scrubbing the steps, and this was entertaining to Julia because she thought that Bertha's body language in her frustration was comical.

Bertha was not aware that Julia was watching as she continued to work. Before Bertha could notice that she was being watched, Julia pulled her head back inside the room and closed the door quietly. She put her back to the door and let her body slide down it until her bottom hit the floor. She sat there on the floor and started thinking of a way to entertain herself. She couldn't think of anything to do, so she got onto her feet and decided to poke her head back out of the door again to watch Bertha in her misery, which provided a bit of entertainment for the moment. That's when she saw something that made her laugh. Bertha was cleaning the steps, and up walked Beatrice and Bernice.

"Hey, Bertha what you doin'?" Bernice had the glimmer of a mischievous child in her eyes.

"Can't you see what I'm doin', you fool?" Bertha let out an annoyed chuckle. "Don't you fools got work of yo' own to do?"

"Oh, we do," Beatrice said slowly and methodically as if she secretly had a trump card in her pocket and couldn't wait to use it.

"You know what?" Bertha said. "I know Agnes was born on a full moon, and she say that's the reason why she ugly, but y'all two must have been born on a half-moon because ya got about half of a brain between the two of you. Now get away from around here and let me finish my job!"

Bertha had unknowingly allowed her sharp

tongue to get her into a jam. Beatrice and Bernice had been out in the garden working after they had finished the laundry, so they were both wearing big black garden boots. These were the kind of boots that had deep ridges on the bottom that seemed to hold on to dirt like a coffee mug holds coffee. Bertha had not noticed the boots. If she had, she might not have been so quick to insult the two of them out of her frustration.

After Bertha insulted them, Beatrice and Bernice looked at one another with giddy looks on their faces and smiled, communicating with each other without words as only close siblings can. Their smiles grew larger, and they started laughing. Bertha just stood there at the bottom of the steps looking at the two of them smile. She was trying to figure out what they were up to. That's when she looked down and saw the grime and mud protruding from under the girls' boots. Immediately, her face dropped.

"Uh-oh," she whispered to herself.

Before she could complete her thought, the girls both quickly jetted up the steps with dirt and mud seemingly being magnetically pulled from their boots and sticking to the damp steps that Bertha had meticulously cleaned. Beatrice and Bernice ran up the steps and then turned around and ran right back down, stomping and clearing as much mud from their boots as they could. Bertha was furious, and she managed to grab the scrub brush and clobber Bernice on the ankle. Bernice squealed in pain, but the two sisters made a quick getaway before Miss May or Mattie could come investigate.

Even though she managed to get a blow of retaliation in on one of the menacing sisters, Bertha was still left with steps full of mud that she had to clean again. Julia silently watched the whole incident happen from the cracked door as she held back laughter. She was amused by Bertha's swift defense using the scrub brush. However, she wanted to get in on the action. She waited for the perfect moment. As she was sure that Bertha was almost all done cleaning the steps of the garden mud that Beatrice and Bernice had tracked in, she made her move. There was a plant inside her bedroom, and she scooped a bunch of soil out and rubbed the bottom of her shoes with chunks of dirt. She then walked calmly up to Bertha, who was at the top step, and stood behind her for a few seconds until Bertha noticed she was there. Bertha was blocking the steps while she was kneeled over cleaning. When she realized that Julia was standing behind her, she quickly moved out of the way and greeted her.

"Hello, Miss Jewels." Bertha had mistaken Jewels as Julia's name.

Julia gave Bertha a glare but did not correct her.

"I'm sorry; I'll get out of the way. I was just finishin' up the steps here, sorry about that."

Julia nodded her head and donned a devious smile before making her way down the stairs. As she walked down each step, she grinded her foot against the wooden steps, leaving a trail of dirt behind. Bertha watched curiously, but she did not have enough anger left in her to get mad. She just stood and watched Julia from the top step as she slowly made her way down each of the steps, intentionally rubbing dirt from her shoes onto the steps. In a strange way, it was comical, and Bertha continued to stand and watch, speechless. When Julia got to the bottom step, she grinded her foot as she had done on all the others. This time, however, there was some moisture on the wood that made it slippery and she lost her tracking. Her legs went flailing out from under her causing her to fall directly on her butt, nearly causing a major injury. She quickly jumped up from the embarrassment that she wallowed on the floor in.

"Do you need help, Miss?" Bertha called out as she prepared to run down the steps to help her up.

"No, I'm fine," Julia replied in her snappy, high-pitched tone.

When she was up onto her feet, she quickly started to walk away. As she did, Bertha yelled out to her.

"That wasn't nice. You know God don't like ugly, Miss Jewels!"

Julia turned her head back quickly to look at Bertha, who was still at the top step wearing a large smile. Julia shot her a frown and quickly turned back around and walked away in arrogance to hide her shame.

Bertha shouted out to her again. "See you later, Miss Jewels!"

Chapter 15

Julia's Curiosity and Plan

Julia was embarrassed after she had taken a spill on the steps while trying to sabotage Bertha's hard work. She knew that she had given Bertha a good laugh, which was the opposite of her intentions. She ran outside to the yard to sit on the swing that hang from a tree. Her uncle had made it for her and Sage when they were younger. When she was sure that she was out of sight of everybody in the house, she sat there and began to laugh. She laughed a good laugh from the pit of her stomach. She rolled over onto her side and continued to laugh. She kept imagining the way she must have looked falling down on the steps. She knew that it was obvious to Bertha what she was up to. She imagined the awkward way her body had landed at the bottom step, and she laughed some more. She knew that she had to redeem herself in her mission to annoy Bertha. She knew that the only way to do this was to come up with a better plan that would not involve her being the butt of the joke in the end. She did not want to do any serious damage; she only wanted to get under Bertha's skin a bit.

Across the large yard, Julia saw Sage who was still wearing her pajamas and slippers as she made her way over. The warm summer wind picked up, and Sage's pajama pants fluttered in the wind as she wiped her sleepy eyes right before she reached

Julia. She took a seat next to Julia on the two-person swing.

"What are you doing out here so early?" Sage asked.

"It's seven o'clock, Sage. That's hardly early. And why do you insist on being seen outside of the house in your nightwear?"

"This is my father's land, and I'll wear what I please." Sage had surliness in her attitude.

Trading banter was something that the two girls did effortlessly. It was their way of communicating, and they almost never took what the other said personally.

"Suit yourself." Julia gave her cousin a gleam of disapproval.

"What were you out here chuckling about?" Sage asked. "I saw you from the kitchen window."

"Oh, nothing really," Julia mocked Sage from last night's dinner.

"Oh all right, suit yourself," Sage mocked Julia.

For a moment, they sat there in the summer wind silently, and then Julia had a burning inquiry. "So who is this Bertha from last night's dinner?"

"Oh, you mean the one you humiliated for no reason at all?"

"Yes, Sage, I'm talking about her."

"She's been working inside for daddy for a while now, and even though she gets into trouble sometimes because the girls pick on her a lot, she does a great job. And she's funny and smart. Why do you care?"

Quickly, Julia scrambled for an explanation that would not make her seem overly concerned about the lowly help as she hesitated to reply. "Well, I actually don't care at all. It's just … well, it's just that I don't know how much of a good job she's doing, because she was cleaning the steps this morning and made them too slippery. I fell and nearly broke my back."

"Oh, really?" Sage knew that her cousin was up to something. "Well the steps seemed just fine when I came down them this morning."

Julia folded her arms. She knew that her cousin was defending Bertha and was suspicious about her curiosity.

"Well does she ever work in the garden?" Julia asked. She knew that garden work was the least favorite task for the house workers and had decided that she would somehow get Bertha assigned to garden duty.

"Sometimes…. Julia, I know you. What are you planning?" Sage knew Bertha hated working in the garden.

"Well I, for one, love to work in the garden, and I believe that you can't be adequate help inside of the house until you perfect the art of gardening. I'll see to it that this Bertha helps out in the garden one of these days."

Sage could see the devious, faraway look in Julia's eyes that she wore when she was concocting a treacherous plan.

Chapter 16

Bertha Gets in Trouble

The hot Mississippi sun was beaming down on Bertha, and it seemed to suck the energy right out of her. However, her anger of having to work out in the field again, albeit for a short-term punishment, was pumping adrenaline into her body as she kept hacking away at weeds. Her thin cotton shirt was soaked with sweat from her collar to her waist, and it became sweatier with each passing minute. As she angrily continued to hack away, dirt began to float up into the air and stick to her clothes. She was a filthy, sweaty mess when she heard the gallop of a horse behind her in the distance. Not even this took her focus away from the weeds and the rusty hooked blade that had a wooden handle attached that she used to work.

She was all alone out there serving a punishment for something she didn't do. She was innocent, but because of the deal that she had struck with the bullying sisters, she had to serve the punishment. The horse galloping grew closer and closer until she finally decided to turn around and look up to see who was approaching. She thought that it would be Master Jackson or one of his workers coming to relieve her of her duties in the unwavering blaze of the sun, but to her surprise, she turned around and saw Julia.

"Oh shucks," Bertha mumbled.

The sight of Julia brought a flashback of anger to

the pit of her stomach. "Just when I figured the day can't get no worse."

Bertha and Julia did not have a civil relationship at this point, and Bertha was still offended at the mere sight of Julia, but there was nothing that she could do about it. She turned and awkwardly smiled and then turned back around to resume working on the weeds, which were almost as tall as she was. She did not know what Julia wanted, and for a while, she ignored her presence. Bertha figured that Julia was there to monitor her work and continued. Julia sat on the horse looking on as Bertha hacked away. She and the horse were a few feet behind Bertha, and Julia said nothing initially as she continued to watch. After a while, she decided to say something as she took her umbrella out to block her delicate skin from the sun.

"How long have you been out here?" Julia yelled to Bertha loud enough to get her attention. "You know it's not good to work in these conditions. Even the field workers aren't out here now. They've been given the word to rest until the sun subsides. It's dangerous to be out here like this, you know."

Julia gradually made her voice louder, and the pitch of it climbed with the volume after she realized Bertha was ignoring her. For a few seconds, there was silence, but Bertha eventually replied.

"I don't have no choice." Bertha's voice was low and nearly sounded like the growl of an angry bear. She spoke through her clinched teeth.

"I'm sorry. What did you say?" Julia yelled back from atop of the horse.

Bertha spoke up louder. "I said, I don't have no choice!"

"Well why not?"

At that moment, Julia was seemingly oblivious to the fact that Bertha was a slave and might sometimes have to do things that she did not want to do. Bertha stopped hacking away at the weeds and turned around to look Julia in the face.

"Because I'm Bertha. I'm talented. I'm smart. I'm pretty. I speaks my mind," she said, starting an emotional rant.

"People don't like me for no reason at all. I do the best that I can with what God gave me in this life, but even that ain't good enough to keep folks off me. I works hard, and I mind my own business, and I still find myself, day after day … I be havin' to answer for someone else's wrongdoin' or havin' to defend myself and my doin' all the time and all by myself. I don't have much family on this land, and I have to make my own way."

Tears were in Bertha's eyes. Julia just looked on from the horse and listened with her eyes focused on Bertha as she spoke passionately.

"So today when Mattie come in the kitchen and there was two pieces of chicken missing, she comes to me first." Bertha continued as she wiped a loose tear from her face, and then she turned around and proceeded to angrily hack away at the weeds.

"I said, 'I don't know what happened to the chicken, Mattie.' She said. 'You's a lie, because you and the sisters the only ones who been in here so one of you did it.' I didn't say nothing, so she came and got in my face and started hollerin' because I wouldn't speak up. She told me to get out.

"I said. 'Fine, I'll get out' and she said, 'Don't be givin' me no lip.'

That's what she always say: 'Don't be givin' me no lip,' " Bertha repeated, mocking Mattie.

"She said, 'You was the one that was supposed to be watchin' this kitchen,' " Bertha mocked Mattie again.

"She told me to come out here and hack the weeds until the sun went down and not to come back until I was nearly dead. So I grabbed the weed chopper, and I been out here chopping for about forty-five minutes. I figure I'll stay out here until I pass out dead, because I just can't take this anymore."

"Oh don't be silly; you don't really want to die. Do you?" Julia was trying to calm Bertha and talk some sense into her.

"Now stop overexerting yourself, because it's hot enough out here that you could pass out from heat exhaustion."

Bertha started chopping weeds again, but this time at a slower pace. Julia got off of the horse, put away the umbrella, and then walked with the horse a few yards away from where Bertha was chopping weeds. She found a tree with a generous amount of shade and pulled a large bag from the horse before tying the horse to the tree trunk so it wouldn't wander away. Inside of the bag were a picnic blanket and two canteens of cold water. Julia sat down under the tree in the peaceful and seemingly deserted land where no one was roaming because of the heat. She stretched out the blanket and placed it in the perfect spot in the shade. She pulled out a book that she had taken from Sage's room without Sage knowing. The book was titled *Romeo and Juliet* by William Shakespeare, whom Julia had yet to read the works of. Julia started to read, but she was distracted by

Bertha in the distance still chopping down weeds and growing more and more tired, as Julia could tell even from yards away. Julia decided to put the book down and then walked back over to Bertha carrying a canteen of water. She took two sips from it before she reached Bertha. When she got close enough for Bertha to hear her clearly, she yelled over to her in that high-pitched voice of hers. She was desperate to get Bertha's attention.

"Excuse me. Excuse me!"

Bertha turned around slowly, barely able to hold her own body up.

"Would you care to have some water?" Julia asked.

"No, I'm fine," Bertha replied proudly and stubbornly.

"Please, I really think that you should." Julia walked closer to Bertha and insisted that she have a drink.

Bertha looked up at Julia as Julia came closer to her, and she could see the concern in her eyes. She thought that to Julia, she must have looked to be in dire shape because she could almost sense fright in her eyes. That was when Julia reached her arm out holding the canteen in her hand, and Bertha reached her arm out in return to grab it. Bertha drank the first few sips in gulps as Julia stood there and watched her. She took one last gulp and then reached back out to return the canteen with the rest of the water in it to Julia.

"Oh no, don't worry about it. You keep it. It's all yours. Look, I'll be over there sitting under the tree. When you're done, you can bring it back. I have another one over there with the rest of my things.

If you want, you can come rest awhile in the shade and get back to your work after you've had a little break from the sun."

"Oh no. I'll be fine here, Miss Julia. Thank you for the water." Bertha awkwardly thanked her and was still obviously exhausted.

Julia was happy that Bertha accepted the water and decided to return to the shade. As she walked about a dozen steps back in the direction of the shade tree, she heard the clank of something metal hitting the ground. It was Bertha tossing down the hooked blade, relieving herself of its weight, and she was heading in the same direction as Julia walked. Bertha caught up to Julia with a jog, and the two of them walked silently over to the tree and sat in the shade. At that moment, the wind picked up and the weather became slightly cooler. Bertha sat next to Julia in silence as Julia opened up the book again and read, pretending to forget that Bertha was sitting next to her. As she read, Bertha drank more water, and the wind picked up again, giving them both a refreshing breeze. Julia turned to look at Bertha and broke the silence of the moment.

"Would you mind scooting over a bit?" Julia looked as if something was bothering her.

"No, Miss Julia. But why?" Bertha was confused because she thought that there was more than enough space between the two of them.

"Because you stink," Julia told her without hesitating.

Bertha, not taking offense, giggled a bit and scooted over, happy to be out of the scorching heat. They sat there on the soft blanket under the shade of the tree until the sun began to set on the day. They said next to nothing in comfortable silence as the warm wind breezed gently across their faces. Bertha stared straight ahead in contemplation, reflecting on her terrible day and occasionally turning her head away from Julia to create more perceived distance. Julia sat by her side as her golden locks blew softly in the wind. Every now and then Julia would glance up from the book, and out of the corner of her eye, she would quickly and very discretely look at Bertha, who was lost in her thoughts. Bertha would not even notice the occasional glance from Julia.

That day as they sat there, the wind continued to blow softly and the sun came down and rested in the horizon. Once, Bertha looked over at Julia reading and saw that she was nearing the end of the book. Then Bertha looked away before Julia noticed that she had taken an interest in her reading. The silence continued, and after a while, Julia suddenly shut her book and got up off of the blanket before the evening could grow older. She knew that the quiet time in the shadow of the shade tree with Bertha had to end at that moment. She knew that they both had to get back to their normal daily roles with Bertha as a piece of property and her as a young, privileged, and ambitious woman trying to find her way in a world that limited her success.

When their shared moment was over that evening, Bertha returned to the small cabin in the field slave living quarters where her family resided. Julia returned to the big house to join Sage and her uncle where dinner was waiting. This was normal. This was what they were born into. However, for those short hours in the shade of the tree, all was calm and all seemed to be fair. During that time, they were just two young women sitting under a shade tree in a perfect world, seemingly created for them at that moment.

Chapter 17

Logan and Julia

It would be a few years before Julia returned to Master Jackson's for an extended stay and actually had the chance to fulfill her mission of torturing Bertha with garden work. The family's Fourth of July celebration that year was cancelled at the last minute because of a rift between Julia's dad and Master Jackson. The rest of the family never showed up to meet Julia at Master Jackson's home that year. She stayed there about a week with only Sage, Master Jackson, and Aunt Margaret and then headed back to boarding school straight from her uncle's home.

Upon graduating from boarding school, Julia traveled to the North and worked at a small hospital in Philadelphia, Pennsylvania, helping to care for female patients. At the time, women were not allowed to care for men. She planned on staying in the North, because she had grown very comfortable with the life of Northerners, and her father approved it as long as she would marry and establish a secure life soon after. She thought that marriage would be a drag and an inhibited kind of lifestyle. She thought being married would turn out to be very much unlike the life that she had imagined for herself as a child when she envisioned traveling the world as a doctor and missionary and healing the world's sick. However, she loved the North so much that she agreed to marry a guy that her father approved of and live a much more settled and stationary life away from the slaveholding states of the South.

She started seeing a guy a few years older than she was whom she met in the public library while studying techniques for her job as an assistant at the hospital. He was from an extremely wealthy family. His family was part owner of one of the first companies to build an intercontinental railway system that transported economic goods and human cargo across multiple states in the South. His name was Logan Thompson. He had brown hair, a masculine and attractive jaw line, and a tall and skinny frame, standing about six feet, two inches. Julia loved tall men. He had pasty white skin, and she was amused by his aloof and goofy demeanor. He made her laugh, and she loved to laugh. He was a good guy who was smitten by her the minute he saw her for the first time sitting quietly and all alone in the library. She was sitting at a circular table that day and twirling her hair with her fingers; her head was buried in a large, thick book while she seemed to be taking tedious notes.

That day Logan walked confidently through the aisles of the library while searching for materials for his mechanical engineering class at the University of Pennsylvania. He was extremely handsome. Women at the university flocked to him, but almost none of them seemed to interest him; he turned many of them down for dates. He was picky when it came to women. He not only loved a beautiful face, but he would fall in love with a beautiful personality. He had everything he ever wanted except for a woman to love. He thought that he wouldn't find what he was looking for in a woman until late in his life.

However, this would change when he first saw Julia in the library. That moment was pure serendipity for him.

It was a Friday afternoon in March, and being so accustomed to the outdoors, Logan would have rather been doing something in the open air as opposed to being in a dimly lit library that smelled of old books and aged wood. However, he was a procrastinator and a bit of a lazy student. Of course, he had waited until the last moment to finish up an important paper on railroad engineering, which was due Monday. Logan was extremely bright, so he was not worried about not doing well on the assignment. He knew that he had given himself just enough time to finish and still a good grade if he worked on it the entire weekend.

For a second, he discretely stared at Julia from across the room, watching her through the small spaces in one of the very tall bookcases that towered in the library. After a while, he began to feel like a creepy stalker watching her, so he grabbed two of the books that he needed, walked over, and took a seat at a table very close to where she sat, still captivated in her studies.

Logan removed his backpack and opened it to retrieve his notebook. He sat down and opened the first of the two books that he'd picked from the stacks. Before starting his studying, he looked over at Julia, who still had not looked up from the pages of the book in front of her. Again, he discretely watched her, but when he was unable to make friendly eye contact with her, he looked away.

The tables were not equipped for a guy of his size, and as he sat down, his knees and thighs bumped the bottom of the table slightly. This left him sitting a bit awkwardly. He tried to reposition himself to appear a bit more comfortable and relaxed just in case the girl with the beautiful long locks ever glanced up from her note taking. As he adjusted himself, he made more noise, and the thud of his knees hitting the table caused Julia to casually glance over in his direction, which caught him off guard, and he quickly looked away nonchalantly. He was very nervous and cracked a nervous, crooked smile, the kind of smile that he never failed to make in embarrassing situations. His heart was pounding at the thought of his embarrassment, but he did not want to let the fact that he was a little rattled show.

Logan gathered himself and focused on his work. About fifteen minutes passed, and he could not help but to continue to stare at the pretty girl sitting nearby, enveloped in her studies. He was intrigued. She was wearing a pastel blouse with elaborate detail that made her skin appear soft and delicate. She wore an earth-toned skirt that reached her ankles and made her appear sophisticated and professional. Across the back of the chair was a spring jacket that appeared to be made of expensive material. He loved a well-dressed woman, and this made it even harder for him to focus.

He concocted a plan to get her attention. He tried walking past her a few times, and luckily for him, the path to other books took him right past Julia's table. He periodically made his way past her table without succeeding on getting her to notice him. On the first trip, he coughed as he past, but she didn't look up. On the second trip, he dropped a pencil and then cleared his throat as he bent down to retrieve it, and she still did not notice him. On the third trip, he dropped his notebook. As he did this, she got up and walked away from the table to return some material that she no longer needed but still did not acknowledge him. By then, he was all out of ideas and was ready to give up. It had been four hours since he had made an unfocused effort to finish his work, and he knew that making any more progress on the project was a lost cause. He decided to pack up and head back to his dorm room. He threw some books into his bag and decided to carry the rest of his things in his hands. That turned out to be a bad idea.

Logan was frustrated by the lack of success in sparking up a conversation with Julia, so he tried to quickly pass her on his way out, this time, without her noticing. In his effort to do this, just as he past her table, another student carrying several books nearly stacked to the ceiling brushed against him. He tried to move out of the young man's way to clear a better path for him as they both passed Julia's table. In his effort to do this, he tripped over his foot and a chair leg that had been protruding from under the table where Julia sat. At that moment, he fell clumsily on his face, causing his paper notes to scatter all around the floor near the table. Meanwhile, the student with the large stack of books looked back at him lying on the floor and chuckled before continuing on his way unscathed and without offering any help. The other young man had noticed Julia too, and he had also tried to get her attention by impressing her. He had grabbed as many books as he could and walked past her table just as Logan was leaving.

With Logan on the floor and paper scattered all around him, Julia looked over at him with mild interest but didn't speak a word. As he embarrassingly crawled around on the floor to gather his things, she decided to ask if he needed help. He quickly said no as he picked up the last of his belongings and pounced to his feet, brushing himself off with his free hand.

"I-I'm fine," Logan stammered. "Thanks for offering to help."

Julia tried not to look overly concerned, so she looked away to ease his embarrassment. When he got to his feet, he left swiftly without looking back, and Julia continued her work. That night Logan lay in bed restlessly tossing and turning, because he could not get Julia off of his mind. He felt ashamed that he had not mustered up the courage to talk to her or at least ask for her name. He thought that if they met again, she would never take him seriously after witnessing him fall flat on his face. He could not sleep and decided to work on his project through the early morning hours. He managed to focus this time and completed most of the assignment. Later in the day, he decided to go back to the library to return some of the books he had checked out and hoped that he would see the beautiful girl there again. He returned his books at the front desk and made his way back to the same seat that he'd sat in the previous day.

Logan was there for hours studying and hoping to see her again, but she didn't show up. Soon the sun began to go down, and he became exhausted from studying. He managed to finish his assignment, which would later be acknowledged by his professor as the best paper that he had ever had the honor of grading. Logan finished that assignment swiftly and even had time to begin his next assignment for another class soon after. He worked a bit longer and decided to call it a night. When he had his backpack all packed up, he yawned and made his way to the exit. At that moment, he saw the guy who had been carrying all of the books the previous day and had caused him to trip over the chair leg. He turned around in the doorway to confront him.

"Hey there, you made me fall on my face yesterday," Logan snapped.

"I'm sorry, feller!" The guy continued walking, never coming to a complete stop when he turned his head to respond to Logan. Just as Logan was staring him down, he backed out of the door and bumped right into someone who was coming through the door with a stack of her own books. Logan crashed right into her, causing her to drop all of the materials in her hands. He turned around to see whom he had just rammed into. It was the girl from the library, the girl he'd been thinking about all night. His cheeks turned bright red. Again, he was embarrassed.

"Goodness!" Julia blurted out loud, wanting to rip Logan apart. She quickly bent down to retrieve her things.

"Wow. I'm so sorry."

Logan couldn't have been more nervous, and the word *nervous* may as well have been written on his forehead. He searched for words to rectify the mistake. He quickly bent down and helped Julia gather her things.

"What's the matter with you?" she asked. She was frustrated as she brushed her hair out of her face and bent down beside him. "Do you need to wear an armor suit or something?"

Julia remembered him from falling on the floor the previous day.

"No, no. I-I ... I just. Tu ... well, you see ..." Logan stumbled over his words and tried to explain, but he couldn't find the words.

"It's all right." She had calmed down and took some sting out of her tone in a moment of trying to be understanding. She realized his uncomfortable and apologetic demeanor and actually became charmed by his nervousness and willingness to try to rectify the situation and appease her.

Julia and Logan gathered her things from the floor, and she thanked him for helping her. Then they went their separate ways. Just as they were headed away from one another inside of the library, Logan took a deep breath and decided to make his move. He jogged desperately back over to her before she was out of sight. He knew that this could be his last opportunity to ask her out, and he didn't want to let it pass. When he was near Julia, he called out to her.

"Excuse me! Excuse me, miss! I just can't part without ... well, without at least asking you what your name is." Logan was still nervous and slightly winded.

When Julia turned around, she was surprised to see that it was the clumsy, tall guy standing there again. She looked at him breathing hard and trying to catch his breath while trying not to let it show how winded he was. He had nearly jogged all the way across the large library. She looked at him trying to catch his breath and stumbling over his words and at the same time trying to sound self-assured. He wore a shaky smile, and there was vulnerability in his deep dark-brown eyes that she could not resist as he stood there and waited for her to answer. Somehow she knew that the moment was special, but she did not want it to show.

"My name is Julia." She displayed a nervous smile.

"I just think that you are the prettiest girl that I've seen around here in a long time. I wanted to tell you before, but I haven't found a way to say it to you in a situation that doesn't end with me on the floor."

He tried to calm down and gained a bit more confidence as he noticed her smile.

That moment would be the beginning of a relationship that Julia found more fulfilling than any other relationship she had been in during her young life. They laughed and joked together and took long walks in the park. They became very good friends along with their romantic bond, and Julia felt that the relationship was satisfactory. She knew that if her father met Logan, he would immediately approve. She was sure that somehow and somewhere in the future the two of them would get married and start a life together. To marry a man she could stand and also enjoyed to spend time with was a wonder to her. To be with a handsome guy who she could honestly say she was in love with was a great discovery. Most of the young men Julia had met before did not understand her strong will and ambition. They often began to resent her for it, but Logan was different. He encouraged her to go for her dreams, and he listened intently to all of Julia's superfluous life goals. Not only would he listen, but he would not judge her for wanting things that seemed to be ahead of the time that they lived in.

During the time they became a pair, Julia worked in the hospital, and Logan went to school. They both agreed that when Logan was finished with school, they would take their relationship to the next level. Julia was happy with Logan, but she wanted to keep it to herself, which was why she never brought him to meet her family while they were an item. During the holidays and at family gatherings, Julia would keep things mum when she was interrogated by her mother and father about the mystery guy she was seeing. She never even let Sage in on the details. She was obviously pleased with him, and her family knew it, but she was still the same old ornery Julia she had always been so they did not think much of the situation. The family was patient with her and knew that when she was ready to talk about it more, she would.

Julia wanted to bring Logan to a holiday dinner, but she knew that the Jackson family dinners around the holidays could be a bit tense with the rivalry between Julia's dad and Master Jackson. She also knew that being around her family could be a bit bothersome, and this always tended to bring out the worst side of her personality. She did not want to introduce Logan to that side of her just yet, even though she knew he was the type of guy who would still love her even if he saw that side of her.

Chapter 10

Julia Returns

After two years of working in the North and being with Logan, Julia made a tough decision to return to the South. Aunt Margaret's illness had lingered for years. She was barely eating and began to lose a lot of weight because of her poor appetite. She would be out of bed for about two hours every day, and during most of that time, she limped slowly over to the rocking chair in the bedroom and sat. Many of the best doctors in town had come to offer their expertise, but none of them knew what exactly was causing the illness.

Dr. Johns was the only medical professional who could give Master Jackson and the family a true understanding about her condition. Dr. Johns studied microbiology and led some of the first nineteenth-century studies on immunology. He knew there was a malfunction in Margaret's body causing her to be susceptible to many illnesses, but this type of study wasn't advanced enough to treat her or provide a chronic diagnosis. Margaret had been affected by symptoms of fever, diarrhea, coughing, and severe aches and pains. Her symptoms would improve many times but later come back worse. She had a bout with the measles that nearly killed her, but she recovered; however, she would soon face other illnesses.

Dr. Johns prescribed pain suppressants, suggested some herbal remedies such as tea with larch that seemed to work many times, and advised Margaret to drink a lot of water. There wasn't much else that could be done. He also advised Master Jackson to hire an in-home caregiver to give Margaret the type of medical attention and end-of-life care she needed. He knew that this would be best for the family, giving them someone who would be there regularly to monitor the dosages of the highly potent medicine that Margaret would require and to comfort her.

Master Jackson knew Julia had been working in a hospital. He offered her the job to care for Margaret, and she immediately accepted. Surprisingly, she was excited to return to the South. It took several days on the train to get to Mississippi from Pennsylvania. During the long ride, she thought about helping Margaret get better and was optimistic about it. She also found herself thinking about Bertha Oliver. She got a few good laughs from reminiscing about the previous time she visited. She was interested to find out how Bertha was doing even though she did not want to admit it to herself. Exemplifying her loneliness throughout her life, Bertha was the closest thing to a friend that Julia had other than her cousin, Sage. Somewhere deep in her subconscious she really missed her. Bertha made her laugh even when she didn't want to laugh.

When they had met during the Fourth of July holiday a couple years ago, when the family celebration was canceled, their bond had blossomed without them even realizing it. It was a human connection that they'd made that year; they understood it but could not explain it.

Julia remembered when Bertha had served her

food a little while after she berated her about her hands the day that they first met. What Julia didn't realize that day was that the girls in the kitchen were all cackling quietly in the back, standing between the door that divided the kitchen and the dining room. Lucille had shoved the serving bowl into Bertha's chest and pushed her out into the dining room with it as Bertha tried to overpower them and protest serving Julia. The girls were to serve a small dinner to only Sage and Julia, so Miss May had let Sue be in charge of the dinner prep that night while she attended to other business. Bertha had no choice but to go out and serve her at that point. She gave Sue and the girls a scowl and clinched her jaw. Then she turned around, straightened herself up, and walked over to Julia with pride and dignity as the girls all snickered in the back, waiting for her to be defiled.

Julia recalled the conversation that followed.

"Miss Julia, I'm sure you don't care for the likes of me, and ya didn't look too happy sittin' here waitin' on us to serve up this dinner, but the girls in the kitchen made me serve tonight. Yes my hands a bit rough, but I can't help that. I mean, to keep you from hollerin' at me like you did the other night, I reckon I would cut my hands off and serve this to you without them, but I don't think that's anywhere doable."

"What are you serving tonight?"

"Miss Julia, they gave me corn."

"Corn is my favorite. You can proceed."

Julia remembered the relief on Bertha's face that moment. Bertha was thankful not to be scolded again. It was something about Bertha's personality that she was drawn to. It was something about her that she found amusing.

Julia arrived back on her uncle's land to care for Margaret on a bright summer day in 1861. She was looking forward to being able to help care for her aunt, and although she knew the prognosis was grim, she was hopeful that she could help Margaret's comfort level during her sickness. A carriage was waiting at the train hub to take Julia to the Jackson plantation, and as her carriage made its way onto the land, Bertha was out in the field hacking away at weeds. It had been awhile since they had seen one another, and Julia felt that it was necessary for her to go over and bother Bertha while she worked. She knew that the only reason that Bertha was working outside was because she had somehow gotten herself into trouble again, and Julia wanted to get a firsthand view of Bertha's misery for old time's sake.

Everybody knew Julia was coming to care for Margaret except for Bertha. The girls in the house knew that Bertha and Julia had a peculiar and combative relationship and thought that it would be funny to see Bertha's face when Julia walked in the door. However, their plan did not work, as the two of them connected outside in a field of weeds on Master Jackson's land, as Bertha completed yet another punishment.

"Well I see that nothing has changed around here." Julia spoke from her carriage. "You still get in trouble, and you still smell of feet and dirty linen."

She had been overly anxious to take the first insulting crack at Bertha.

Bertha turned around at the sound of Julia's

voice and donned the palest look that a Southern Negro could possibly wear. It was as if all of the blood had drained from her face. Inside, her heart pounded. They were both happy to see one another again after so long, but they were both too stubborn to give the other the satisfaction of showing it. They certainly did not want anyone else to know.

"Hi, Miss Julia."

That was the only thing Bertha could think to say. Julia said nothing more and turned her head and motioned for the horses to continue pulling the carriage. Off she went to park her carriage at the front door of the big house, leaving Bertha behind in her dust.

Just as the girls in the house imagined, the Julia versus Bertha saga continued to their entertainment. One day when Julia was cleaning out the kitchen, she found bottles of spoiled milk and honey that had been inside for some time. She developed a plan to torture Sage, so she filled a bucket with the gooey milk and then dumped in the old honey that she had found in the pantry into the mixture. She added water and had a recipe for a great prank on her cousin. However, Sage walked in and caught Julia in the action of mixing up the concoction, which killed the plan.

"What do you think you're going to do with that, Julia?" Sage questioned. She knew that Julia was up to something, and this time, she was not going to be the victim.

"I'm not up to anything." Julia had the bucket in her hand as she eyed Sage.

"Julia, don't think about it!" Sage yelled as she

ran a few steps and grabbed a large wooden spoon for her own defense.

"What are you going to do with that, Sage?"

"You will find out if you try to dump that bucket on me."

At that moment, Julia knew that her plan had been thwarted. Even if she threw the contents of the bucket on Sage, it would not be as fun as it would have been in a surprise attack. Julia gave up and placed the bucket on the kitchen counter. She went to the kitchen window and saw Bertha outside working alone. Julia strained her eyes to get a good look. Then she turned around to Sage, who had hopped up on the counter and taken a seat next to the bucket of slop.

"You should get rid of this crap." Sage crinkled her face and covered her nose at the smell of it.

Sage eyed the bucket and then grabbed an apple from a nearby basket and took a bite. Her comments were ignored by Julia, who was still looking out of the window.

"What's she doing out there again?" Julia's lips tightened from disappointment.

"Who?" Sage questioned.

"Is that Bertha working out in the field again?"

Sage hopped down off of the counter and looked out. "Yes, that's her. She must have gotten into trouble again. She does this every once in a while. Poor Bertha. She's too smart for her own good sometimes."

"Well I'll teach her a lesson. If she keeps getting into trouble, I'm going to make reprimands worse for her." Julia looked over at the slop in the bucket.

"Julia, don't think about it!"

"Well it's really hot out there, and she needs to be

careful in the sun. This will actually cool her down a bit." Julia had a mischievous grin as she looked over at Sage, who was still protesting. "Look, it's either her or you. Now get out of my way."

Julia quickly grabbed the bucket and stormed out of the door. She boarded Master Jackson's carriage and rode a short distance over to Bertha.

"What are you doing out here, Bertha?" Julia yelled to her from atop of the carriage as she looked down at Bertha working in the field. She didn't reply and kept working.

"Well are you hot? It's easy to get exhausted from the sun in this kind of weather, Bertha."

Bertha continued to ignore her, which immediately annoyed Julia.

"Excuse me! I asked you if you were hot!" Julia yelled.

Bertha turned around in her frustration and yelled back. "What do you mean am I hot? I've been out here in this hot sun for thirty minutes! Yes, I'm hot!"

Just before Bertha could get another word out of her mouth, she felt a splattering of liquids coming across her face. She was stunned. She screamed a loud shriek as she backed away, gasped, and tried to wipe her face. It took her a few seconds to figure out what had just happened as Julia rode away laughing. Sage watched from the kitchen window shaking her head in disbelief that Julia had the nerve to do such a thing.

After being doused with spoiled milk, honey, and water, Bertha was irate and sat down on the hot, sun-beaten soil to think of a plan to get back at Julia. She had sticky milk and honey all over her clothes, and flies and insects were starting to swarm her. She was even getting stalked by bumblebees. She had to stay out in the field for the rest of the day in that condition, and there was nothing she could do about it. As she sat there and took a break from her duties, Bertha continued to plot.

She knew that she would probably get put on the whipping post for her plan, but she was so upset that she thought it would be worth it. It was almost two o'clock in the afternoon, and she knew that it was time for Julia's weekly trip into town for shopping. She knew that Julia would be taking Master Jackson's carriage, the one with the wobbly back wheel. The wheel would tend to get stuck in a ditch if the driver wasn't careful. Bertha developed her plan of revenge against Julia with that thought. There was a garden shovel nearby. Bertha walked a distance and started to dig a small hole in the path that she knew Julia would be crossing. This area was not far from where Bertha was working.

Bertha knew that she had to work fast, and she had just enough time to dig. She dug a hole steep enough to trap the wheel and cause a huge problem for Julia if she rode over it at the right speed. She was pleased with her work and disguised the hole with some loose plants, leaves, and dirt that were lying on the ground. After that, she waited in the distance for a speeding Julia to get stuck. Sage would always advise Julia to watch her speed while driving the carriage, but Julia never listened. Finally, Bertha saw Julia riding by, but this time, she was actually going a reasonable speed. Julia looked over at Bertha who was still soggy and sticky and laughed at her. She waved at Bertha and kept on her path. Bertha waited and waited for the big moment, but Julia made it by without going over the ditch, and Bertha thought that her plan had failed. She was soaked in filth just for Julia's own amusement, but she kept working out in the field and serving her punishment.

Soon the day grew old, and it was time for Bertha to head back into the house and check out with Mattie. As she headed toward the house, she heard a rumbling in the distance. It was Julia speeding on the carriage. Bertha turned and curiously looked over her shoulder, and then she watched the magic happen. Julia speeded up to the area where she had dug the ditch. Bertha paused in shock as if her body were frozen there in time. Her mouth was gaping because she knew that this moment was almost too good to be true. She knew that she might finally get revenge on Julia.

Sure enough, Julia's speed got more rapid as she neared the hidden ditch. Then, and executed almost perfectly with a loud thud and crash, the wobbly back wheel got stuck in the small ditch Bertha had dug earlier. Not only did the wheel get stuck, but because of Julia's high speed, the wheel popped off, leaving the carriage skidding out of control with Julia still on board. The horses pulled back to stop the motion, but one horse fell over onto its side. This calamity sent Julia flying through the air before landing in a field of dirt and dust, with only dried weeds to cushion her fall. It was such a beautiful sight to Bertha that it almost brought a joyful tear of laughter.

Bertha could no longer hold in the laughter, so she let it loose and ran the distance over to the wreck to see if Julia was all right. Julia quickly pounced onto her feet, trying not to look foolish in front of Bertha, who still wore the soiled clothes that had dried to a crust.

"Are you all right, Miss Julia?" Bertha asked.

"I'm fine."

Julia tried to catch the air that had been knocked out of her when she landed. Somehow she knew that Bertha had something to do with the accident, but she never confronted her about it. They left the wreckage of the carriage out in the field along with the scattered goods that Julia had purchased during her trip into town that day. They both slowly crept back to the house like crippled senior ladies.

Bertha held Julia up by throwing her arm around her shoulders because she had begun to limp badly. Julia was a bit battered and scraped from her accident, but she moved slower to exaggerate her injuries for extra sympathy. Bertha was worn out from her day of hard labor in the Mississippi sun, so she had no problem moving at a slower pace. Master Jackson and Bob Jenkins would later retrieve what Julia left behind in the wreckage.

Chapter 19

Working in the Garden

Julia knew she would eventually get Bertha back for the carriage accident, and she knew garden work was the best way to do it. So when the right time of year came, she put Bertha to work in the garden, which was something she had been waiting a long time to do.

It was a perfect day to start gardening, and Julia was standing in Master Jackson's expanded garden that now covered about a quarter acre of land. It was the time of year for turning over the ground and planting seeds so that the vegetables could mature enough to be ready for picking during the fall harvest. Julia stood there patiently with her arms folded, waiting for a slow-moving Bertha, who was making her way across the field to the area where Julia was standing. Bertha was carrying gardening tools in both hands, and the bulky items were weighing her down. Julia stood there in the distance and watched, very amused at Bertha's expended effort. She felt bad for her and wanted to help while simultaneously enjoying Bertha's struggling as more entertainment.

Bertha made her way to the garden carrying the unwieldy garden tools, and the minute she reached Julia, she dropped everything on the dirt ground in exhaustion. The ground was bare and cold with no seeds yet planted. Bertha hid an intense anger with a forced smile that made her facial muscles tighten. She hid her lower back pain with an erect posture as she stood up straight and placed her hands on her hips. She wanted to appear strong and did not want to give Julia the satisfaction of seeing her miserable.

"All right, Miss Julia, I'm here now just like you wanted me."

Bertha looked Julia in the face. There was a burning anger in the bottom of her stomach that she had to hide with every muscle in her body. She was furious, not because of the garden work, which she hated, but because she knew that Julia was doing all of this just to annoy her. She knew that she was powerless against Julia considering the circumstances, so there was nothing she could think of to do to stop the harassment or to get revenge again. Julia paused for a moment and looked Bertha over from head to toe. Bertha was standing there with her hands on her hips and a light gloss on her face from sweating.

"Well ain't you a bit of a sweater, my dear?" As she spoke, Julia looked at Bertha and grimaced in disgust.

"Well, ma'am, I am, and I'm sure it's how I keep this pretty figure," Bertha replied with a smirk not making eye contact with Julia.

"Huh?"

Julia was bewildered by the response, but very amused.

"I eats a lot of junk—pig guts, pie, cornbread—but I reckon I sweats it all off by the way I sweat. It gets even worse in the summer days, around late July."

Bertha was now looking Julia in the face and noticed that she was wearing her hair down and not up in the ponytail she normally wore when she worked. As Bertha was trying to make sense of why Julia had her hair down to work, her thoughts were interrupted by Julia's high-pitched voice.

"All right, this is what we're gonna do." Julia started giving directions as she bent down and grabbed a hoe. "My daddy always said that you can't be good house help until you learn how to grow the vegetables that we need in the kitchen. Now I'm gonna be here awhile helping Auntie Margaret get better, so you just better get used to the likes of me. Uncle has expanded his garden, and since you and I are alone today, we can't get to it all, but we are gonna work on a small portion. We'll be planting tomatoes, potatoes, and cucumbers. Tomorrow we will start with tomatoes. This will be a few days' worth of work. I figure by the time we're done, you should be broken in good enough to figure your way around any garden."

"Miss Julia, I know my way around any garden now, but that don't mean I like to do it. And besides, if we ain't plantin' nothin' today, then what we doin'?"

"Today we have to get the ground ready by turning it over. Don't you know anything about gardening?"

"I do.... Well, actually, not much."

An idea popped into Bertha's head. Since Julia was forcing her to do garden work to get back at her, she would act as if she had no idea about gardening just to make Julia explain things more than once. Bertha knew that this would get under her skin.

"I don't works in the garden very often, Miss Julia. You know I can be dumb as a ox sometimes. Now, what we gonna do again?"

Bertha and Julia worked all day getting the ground hoed and the soil fertilized. Bertha asked a thousand questions and just about drove Julia crazy. They used cow manure for fertilization, which was Julia's favorite part of the evening because Bertha was squeamish at the odor of the manure. To fertilize the ground, they had to get down on their knees and massage the manure into the soil with their bare hands. After Julia saw Bertha's squeamishness at the smell, she insisted that this was the best way to do it. Bertha's eyes watered, and she gagged until some of her partially digested food came up. She held it inside of her mouth, not knowing if she should spit it out on an area of the ground where food would be grown.

"Oh just spit it out, Bertha!" Julia hollered. She felt sorry for Bertha but pretended to be annoyed. "You're like an overgrown child or one of those city slickers in the North who don't know jackrabbit when it comes to the countryside."

Bertha spit out the small amount of puke, and it nearly landed on Julia's boot.

"My goodness, Bertha! I didn't tell ya to spit it on me!" Julia threw a dramatic fit as she usually did.

"Well I'm sorry, Miss Julia, but yo' foot was in my way. Had it not been there, that wouldn't have happened"

Julia gave her a look, a look that was backed by a sharpness that could shoot right through a person and this made her feel small and transparent. Bertha immediately switched up her tune.

"So, Miss Julia." Bertha was polite as possible after the sharp look she got. "When are we gonna be done with this for the evening? We been workin' out here all day long, and we's ain't even started plantin' nothin'. In a few more hours, I reckon that the sun be goin' down."

"Oh, Bertha, stop your whining. We've only been out here for about five or six hours. We still have a bit more work to do, and then we will call it a day."

Julia got on her knees again to finish working with the soil. Bertha immediately followed her lead and got on her knees to continue working alongside of her. They continued to work the fertilizer into the soil with their hands, but eventually, Julia was nice enough to let Bertha wear a pair of gardening gloves that she had stashed in her overalls the whole time. When Bertha found out that Julia had been holding out on the gloves, she was completely aggravated at the fact that she had been letting mud and manure touch her bare and already rough hands unnecessarily.

"Well ain't you gonna wear a pair of gloves too, Miss Julia?" Bertha asked. She thought that no woman in her right mind would touch mud and manure that smelled so horribly with her bare hands if she didn't have to.

"No, I'm not. I've been doing this all of my life, and you know what? This mud is actually good for your skin. Every time after I've spent a day in the garden with it, my hands feel like a baby's bottom."

"Well I understand ya reckonin', Miss Julia, but why you let me touch the crap?"

Bertha did not get an immediate response. Julia just ignored the question and busily kept herself preoccupied with massaging the soil. Bertha, still not understanding Julia and waiting for a reply, finally decided to put the gloves on so that she could continue to help with the soil. She placed her right hand into the glove and was amazed that it was a perfect fit.

"Oh my," she exclaimed, "I never had on a glove that fit this well."

Bertha had a candid outburst of joy from discovering how a glove that fit perfectly felt on her hand. Julia glanced over at her nonchalantly, but inside, she was pleased that the glove fit Bertha and pleased that Bertha appreciated such a trivial thing. This was a heartwarming feeling for Julia, but she managed to maintain her stoic demeanor.

While putting on the other glove, Bertha took a good look at her right hand and realized that her skin was dry. The small amount of flesh between her right index finger and her thumb had become visibly hardened and flaky. She shamefully put on the second glove, and Julia glanced over and saw Bertha's expression. She pretended not to notice the shame on Bertha's face and didn't comment on her rough hands that day as they continued to work side-by-side in the garden before heading back to the big house for the evening to end the day.

Chapter 20

Stuck in the Mud

In less than twenty-four hours, Bertha and Julia returned to the garden to continue to work. It had rained all night, and the ground they had hoed and fertilized was nice and moist and ready for the seeds to be planted. On one edge of the garden was an incline. When they were younger, Sage and Bertha would often roll down the small hill for fun. Every time Bertha would walk up that side of the garden she would remember all of the fun she and Sage used to have just a short time ago. However, she never mentioned this to Julia, because she knew Julia would be envious. Bertha realized that Julia was a bit envious of Sage because of the way she was able to bond with everyone.

Julia and Bertha took a lighter load out to the garden this day. They brought seeds and digging tools. Bertha was not pleased at being out in the mud, but again, she did not want to give Julia the satisfaction of seeing her miserable so she put on a happy expression and did what she needed to do. They measured out each spot for planting the seeds on a grid, and Bertha was good at that.

"Today is the day that the tomato seeds will be planted," Julia announced.

Bertha did her best at staying focused on the task at hand, but soon, she started to become a victim of her own short attention span. As she was digging with the garden shovel, she quickly became bored and decided that she needed to use the outhouse. There was an outhouse was close to the garden, and Julia gave her permission to take the very short walk over to it. She really didn't need to use the outhouse, but she could not think of any other way to be excused from garden duties for a while.

"All right, Bertha, you can go, but hurry back because we have to get all of the tomato seeds in the ground by the end of the day."

"I'll be back really quick, Miss Julia."

Bertha took off in the direction of the outhouse as if she were in a hurry to get back. She quickly made it over and was planning on hiding there for a while, but she soon grew tired of the smell of urine and feces. She had nothing else to do, so she slowly made her way back to the garden. When she got back, she decided to go up the sloping area that was still very slippery and muddy from last night's heavy rain. As she made her way up and was near level ground, where they were planting seeds, yet another ingenious idea to get revenge on Julia popped into her head. She slowly trotted up the slight slope and then suddenly fell to the ground.

"Help me, help me. I can't get up!" she called out.

Bertha seemed to be in despair, and Julia was a few feet away still on her knees digging and planting tomato seeds. She looked over her shoulder to the area where she heard Bertha's voice and spotted the top of her head and an arm waving desperately for help. She ran over quickly. Her natural instinct to help those in need kicked in and sent a rush of adrenaline through her body. She reached the edge of the slope and yelled to Bertha.

"Bertha, are you all right?"

"Yes, I'm alive! Just help me. I fell down. Grab my hand."

Julia was about an arm's length away standing at the top of the slope. Bertha was lying on the sloped ground on her belly with her face down and was covered in mud. She reached out with her muddy arms for Julia to help pull her up. Julia bent down and reached out to grab Bertha's extended arm. She tugged at her to pull her up and thought that this would be all that Bertha needed to regain her balance and win the fight against gravity. However, she noticed that as she tried to pull Bertha up, she was not getting up as easily as she'd thought. Julia was confused at this because the slope wasn't that steep. She didn't understand why it was so hard for Bertha to get onto her feet.

"Hey, what's going on, Bertha? I'm pulling you as hard as I can. Did you break your darn legs?" Julia was clearly frustrated at the lack of progress with helping Bertha off of the ground. "Get your behind up!"

Bertha continued to slip and slide on the mud, getting halfway to her feet but falling down again numerous times. She was pretending the whole time. Suddenly and right before Julia, who was hanging on to her arm, could get another word out, Bertha yanked Julia down to the muddy sloped ground as hard as she could, causing her to land on top of her. That's when the both of them went tumbling down the slope, alternating one on top of the other like an intertwined ball of mud and goo, getting more slop piled on as they rolled farther down the hill.

"Ahhhh!"

They both screamed. There was a thud and a

splash over and over as their bodies kept hitting the wet ground on the way down the hill. Finally, they reached the bottom of the slope, skidding a few inches on some gravel before coming to a halt. They landed on their backs facing the sky, lying about a foot apart. That's when Julia screamed at Bertha.

"What the hell were you thinking? You did it on purpose!"

Julia sat up. Her eyes were burning with fire. Bertha was still lying flat on her back trying to catch her breath, her mouth wide open.

"I'm sorry," Bertha said. "I just couldn't get to my feets."

Bertha spoke through inhales and heavy exhales as she continued to catch her breath. That's when Julia, in her quick thinking, reached down and discreetly grabbed a handful of mud as Bertha still lay on the ground looking up at the sky gasping.

"Bertha!" Her shrill, high-pitched voice had been put on display. "Apologize now!"

"For what, Miss Julia?" Bertha spoke out boldly as she sat up quickly.

That's when Julia shoved the handful of mud right into her face, with the majority of it going into her mouth. In shock, Bertha jumped up gagging and coughing, and slobbering and spitting, and screaming and freaking out, and running around like a decapitated chicken. After a while of watching this, Julia burst out into uncontrollable laughter. Soon Bertha pulled herself together and was bewildered at Julia's laugher. She paused to watch her laugh, because she had never seen Julia laugh so carelessly before. Even though she was still offended at the taste of grime in her mouth, she was amused as Julia continued to laugh.

Bertha was still a bit embarrassed, so she shouted at Julia. "Stop yo' laughin', Miss Jewels!"

"No, I won't." Julia continued to giggle and laugh. "You should have seen yourself. You did this ... 'Ahhh!'" Julia stuck her tongue out and patted it franticly, imitating Bertha. After that, she burst out into laughter again and lay back down on the damp ground.

Bertha sat down beside her, and pretty soon, she started laughing at herself as well. She found it hysterically funny how silly Julia looked doing the impression of her. They both laughed and laughed together, forgetting all about the task that they had come to complete that day. In their own way, they were enjoying one another's company, as they always would but would never admit.

When they stopped laughing they were pooped from all of the excitement and hard work and soon found themselves lying there looking up at the sky as the wind whipped and made a swooshing noise through their ears. They found themselves together side-by-side, enjoying the symphony of nature, so they continued to be silent.

Bertha was the first to break their silence. "Jewels."

"What is it, Bertha?"

Julia found comfort in Bertha's voice. It was a break from the sound of the wind. However, she answered in her normal, petulant tone that Bertha had begun to disregard.

"That day you offered me the water and we sat

under the shade tree together ... you remember that?"

"Yes, Bertha. I remember that day."

"I suspect God saw that as a mighty thing to do for another person. Thank you."

"Oh ... don't mention it."

Julia brushed off the thank you for her past gesture as if it were no big deal and they ended up having a good time that day, even though they were muddy and still hadn't regained all of the wind that had been knocked out of them when they tumbled down the slope. They had a few laughs to make them forget about the reality of their circumstance. The next day they would revert back to the same hostile treatment toward one another.

They would eventually finish planting the seeds in the garden. With each day working there with Julia, Bertha improved upon her gardening skills and learned more about gardening than she already knew. One day when they were quietly digging in the garden and planting more seeds, their silence became awkward, so Bertha decided fill it with conversation.

"Miss Julia." Bertha's eyes glimmered meekly, bursting with a question.

"Yes." Julia looked over at Bertha in anticipation but still focused on planting seeds.

"What was that book you was readin' that day under the tree?" Bertha asked.

"*Romeo and Juliet.*" Julia didn't hesitate to respond.

"Huh? What's that about? You know my kind not allowed to read, but I do enjoy a good storytellin'. You mind tellin' me about it?"

"It's a play that was written a very long time ago by a man named William Shakespeare. It's a love story about two star-crossed lovers."

"Star-crossed?" Bertha questioned. Her mouth was gaping open and was accompanied by the most vulnerable eyes staring back at Julia as she waited for an explanation.

"Well, the two main characters are Romeo, who's the guy, and Juliet, who is the girl. They are from families who don't get along. Their families have a rivalry, and against the odds, the two of them fall deeply in love."

Julia explained the story as her eyes gazed in the distance, imagining the love of Romeo and Juliet.

"Well do they fall in love and stay happy forever?" Bertha became trapped in the imagination of her own romantic daze.

Julia could see the wonder in her eyes. She was done reading the play and knew that there was a less-than-perfect ending. However, she didn't want to take the joy away from Bertha, so she circumvented answering the question.

"Umm ... well, maybe they do. Maybe there is true love that still exists in this world. I don't know what happens at the end, because I never finished reading it."

"All right."

There was silence for a moment.

"Miss Julia, you don't seem like the type to leave something unfinished. Mattie always say that you always gotta finish what you start."

"Yes, Bertha, that is very true," Julia agreed. "You should always finish what you start."

Julia looked at Bertha as she worked and noticed

that she seemed to carry hope in her eyes of one day finding out the ending to a love story that seemed so fascinating. They continued to work there in the garden silently, both lost in their thoughts. In time, the fruits of their hard labor in the garden would begin to show.

Chapter 21

Aunt Margaret's Journey

It had been several months since Julia had arrived back in town to care for Aunt Margaret, and with her loving care, Margaret had lasted longer than Dr. Johns had predicted. When she first took over as Margaret's caregiver, she found an ailing woman on the verge of death, and she knew that Margaret didn't have long to live. However, Julia was a fighter, and she was not going to give up on Margaret easily.

On her first day as caregiver, Julia walked into a darkened room that was ominous with the threat of death looming, even though the scenery outside was rich and vibrant. Inside the room the beauty of day could not be appreciated, because the curtains stayed closed at the request of Master Jackson. He wanted to give his wife privacy in her sickened state.

The sun was shining and the colors of nature were vibrant and inviting, but there was a grim ambiance inside the room that disgusted Julia. She took over from there. She rearranged the room immediately, as Margaret lay there not able to object to any of the changes even if she wanted to. Julia began grabbing and tossing things out of the room that did not fit the feel of the space that she wanted to achieve. She wanted to spruce it up by bringing brighter things in that she felt would bring a better vibe. She spent most of her first day caring for Margaret shuffling things around and getting rid of old things that she found no use for.

In her mission to change the aesthetics and décor, she looked over her shoulder at the large bedroom window that had thick curtains hanging down covering them, and she was appalled. The curtains did not pose so much of an issue to Julia as the fact that they were pulled shut, doing an injustice to the natural lighting of the space and blocking the bright and warming shine of the sun. When she realized this, she immediately brushed her hair out of her face, walked over to the window, and quickly drew the curtains apart. At that moment, with the most perfect timing, the sun was the brightest it had shined the whole day and maybe even the whole month. It was at a point in the sky where it seemed to hover a few feet right above the window. When the potent light beamed in through the window, Julia immediately turned away from it to wince; it was more than her eyes could bear. The warmth of the light seemed to grab hold of her like an embracing hug. In the background, Margaret began to smile a smile of relief when she felt the warmth come into the room.

Margaret had been lying there with her eyes shut the whole time, and when she smiled, her eyes remained shut. She did not have to open them to recognize or to enjoy the wonder of natural light. This was a feeling that had been kept from her for so long for two reasons. One of the reasons was a protective husband guarding his wife's image in her vulnerable state. The other reason was a husband's shame and will to keep his wife's illness from being a spectacle to inquiring minds who wondered just how much of a toll her lengthy illness had taken on her physical appearance. Because of that,

Master Jackson kept Margaret in the room with the curtains shut, creating as much privacy as he could. However, Julia knew how important sunlight was for recovery. Not only was it good for Margaret's physical well-being, but it was good for her morale, so Julia and Margaret began to bathe in the sunlight that welcomed itself into the room.

In the following days, opening the curtains became the very first thing that Julia did in her routine of caring for Margaret. She would open up the curtains, help take care of Margaret's hygienic needs, feed her, and distribute her medication. Then she would try to get Margaret to do as many physical activities as her weakened body could.

One of Margaret's physical activities consisted of lifting her limbs under her own power while lying in bed. Julia would also try to get Margaret to partake in various stretching exercises, and pretty soon, Margaret was even sitting up in bed with no help. Soon after, Julia got Margaret to walk around the room with her assistance and the aid of Master Jackson or one of the house servants, which was usually Bertha. Bertha was the most afraid of Margret's illness. The girls all thought that because she didn't get along with Julia and was so afraid of Margaret, they would get a good laugh from sending her up to help Julia during Margret's walks.

Margaret's physical health improved steadily relative to the condition that she was in before Julia's care, but her mental state lagged far behind. Many times she was delirious because of the medication that she had been prescribed, and her communication habits and speech patterns were often incoherent. She developed a motor tic where her head would jerk quickly to the side and spring back. She would frequently blurt out words that did not fit into any conversation, and oftentimes, her outbursts would come with no warning at all.

Sometime during the course of lingering in her illness, Margaret lost every care in the world that would motivate her to filter herself before she spoke. As a result, she said whatever she felt. She had been ill for so long that she was happy to be healthy and strong enough to speak and hold a conversation regardless of how much sense she was making. When she regained her speech, it was hard to get her to stop talking. She talked and talked and talked, and this all became a comical spectacle to Julia and Bertha whenever they were able to witness it. They were thoroughly entertained by it.

"This fucking hallway smells like crap!" Margaret yelled.

She became vexed as she walked fragilely down the hall under the assistance of Julia and Bertha. She was being held up on one side by Julia, who had hoisted Margaret's right arm over her shoulder and around her neck. On the other side was a terrified Bertha, who had Margaret's left arm hoisted over her shoulder and around her neck. Bertha was terrified and praying that she didn't catch whatever illness Margaret had, because she was sure that if she did become ill, her care would not be as thorough as the care Margaret was receiving.

"Oh please don't let her cough on me, Lord. Oh please don't let her cough on me, Lord," Bertha mumbled to herself.

"I said the hallway stinks," Margaret repeated. "Or is it this young Negro boy that smells?"

Margaret was referring to Bertha and trying to get to the bottom of the origin of the foul odor. Julia smirked and tried to keep from bursting out laughing, because she did not want to lose her grip on Margaret, leaving a struggling, skinny little Bertha to bear the brunt of Margaret's dead weight. Bertha rolled her eyes and kept up the pace of their slow walk, and Julia glanced over at her just to see the look on her face. Then Julia quickly turned back around and looked straight ahead.

"There is no foul odor, Margaret," Julia answered. "The morning meds must have your senses in disarray. Please focus on walking. You're doing well."

"Tell the boy that he's gripping my back too damn tight for heaven's sake!" Margaret yelled out, and again, Julia had to wipe a smirk off of her face.

"Margaret, that's not a Negro boy. She's a Negro girl, and her name is Bertha. I'm sure that you're just a bit confused by the hair on her upper lip."

Bertha hated being called a Negro. It annoyed her, because she always saw it as a polite way to say nigger. Politely degrading a person was much worse than flat out degrading them in the first place according to Bertha's reasoning. To Bertha, the former was an insult, not only to who she was as a person, but also to her intelligence. Julia knew that Bertha hated the word, and she used it around her just to annoy her.

When Bertha became aggravated, Julia found it humorous. Bertha would make the weirdest faces in those situations. She would often and unconsciously display awkward grins or frowns. The discomfort of these expressions showed that even though she was upset, Bertha would rather not show how she felt. Those moments would create the most uncomfortably awkward faces on Bertha that Julia had ever seen. Those inconspicuous grimaces or head rolls that Bertha would do were some of the many idiosyncrasies that characterized Bertha in Julia's mind. She missed those sorts of things whenever she did not see Bertha for a while.

When Julia looked over at Bertha again, she had one of those looks on her face after being called a Negro and a boy, especially after Julia pointed out her embarrassing upper-lip hair. Bertha loosened her grip on Margaret almost completely, letting her fall off balance out of retaliation. Margaret's weight started to tilt and Julia shot Bertha one of her corrective glares to get her in line. That's when Bertha quickly grabbed Margaret again, stabilizing her weight before a disaster could occur.

"All right, we've walked long enough, and we even made it to the end of the hallway today. Let's turn around right here and go back to the room," Julia announced.

"Julia, your breath reminds me of the scent of horse manure when I was a girl taking walks with father through the countryside." Margaret said this with the most delightful tone of voice. Her tone did not correspond with her insulting words, but she couldn't care less. That's when Julia loosened her grip on Margaret, and Bertha gave her the corrective look this time. She quickly retightened her grip on Margaret, right before she started to tilt. At that moment, Bertha and Julia looked at each other and laughed under their breaths, similar to the muffled snickers of Beatrice and Bernice.

More days of care went on, and Margaret kept

fighting to get better. On one of the days when Bertha was forced to help with Margaret's walk, they did not take her walking at all. When Bertha got to the room at her usual time, Margaret was fast asleep. Bertha slowly and quietly entered and found the room dimly lit with the curtains shut.

"Shhh." Julia directed Bertha as she entered. "Please come in and shut the door quietly. She's sleeping."

Bertha did as she was told. "Would you like me to come back at this time tomorrow?" she asked. "The girls are really busy downstairs, and I'm sure that they could use my help if you don't need me today."

"No, come in and have a seat. I'm sure that the girls will manage. Uncle feeds them well, so whatever amount of work they're doing, I'm sure that they're well rewarded."

"Don't matter what you eatin' if you a Negro eatin' it on a plantation, Miss Julia." Bertha pointed out.

Bertha could have ignored Julia, but she rebutted her just for the sake of rebutting her. Bertha would often rebut the things that Julia said when she got the chance. The way that she would speak would sometimes get to Bertha. Bertha thought that Julia spoke as if she knew it all and had all of the answers in life. However, Bertha knew that Julia would often speak from the point of view of a limited life experience, and many times her comments would be off base and inaccurate. Even though Julia's arrogant demeanor and know-it-all comments were usually annoying, Bertha was sometimes amazed at how Julia spoke so freely and straight from the heart. She believed that this character trait of Julia's helped to define who she was, and it added a genuine honesty to her. To Bertha, there was beauty in this, but even that didn't stop her from correcting Julia anytime she saw the opportunity.

Julia looked at Bertha and nodded her head in understanding of the alternative perspective. Her eyes could not hide the fact that she was amazed at Bertha's courage to correct her. There was something appealing about this to Julia, and she didn't understand why she secretly liked it. She shrugged her shoulders as if it were no big deal. Bertha took a seat, and Julia changed the subject.

"She may wake up any minute now, and then I will need help getting her out of bed, Bertha."

Inside of Bertha, there was a tingle in her gut. Julia had just spoken her name, and coming from Julia, Bertha saw it as a gesture of respect. Julia hardly called Bertha by her name, and usually Bertha didn't care as long as Julia wasn't yelling at her or insulting her like she had the first time they met.

Bertha knew how ill-mannered and ill-tempered Julia could get. When Julia was ill-tempered, it was really tough to be around her. She had a way of getting to Bertha. Sometimes Julia's mean-spirited words hurt worse than anything the other girls in the house said, and Bertha couldn't figure out why. One time, when Bertha was outside washing the shutters while standing on a ladder, she must have irritated Julia, who was inside of the home sitting near the shutters on the opposite side of the window, and Julia rushed out through the door and came over and screamed at her.

"Must you make so much noise while you do that for goodness sake?! I'm going to kick you off of that ladder if you continue." Julia verbally attacked Bertha with no warning that day.

"What am I doin' wrong, Miss Julia? I'm not makin' much noise."

"You're scrubbing the shutters entirely too hard!"

At that moment, Bertha had to remember again what Mattie had told her about Julia as she struggled to keep herself from yelling back, at the risk of a whipping.

"Well, Miss Julia, I'm sorry."

With that exchange, Julia turned around without saying another word and went back into the house as Bertha stood on the ladder still trying to sort out the reason for the unprovoked attack. Julia had become upset right after Bertha and Sage had spent about a half hour laughing and joking around as Bertha scrubbed the shutters. Bertha actually had to tell Sage to leave because she was not getting her work done fast enough. Julia could hear them the whole time through the window. Soon after Bertha shooed Sage away, Julia burst through the front door and yelled at Bertha, completely blindsiding her. Remembering incidents like that, Bertha was flabbergasted and pleased to hear Julia say her name when she was in the room that day. It almost felt like some sort of an accomplishment, and for Bertha, it was pleasant change of greetings.

Julia and Bertha sat there across from one another as Margaret lay there and slept. Bertha sat in an identical chair that was a few feet to the left of Julia's. There was silence for a period of time as the girls waited, but then Bertha became uncomfortable in the idle moment and spoke up in a whisper.

"So how long do you want me to stay in here, Miss Julia?"

Very dispassionately, Julia answered, "She should be waking up pretty soon. It shouldn't be much longer."

Julia was lonely and had been cramped up in the room all day with Margaret without anyone to talk to. Honestly, she did not know when Margaret would wake up and desperately wanted some company, but she did not want Bertha to know how much she wanted her to stay.

"Okay." Bertha let out a sigh of boredom.

The both of them continued to sit and wait there silently for Margaret to wake up. Margaret, in her playfulness, was not asleep at all. She was pretending to be asleep, lying there as still as she could with her eyes shut. She was enjoying the girls in their uncomfortable and awkward moment.

After another stretch of uncomfortable silence, Bertha decided to speak up again. "So, I think that we've been waiting in here for almost a hour, Miss Julia."

"Look, Bertha, if you want to leave, then just leave. All right?" Julia snapped, wrinkling her nose and forehead.

Bertha did not know what to do or if she should take what Julia said at face value, so she slowly got up off of the chair. That was when Julia looked at her with the eyes that Miss May would describe as polished jewels. There was a subtle vulnerability in them that struck Bertha in a way that she had never felt before. Instinctively, she wanted to do something, and do something fast, to remedy that look. She knew that the expression on Julia's face and the look in her eyes was her saying as best as she could, through the barrier of her pride, that she wanted her to stay. That was when Bertha, who had not made it completely off the chair yet, decided to flop back down and remain seated.

"Bertha, I actually don't know exactly when she'll wake up, so I have another task for you if you'd like to help? I'd like to make Margaret some lemonade, but I need help carrying the ladder out to the lemon tree and carrying the basket back. Would you mind going with me to help?"

"Miss Julia, anything would be better than us bein' in this room all day," Bertha answered.

They started to make their way out of the door, and suddenly, they heard Margaret yell out.

"Father, father please catch the tuna!"

They poked their heads back in the bedroom door to check on Margaret and then realized that she was talking in her sleep, which was normal for Margaret according to Julia. They continued on their way and went down the steps and out the door with the fruit basket heavy ladder, which took the two of them to carry. Bertha was in the back and Julia at the front of the ladder, holding it parallel to the ground. They headed right for the lemon tree out back. Julia carried the basket to hold the picked lemons. The lemon tree was in a location where it could be seen through one of the windows in the room where Margaret lay, still pretending to be asleep.

"You know what, Miss Julia? If you wanted me to boondoggle with you, you should have just asked me," Bertha teased.

"Oh don't be ridiculous. Why would I need to spend time with the likes of you?"

"Because you lonely and I know it. It must wear on you to spend all day with a sick woman. I mean, we all need a little company every now and then, right?" Bertha talked as the two of them fumbled around with the heavy ladder.

"That's none of your business. Just help me get this darn ladder stood up, Bertha."

With Bertha's help, Julia was able to open up the ladder and stand it upright. There was a bit of debate between the two girls as to where to put it, but they eventually worked it out.

"My goodness, Bertha, are you going to push the darn thing way over there?" Julia asked. "How the heck am I supposed to reach any of the lemons from there?"

"Oh c'mon, Miss Julia, your arms can't be that short."

"Just help me slide the darn thing over here, so I can get on with this." The high pitch of Julia's voice reared its vicious head again.

"Fine by me, Miss Julia!" Bertha was irritable and quickly shoved the ladder over to where Julia wanted it. "Please don't yell at me. I'm only here to help, Miss Julia!"

Julia had no response as she quickly took a hostile step onto the first rung of the ladder. Then she took another quick step onto the second rung with Bertha standing at the base of the ladder to hold it steady. With another angry half step, Julia missed the third rung on the ladder, and before she knew it, she was falling backward right off of it. Bertha, in her quick thinking, put both of her arms out and tried to catch her, or at least break her fall. When the full brunt of Julia's weight landed on Bertha, it knocked her down, and they both went tumbling. Soon they both hit the ground and burst out into laughter after they realized that neither of them was seriously injured by the short fall.

In the room where Margaret spent most of her time ailing from her sickness, she had gotten out of her bed and slowly hobbled her way over to the window that was a short distance from the bed. Nobody knew that she was well enough to walk under her own strength except for her. The aided walks down the hall, right outside of the room door, were strengthening her as she continued to heal. The walk to the window was some of the first steps that Margaret had taken in several months under her own power. When she reached the window, the curtains were still shut from earlier when she was pretending to be asleep. She cautiously pulled one of them back a few inches, just enough to see the girls out by the lemon tree. She peeped out just in time to see Julia and Bertha fall to the ground.

Margaret witnessed their laughter as they lay there on the ground, and she laughed softly along with them from the distance of the window. They looked like they were having fun. They looked like they were happy, and Margaret hadn't seen a moment like that in so long that it was hard for her to remember the last time she had. She kept watching from the cracked curtain and saw the girls continue to interact. They stopped laughing and got up off of the ground. She couldn't hear what they were saying to one another, but she didn't need to hear them to realize that these were two girls with a special bond. Bertha said something to Julia swirling her head with sass to emphasize her point. Then Julia returned the sass, adding more sass and flailing her arms to emphasize something that she was trying to show Bertha about the ladder.

As Margaret continued to watch, she saw a full range of emotions that displayed the passion each of the girls had for what they were saying. They argued, they yelled, they spoke calmly, and then they laughed. After that, they would do it all over again until the final lemon was picked and they were folding up the ladder and bringing it back into the home along with the basket of about fifteen lemons. It had taken them a half hour to pick the batch, although it should have only taken them about fifteen minutes.

Before the girls got back into the house and made their way back up to the room to check on Margaret, she was back in bed without anyone knowing that she had walked. When Julia peeked inside of the room door, Margaret pretended to be asleep again, so Julia headed back downstairs, where Bertha waited to assist her with making the lemonade. All of the other girls were outside by then doing God knows what, and Bertha and Julia were alone in kitchen as they squeezed lemons and worked.

In the days after there was steady improvement in Margaret's health, and she and Julia took long walks around the land with Bertha continuing to come along on many of the walks to help. Margaret continued to call Bertha the Negro boy because she didn't care to remember her name or if she offended Bertha by this. Margaret thought that Bertha was very pretty, and she found the face that

Bertha would make when she was offended to be amusing. Margaret continued to make fun of Julia's bad breath, and Julia and Bertha would make fun of Margaret's wig behind her back.

One evening Julia and Bertha took turns putting on the wig while Margaret was asleep. The wig was salt-and-pepper colored and very thick, so the girls looked really silly when they each tried it on in the mirror. They goofed around with it and had the most fun and laughs that they had had in their young lives. They never laughed so hard, and they never bonded with another person as much as they bonded with each other that day. They laughed and lived in the moment. It was a blissful moment that the two of them shared together. Julia even became less ornery during the time she began spending more time with Bertha. The whole family picked up on this, but they could not figure out the source of the change in Julia's attitude.

Margaret had outlasted the life expectancy that she had been given by many physicians who had seen her, and many found it to be an anomaly. However, her luck would soon run out. The medication that seemed to work so well before began to fail her, and once again, Margaret became bedridden. She was not talking as much as she had been, and there were no insults coming from her any longer as she, once again, lingered near death. She had been stricken with typhoid fever.

Dr. Johns was stumped as to what went wrong after examining Margaret when her condition worsened.

"Things were going so well, Julia, but it looks like the medication isn't as effective as it was before," he said. "I wish that we could give you an explanation why, but this is a unique case. We've never seen anything like it. Some people are not meant to live. Maybe it's her time now."

Julia stood there with her arms folded, not ready to give up. "What do you mean some people are not meant to live?" she questioned. "That's the most ridiculous thing I've ever heard. I'm gonna ask you to leave and don't worry about coming for a follow up appointment. Your job here is done. I'm getting another doctor."

"I'm sorry. I wasn't trying to offend you, Miss Julia."

"Well you sure did a poor job of not offending me. Now please leave."

"I'll leave," Dr. Johns agreed, "but I'm going to warn you that I'm one of the most prominent doctors in the area. You won't get a better opinion than mine."

He pleaded and tried to reason with her, but she was unmoved by the apology. "Have a good day, ma'am. I'm sorry for Margaret's condition. Please inform Mr. Jackson that I was here."

"Have a good day." Julia abruptly cut him off and showed him to the door.

Margaret's illness was taking over her body, and she knew that her time was getting shorter as she became weaker. Sage had long stopped her daily visits to her mother's room and became more withdrawn. She began to spend more time alone in her room or away from the house and missed out on spending time with her ill mother.

Chapter 22

Logan Returns for Julia

Julia was sitting in Margaret's room on the window seat reading a book, while Margaret lay there in a deep slumber. It was raining heavily outside, and Julia would occasionally stop reading her book and glance out of the window. It had been raining for several days, and Julia could not remember a year when they'd ever gotten as much rain. She was worried about the garden that she and Bertha had put so much time into.

There was a loud knock at the door that startled her out of her daze. She didn't think much about it and kept reading. There was no one in the house except for her and Margaret, who were upstairs, and the servants, who were in the den. The den was now their normal place of waiting out storms.

She began to wonder who was at the door, because her uncle was out of town with her dad attending a very important political meeting concerning the rights of Southern states. There had been rumors going around town that the affairs between Southern and Northern states were getting very tense, and people all over were fearful of the future of the Union. Julia heard the worries in people's conversations when she would go into town, but she never paid much attention to it until she heard these same concerns voiced by her father and uncle, whose opinions she respected. Her dad was a state representative, so his opinions were highly considered by her.

Miss May made it to the door to open it quicker than any of the others in the house, as she always did. When she opened it, she saw a tall guy wearing a long black coat and a black hat. He was soaked with rain. She didn't recognize the young man, so she was hesitant to let him into the house.

"Hello, sir. May I help you?" she asked.

He took the best glance inside the house that he could get with Miss May standing there blocking the doorway. "Hi, ma'am. My name is Logan Thompson," he said, introducing himself. "Is this the Jacksons' residence?"

"Yes it is, but Massa Jackson is outta town." Miss May couldn't help but notice how polite the young gentleman was as he stood there dripping with rainwater.

"Oh, I'm not here to see Mr. Jackson. I'm here for Ms. Julia Jackson. She's a good friend of mine. I understand that this is where she's been residing."

"Come inside, and get outta the rain. Miss Jewels is upstairs with Mrs. Margaret. Wait right here, and I'll go get her."

"Thank you, ma'am. I really do appreciate it."

The graciousness in his voice motivated Miss May to move faster. Logan hadn't seen Julia in many months. They had stayed in contact through writing letters, and Julia began to feel as if they were growing apart and wanted to end the relationship. Her last letter to Logan had been very bleak. He was worried that she might have found another love interest, so he decided to surprise her with a visit. He had finally made it from the North to the door of Julia's uncle's home, and this would be a complete shock to her.

"Miss Jewels," Miss May called as she knocked on the bedroom door.

Julia gave her permission to enter.

"There is a tall and handsome young man downstairs waitin' to see you, and he all soaked in rain. He said his name is Logan, and he's a friend of yours."

Julia's expression reeked of calamity. She had yet to rid herself of Logan and his memory, and she had buried that on her to-do list of indefinite procrastination. Now he was there inside of the house, and she was forced to confront the task of possibly ending the relationship, even though she had not yet made up her mind. She had been apart from Logan a long time and thought that her love for him had faded. She did not have the heart to directly tell him how she felt, but she had hinted toward it in several letters that she'd sent him. He was beginning to get the hint. However, he was not ready to let Julia get away, and he'd dropped everything to come see her.

Although Julia was initially hesitant to welcome him into her town and into her uncle's house, she eventually gave in to his will and soon remembered why she had fallen for him. Julia was then forced to finally introduce Logan to her family, and Master Jackson insisted that he stay in the home on his visit but, of course, in a separate room from Julia. Master Jackson said that there was more than enough room in the spacious home for Logan to stay a few days or however long he wanted to stay.

Logan and Julia began spending a lot of time together again on his visit. They laughed and cuddled up like they had before. Julia began to see less and less of Bertha, and for some reason, this gave Bertha an empty feeling in her stomach. She would cringe when she saw the two of them together. This is why she would often look the other way or go in the opposite direction when they were around her.

Bertha remembered the looks she would get from Julia when Julia would see her spending leisure time with some of the girls from the house. The feeling that Bertha felt when she saw Logan and Julia together could probably be illustrated by those looks Julia used to give her. They were expressions that buried resentment and discomfort. They were jealous looks.

Something had long been going on between Bertha and Julia, and although it was very innocent, they did not understand it. They had bonded, and neither one of them was ready or willing to let go of their special bond, not even after Logan came back for Julia. This, of course, created an uncomfortable moment when in a short time Logan and Julia would be married. Bertha felt like she had lost a friend, and it came simultaneously as Julia was given a large diamond engagement ring.

Chapter 23

The Wedding

During his visit, Logan informed Julia that he was nearly finished with school because he had worked harder and took more classes than normal, although he had put that on hold to come for her. She was very impressed by this. He said he wouldn't go back North without her and worked hard to convince her that their love was still strong. He did all he could to win back her favor. Soon, she would give in to him.

During this time, she still wanted to spend time with Bertha working in the garden, but oftentimes, Bertha was nowhere to be found when Julia came looking for her. She was avoiding Julia, and Julia knew it. However, Julia was not one to give up. One day she searched for Bertha with intensions of forcing Bertha to work in the garden with her like they had before Logan arrived. She found Bertha scrubbing floors in the girls' sleeping area.

"Listen here, Bertha," Julia began, "it's been a while since we worked together in the garden, so stop what you're doing here and come with me."

"Where's Logan, Miss Julia? I'm sure that he can help you."

"Bertha, I don't want no lip outta you. These are orders. Come, or I will grab you by the collar and drag you out there."

Bertha could no longer object. They spent that day picking weeds and doing other aimless tasks in the garden. Julia knew that Bertha was upset at her for something. She even had an idea about why she was upset, but that conversation would have been much too uncomfortable so Julia pretended not to notice that she was getting the cold shoulder.

By the end of the day, when the sun was setting on the brisk evening, the girls hadn't said more than two words to one another, and the silence was heavy with tension. Bertha was told that she was free to go for the day. She looked down at Julia who continued to pick weeds from the garden on her knees. Julia was wearing the same gloves that she let Bertha use the first day that they worked together in the garden—the day Bertha didn't want to get her hands dirty.

"I thought you woulda thrown them away by now, after a Negro wore them."

Bertha stood there as Julia stayed silent and brushed a straggling piece of hair out of her face and continued to work. She was extremely hurt and frustrated by what Bertha said. She never even looked up at her. Her frustration showed in her flushed, red cheeks. When she finally decided to look up, Bertha, who was standing over her trying to figure out why she was still working if their job for the day was done, could see that Julia's eyes were misty, but she made no mention of it. Julia continued to aimlessly work on the ground beneath her. Then Bertha silently walked away. Julia heard the footsteps of Bertha's departure, ignored them, and continued working.

After a few seconds, she could not resist watching Bertha walk away. She looked up and realized Bertha was not heading in the direction she should have been. Julia became even more interested in watching Bertha to see where she was headed. Bertha had taken off in the direction of the shade tree, the tree that they had sat under on the scorching hot day when Julia rescued her from the relentless sun. Bertha took a seat under the tree and stared straight ahead. Julia stood up from her kneeled position in the garden so she could get a better view. Soon, she dropped the handheld shovel she had been working with and headed toward Bertha to have a seat next to her. She quickly walked over and sat beside her. Bertha was glad that she had decided to join her but pretended that she was unaffected by the gesture. They sat there in silence for a while as the wind breezed until Julia could not be silent any longer.

"Bertha, I know that you're upset that we haven't been spending as much time together since Logan has come back, but I still miss spending time with you every day. Sometimes when I'm in bed at night, I laugh to myself thinking of some of the things that we use to do together. I don't want to lose that, and I know you don't either."

"Yeah, but that's life, Miss Julia," Bertha responded. "I'm not mad. I just need some time to get used to it. That's all."

There was silence again until Bertha's thoughts and questions about Logan took over, and she had to get some answers.

"So what he like?"

Bertha noticed a look of joy come across Julia's face after her inquiry.

"He's smart, he's funny, he's really, really nice, and I've never met a guy like him before. I guess he makes me happy."

For some reason, Bertha couldn't completely stand to hear more or to see that look in Julia's eyes, so she got up slowly and brushed herself off as crumbs of dirt landed on the ground next to where Julia sat.

"He make you happy, and you should to be happy, Miss Julia." Bertha forced a smile, and then there was another very short moment of silence as they looked at one another. Bertha was standing and looking down at Julia for a while as Julia remained sitting and looking up at her. Julia began feeling terribly guilty for some reason or another.

"Be happy. That's what we all want, Miss Julia." Bertha struggled to find sincerity as she turned her back and walked away. Before she was out of earshot, Julia stood up and yelled.

"Bertha, wait!"

Bertha turned around, startled to hear Julia call out to her.

"We're getting married!"

"Huh?"

"Logan and I—we're getting married, and I wanted you to be the first to know," Julia shouted. "I haven't told anyone yet."

"Oh, that's good." Bertha nodded her head as she yelled back at her. She forced herself to keep up the false sincerity of her support when she really felt as if someone had socked her in the gut. She turned around and walked away to return to the house so she could check out with Mattie for the day.

The wedding of Logan Thompson and Julia Jackson happened on a beautiful day during the time when the harvest was near and the garden that Julia and Bertha had worked on was fully mature.

Not long after Logan had come to town for a surprise visit, he and Julia were walking down the aisle in a private ceremony that was elegantly set in the large yard of Master Jackson, with two hundred of the couple's closest friends and family.

Just like the rest of the house workers, Bertha was to help out with the wedding. For a reason she didn't understand, this would be the most difficult task she had done in her life. She would have much preferred to work out in the field on the worst day carrying pail of water rather than seeing Julia put a dent in their bond when she accepted Logan in marriage.

Bertha felt so alone; their bond was the only thing she had grown to look forward to in her misery. She knew how she was feeling, but she did not admit it. She pretended as if everything was fine, but deep down, there was something wrong with her that day. The other girls in the house, who had come to know her well, could sense something too. She was not her usual, happy-go-lucky self and seemed to be unfocused during the preparing of the food. She had burned three dishes she had been assigned to cook. She was working on the last nerve of Mattie and Miss May with her lack of focus, so they excused her from cooking duties and made her help set up the dinner tables outside for the guests that were to arrive soon. She spent hours helping with preparing and decorating the yard for the guests along with the other girls.

"Look at her over there lookin' dazed and confused. What's gotten into her?" Lucille asked. She just had to speak on Bertha's demeanor that day.

"I don't know. You would think Bertha would be

happy that somebody gettin' that crazy hen Julia out from under our noses. Lord knows I can't put up with her for much longer." Bernice looked over at Lucille for confirmation.

"You can say that again, Bernie. She may be pretty and have the best head of hair I seen on a white woman, but the girl got the worst attitude, and her breath smell like spoiled hog guts."

"Come on y'all she ain't that bad but her breath smell worse than I look." Agnes inserted herself into the conversation. "And she got the nerve to get in somebody's face, yellin' and whatnot."

"If her breath smell worse than you look, then it smells really bad, because you sho' is ugly," Myrtle blurted out and threw in her two cents as she walked up from behind. The girls all burst out laughing.

"Myrtle, that's the truest thing I heard you say in a while," Bernadette announced as she casually looked over at Myrtle. They all stood among one another looking on at Bertha.

As Bernadette, Lucille, Myrtle, and Bernice watched Bertha work from a short distance away, they continued to whisper and speculate about Bertha's body language and attitude.

By two o'clock that afternoon, the newlywed couple had said their vows and was now Mr. and Mrs. Logan Thompson. The celebration after the ceremony was lively. Guests were dressed in their best garments. Even the help had received special new clothes to wear that evening to serve. There was an endless supply of drinks and food. The celebration was very extravagant, and Julia's dad and Logan's parents had each competed to see who could spend the most money on the wedding. There was a live band, there were fireworks, there were white doves released, and there was the best of the best in every aspect of wedding celebration for its day.

Bertha's awkward demeanor continued throughout the evening and seemed to get worse as the night went on. Things got really bad when Bertha began to serve champagne and wine to the guests. She had been sneaking in the back and drinking out of each bottle of wine and champagne. She thought that the alcohol would help her relax, and the first couple of drinks did; however, she started to lose count of her alcohol intake, and the drinks started to catch up with her. The other house workers had also stolen a few drinks, but most of them quit drinking before they became noticeably drunk. Bertha did not make this wise decision. The girls knew that she was continuing to drink, and they found it entertaining. When they were told that they were done serving guests at ten o'clock that night, they decided to stick around and watch a drunken Bertha subtly stumble around, carrying wine glasses on a tray. She continued to serve, not getting the message that they were done for the night. Bertha had chosen to work alone and stayed away from the girls that whole night. She didn't speak to them or offer any help. They thought that not telling her that they had received orders to stop working for the night would repay her for her antisocial behavior. By this time of the night, Mattie was busy with the large crowd of guests, so she couldn't keep her usual tight leash on the girls.

"Whew!" Bertha yelled over the loud music of the band. "Anybody wants some mo wine?"

As she tried to intrigue the guest with the

selection of wine she was serving, she did a little dance. One of the glasses on the tray slid, but she regained the equilibrium of balancing the glasses and kept them from falling off and shattering. She was quite proud of herself for this recovery until an equally drunken man bumped into her, and red wine spilled all over his white shirt.

"I'm sorry about that, mister," Bertha said.

He looked down at his shirt and started to stumble away, not too concerned about the spill or his partially alcohol-soaked shirt.

"Let's keep up the festivities!" The man yelled out, immersed in party mode, and stumbled away from Bertha as he wiped himself off with a white napkin.

Julia had been discretely watching Bertha from the table where she sat with Logan and the other guests. She had figured out that Bertha was drunk after a few minutes of watching her erratic behavior. Julia was on pins and needles trying to figure out a way to save Bertha from her drunkenness without bringing too much attention to the situation. After Bertha spilled the wine on the guest, Julia had seen enough. She waited for the perfect moment to intervene. She watched Bertha walk back into the house, probably to grab more wine, and she slowly rose from the table.

"Honey, I'm going to go inside for a while. There is something I want to fetch to show our guests."

Logan was consumed in an effervescing conversation with the male guests at the table. He stopped what he was saying and turned to Julia. "That's perfectly fine, honey."

He stood up and gave her a huge hug and newlywed kiss. Then he sat back down and continued where he left off. Julia walked away with a strained smile to be as inconspicuous as possible, careful not to show too much concern. Then she quickly shimmied off after Bertha.

Bertha had spilled a couple of glasses of wine all over herself and was sitting up against the kitchen wall in the midst of the mess not able to get up off of the floor and pull herself together, and she had given up trying. Bertha knew that she would soon be discovered there on the floor. At that point, she did not care because she was too drunk. She had gulped down the wine too fast, and now it was taking its toll on her. She sat there and closed her eyes and waited. She thought for sure that this incident would lead to her first whipping, and then she passed out on the kitchen floor.

As Bertha was passed out she was not aware that all of the other girls who worked in the house were all hiding in a nearby pantry, peeking out at her, and laughing their guts out while trying to be as quiet as possible. They found the moment to be one of the most entertaining things they had ever seen, and they continued to peek out at Bertha there on the floor, muffling their own drunken giggles. They laughed and watched even though they should have been helping her.

"All right, I seen enough. I reckon we go out there and get the stupid thang up off that floor." Lucille took leadership and tried to rally the girls to go help Bertha.

She stumbled over her own foot trying to make her way through the crowd of girls hiding in the pantry, and they all burst out laughing.

"Shhh! You fools! We can't let folks know we in

here like this." Pearly demanded the girls to quiet down.

"That's right!" Agnes slurred her speech.

"Oh shut yo' ugly self up! Ain't nobody gonna know we in here. They all drunk too." Beatrice stared Agnes down to show her up.

Suddenly, they all became distracted by Bertha's coughing and saw that she was slumped over and puking.

"Oh goodness! We gotta go get her or she gonna choke on her own mess." Lucille now had a sense of urgency and made a brave break for the door.

"I'm not goin' out there with you!" Isabelle shouted. "No, no, no. Not me."

Lucille opened up the door to walk out and rescue Bertha from her drunken stupor, but before she could push the crowded group of girls out of the way and get to Bertha, she saw Julia burst through the door in her wedding dress. The white dress had a long train that was now off-white in spots from dragging on the ground and celebrating in the outdoors. Lucille's eyes widened when she saw Julia, and she quickly ran back into the pantry and shut the door before she could be seen.

"Oh my God." Lucille blurted as she tried to warn the girls. "She out there!"

"Who out there, Lucille?" Isabelle was frantic and even more terrified than before.

"Jewels is out there!" Lucille was in official panic mode.

"Well it was nice knowing you, Bertha." A drunken Bernice found it to be a good idea to yell out from their hiding spot giggling.

"Oh my God! This is bad." Agnes yelled to the girls

and Pearly told her to shut up. Agnes and Pearly were not as drunk as Bertha but much drunker than the other girls. Pearly was worried but Agnes began panicking as much as Isabelle.

"It was nice knowing yoooou, Bertha." Pearly almost yelled through the door, right before Bernice roughly tapped her shoulder to quiet her down.

Julia had made her way into the kitchen and heard Pearly's indistinguishable voice come from the pantry. She turned and looked, but at that moment, she saw Bertha on the floor coughing and quickly ran over to her and kneeled down, ignoring the voice.

"What do you think you're doing? Are you trying to ruin my wedding?" Julia reprimanded Bertha, whose eyes were still shut.

She slapped Bertha across the face just enough for the sting of the blow to wake her up. This jolted her out of her drunken stupor, and she opened her eyes. Julia's shimmering eyes were the first thing that she saw, as Julia was kneeled down nearly nose-to-nose with her.

"Well gosh damn, Jewels. I've never seen you up this close before. Ya skin look a mess up this close today. Have you been stressed out, Jewels?"

Bertha was filter-less with her line of questions in her drunkenness. Then she started to cry.

"You don't deserve skin like that, Jewels. I'm so sorry. Nobody deserve skin like that. You know them girls say that ya momma drank rum when she was pregnant with you, and that's why ya skin look like a old banana peel. Darn that momma of yours."

Bertha wiped a tear from her eye and then started laughing at Julia's blemishes.

Ignoring Bertha's insults, Julia reached down

and placed Bertha's arm over her shoulder and tried to pull her up off of the floor. Julia got Bertha about halfway up before she lost her balance in her high-heeled shoes, and they both tumbled over. Julia nearly twisted her ankle, and Bertha fell back and bumped her head against the wall.

"Ouch!" Bertha yelled out after her head made a thud against the wall.

The girls hiding in the pantry were peeking out through the slightly cracked door and nearly blew their cover laughing at Bertha insult Julia and watching them tumble to the floor. They quieted down and continued to watch. They saw Julia kick off her shoes and finally successfully attempt to pull Bertha up. Julia knew that Mattie was around the place somewhere, and she decided that she would take Bertha to her so that Mattie could handle her. She found Mattie on the other side of the house cleaning puke off of the floor.

"Mattie, please get her and keep her out of my sight for the rest of the night!" Julia demanded. "I'll have you know that she's been drinking a lot, and I'm sure you're happy to know about that!"

"Oh my. What was you thinkin'? I'll kill you myself!" Mattie rose from the floor and stared directly at Bertha who was barely standing under her own strength, wobbling and tilting as if the room were spinning right under her feet. Mattie slapped Bertha's face to make sure that she was alert.

"Will ya all stop slappin' me across my face?" Bertha yelled.

"Miss Julia, I'm so sorry. Do Massa know about this?" Mattie asked.

"No he doesn't, but if you can't control your

subordinates, then there will be no place working in this home for you or her in the future."

"No, no, Miss Julia. I'll take care of this right away!"

"Good."

Julia walked away and headed back outside through the kitchen. As she walked to the door, she looked over her shoulders and saw the rest of the girls nearly stacked one on top of the other, peeking out of the pantry door trying to be discrete, but she had seen them. They quickly shut the door as a last-ditch effort to not get caught. They were quite sure that they had been seen, but they did not know that Julia had merely shook her head in disgust but continued to make her way out of the door to return to her husband before anyone could get suspicious about her whereabouts.

The girls became quiet and as still as they could. They were all terrified of being caught, and they anticipated Julia opening up the door and having them all whipped mercilessly for a number of reasons and a number of rules that they had all broken that night. However, this never happened. Instead, they waited until they could hear nothing. When they were sure that the coast was clear, they ran through the kitchen and made it down to their bunks where they slept the rest of the night.

While they were safe in their designated areas, Mattie was dealing with Bertha. Bertha and Mattie left the house. Mattie put Bertha's arm around her shoulder and nearly dragged her down the darkened dirt road in the direction of her home. She was still delirious, and Mattie did not want to bring her home in that shape. She decided to make the turn that led them to the pond where the moon lit up the area, and they could sit there for a while until Bertha sobered a bit.

Mattie helped lower Bertha down as slowly as she could, but Bertha still managed to land with a thud right on her bottom. The drinks that she'd consumed that night had robbed her of her balance. Mattie looked at her in disappointment, but she also felt bad for her. She stared at her for a moment, and that's when she saw a young girl with a lot of potential. She saw a girl who could possibly grow up and make a difference in the world but was born a slave and would probably grow old as one as she was doing. She could see her younger self in Bertha. She knew that Bertha was like an injured bird unable to fly because the heavy burden of slavery had crushed her wings. Mattie knew that there was nothing left in this life for a bright girl like Bertha except to get into trouble and make mistakes like the one she had made that night. Because of this, Mattie refrained from scolding her any longer and sat silently beside her.

In her drunken daze, Bertha looked up and realized where they were. She began to think about Bubba. Her expression became filled with sorrow, but she quickly let go of the memories. They were not helping her with pulling herself together, and she didn't want to start crying again like she had done in front of Julia. Suddenly, Mattie reached into a small sack that she had been carrying and pulled out a large piece of chicken she'd swiped from the kitchen before they'd headed out. She gave it to Bertha.

"Here. Eat this, will you? It will help ya feel better, Berda."

Bertha couldn't figure out why Mattie could never seem to get her name right. When she didn't call her "child," it was usually Berda. Bertha was smart enough not to correct Mattie like she had corrected Bubba a time ago.

Bertha took it and quickly devoured it. She was hungry, so she stuffed her mouth and chewed quickly. As she chewed, she began to speak through partially masticated pieces of chicken.

"You know what, Miss Mattie? I love ya cookin'. I always did. That's why every time you cook I sneak and eat a piece when ain't nobody lookin'." Bertha admitted. "I never understood why you could always eat in the kitchen, and we not allowed to. Sound like a unfair rule to me."

"Well, Berda, you should know by now that life is unfair sometimes, and sometimes you have to live with things that you don't think is right," Mattie explained. "That's what I been tryin' to teach you girls. The quicka you learn that, the quicka you will learn to survive in this cold world without goin' mad."

"Yeah, you right, Mattie."

At that moment, Mattie felt the need to tell Bertha a story. "Berda, I been workin' here about twice as long as you been alive. I know what it's like to be that age. I seen many things happen workin' here. In a way, I feel like I'm part of the family. We all are. We black women have to mother the children of these white families more than the real mothers many times. I been helpin' to raise Sage since she was born. I can still remember the little ol' thing when she was a baby. She was a big, healthy baby with a

large smile. She came into this world smilin'; that's
how I knew she was gonna be somebody special.
Mrs. Margaret didn't have the first clue about how
to take care of a baby when Sage was born, so Miss
May and myself shared the duties of takin' care o'
Sage.

"That Sage was a child movin' around all the
time. She was never still. She learned how to walk
when she was eight months old, and she couldn't
stop movin' around when she did."

Bertha sat there silently and listened to the story
as she tried to picture Sage as this energetic young
child.

"One day me and Miss May had trusted Margaret
to care for Sage on her own while we completed our
other house duties for the day. We warned her that
you gotta keep a eye on that baby. That Margaret
a proud woman who never would admit that it was
too much for her to look after her only child, so
she accepted the task. And Lord knows, just after
Miss May had headed back into the house after we
had been workin' a while, I was standin' out back
hangin' clothes and Miss May came out of the house
screamin'. 'Where is Sage? Sage ain't here!'

"Miss May had walked into that house and found
Margaret asleep on the rockin' chair, and Sage was
nowhere to be found. Sage was around two years
old at the time. It must have been help from above,
because somethin' inside of me told me to take off
runnin' in the direction of this here pond. Back
then, I was afraid of a child fallin' in and drownin'.
So that's what I did. I ran right here to this pond.
Before I got close enough, I saw the child fall right
in, and my big self has never run so fast. I'm not

a real good swimmer, and I'm still a li'l bit afraid of water, but that day somethin' just came over me and I jumped in. I grabbed her hand quick before she could breathe in too much water and sink to the bottom.

"Thank goodness for these hips, because they helped the both of us float to the top, and I paddled my way out of the murky wata with Sage still alive and crying and coughin' her li'l lungs out. My goodness, that child was coughin' bad. When we was out of the water, I saw Margaret and Miss May runnin' up to us. Miss May just kept repeatin' 'Oh Lord. Oh Lord,' the whole time. Margaret grabbed Sage and picked her up, and they both was cryin' and huggin'. Then Margaret hugged me, and we all just stood there huggin' and cryin' and tryin' to catch our breath.

"When Master Jackson got home that day, Margaret told him what happened, and he told me that I was welcome to anything in his house and in his kitchen that I wanted. After that, he never complained about me eatin' in the kitchen again.

"How's that chicken sittin' with you?"

"Good, Mattie."

"All right, good. Honey, I think it's time we get you home," Mattie said. "Can you manage to walk on your own from here? Lord knows my back is tired, and my dogs is barkin'. It's been a long day."

"I'll be good to walk, Miss Mattie," Bertha responded.

She then slowly made her way across the short distance leading to Bertha's home from the pond. When Bertha arrived home, Aunt Lola and Cousin Zeke were both asleep. It was early in the morning, and Bertha knew that the sun would be rising in the Southern sky in a few hours.

When Bertha showed up for work the next day, she had a throbbing headache due to the wine. She received her much-expected punishment from Mattie who came down hard on her. Soon as Bertha walked in the door, the other girls snickered and laughed at her disgruntled appearance.

"Take this scrub brush and this bucket, and I don't want to hear from you for the rest of the day until every inch of the floor upstairs is cleaned. Oh, and please don't disturb the newlyweds while you up there." Mattie shoved the cleaning materials into Bertha's chest, not even waiting for her reply.

Bertha was too disoriented to object, so she took the brush and continued on her way. She had about half of the hallway scrubbed when her knees started to ache. She felt nauseated, so she immediately got up from the floor and ran straight into the scrub room where she began to puke in the copper bathtub. The puke flowed from her body like a dam that had given way to flood waters in a storm. There was no stopping the puke as it spewed from her body. Of course, with her luck, she puked down the side of the tub and had to take extra time cleaning it up. As she was trying to clean up the mess in the washroom that she wasn't allowed to use, she heard a knock on the door.

"Is anyone in there?" Logan called out in a very audible voice.

Bertha looked up at the door. "Yes, I'm in here. It's me, Bertha."

"Are you all right in there?"

"I felt a li'l sick, so I ran in here," Bertha explained.

She heard the doorknob twist and remembered that she had forgotten to put the latch on to lock it. Logan came right in.

"I just wanted to make sure that you were all right in here," he said. "I heard you puking from down the hall."

He found Bertha on her knees, leaning over the tub.

"I'm fine, sir. I'm just cleanin' up my mess. I know I ain't supposed to use this room, but I got sick, and I really—"

"You don't have to explain a thing to me. As long as you're all right, that is all that matters. Carry on."

He shut the door and left out.

"Sir!" Bertha called out after him.

Her voice startled him and he quickly turned around. "Yes?"

"Thank you."

He looked back at her, gracious for the appreciation. "Don't mention it."

Chapter 24

The War Starts

In 1859, a religious zealot and abolitionist named John Brown killed five white men in a vigilante effort to take a stand against slavery. Tensions were getting high inside of the country, and there were continued rumors of an inevitable war between states in the South and in the North. John Brown was the first to personally take violent efforts to try and end the institution of slavery that he hated. He was the first to cause bloodshed and to shed blood in this attempt to end what he thought was an ungodly practice. Shortly after John Brown was captured and put to death by hanging, multiple state representatives in the South met to form the Confederate States of America. One by one, Southern states seceded from the Union. They feared that Northern states would infringe on their economic and personal freedoms, including the right to own slaves.

Bertha's home state of Mississippi became the second Southern state to break away from the Union, which included Southern and Northern states. Mississippi seceded and was soon followed by other Southern states. On April 4, 1861, the first shots were fired in a civil war that would leave hundreds of thousands of young American men dead.

War raged on all over the South. Trenches were dug sporadically around Southern landscape in efforts to protect key pieces of land. There was rampant murmuring among civilians about specific death tolls as piles of dead bodies lay in ditches. The deaths were chalked up to the spoils of a vicious war that seemed to rage on longer than expected. These rumors always made their way back to the workers on Master Jackson's plantation. The house workers were always the last to hear the latest gossip about the war for some odd reason, and they could never figure out why. After a while, Bertha became jaded and uninterested in the horrifying tales of the war and seemed to want it to end more than anyone else in the country.

"You know, I heard they found a hundred bodies in a ditch down there off Londer Road headin' into town. None of them had a head, and they had been there for days with flies swarmin' them. I don't know how they gonna identify them boys for they family." Sue informed the girls as she walked into the kitchen.

All the girls heard her, but none of them even stopped what they were doing because they had heard so many stories about the war. At one point, it became a contest between the girls to see who could find the most shocking stories to tell. All the slaves kept an ear and an eye out for any information they could learn, but they all kept quiet around white folks.

Chapter 25

Julia's Excitement

Previously, Julia and Bertha had attended to the garden for several weeks. Shortly after the wedding mishap, Bertha was assigned to other duties, and things around the plantation were slow because of the war. Bertha continued to avoid Julia after the wedding. Julia was left to care for the garden on her own. When they worked together before, the two of them put in arduous labor keeping up the vegetable garden and attending to Margaret together.

One day Julia woke up earlier than usual. She was a new bride, but things had happened so fast that it hadn't yet set in. That day she had nothing to do. After she administered Margaret's early morning care, Sage had given her word to take the day off, offering to attend to Margaret for the rest of the day. Logan was out chopping firewood to prepare for the winter months, so she decided to go have a look at the fully grown garden when she was all washed up and dressed.

She was worried that the crops she and Bertha had planted awhile ago would not sprout correctly because the season had been rainier than usual, and she thought that the extra water might kill them or stunt their growth. When she got out to the garden that day, she was more than happy to see the crops were doing great. It was almost a miraculous sprouting overnight, and Julia was excited to show

Bertha the results of their long weeks of labor as soon as she got the chance. Julia stood there and took in the sight of the garden with its rich, natural colors that seemed to shine brightly in the softness of the sunlight. She was very pleased.

After a while, she turned around and started running back toward the house. She was headed to find Bertha, because she knew Bertha would be just as excited to see how well the garden was doing, especially being that it was her first time being involved in the planting of the seeds. She got halfway to the house when she was stopped by Bob Jenkins. Bob was Master Jackson's main worker. He did all of the dirty work around the plantation that Master Jackson did not want to do. His specialty was discipline, and he took a sickening joy out of inflicting pain on any slave who got out of line. The whipping post was the highlight of Bob's time working on the plantation. Julia found him to be a creep. She never liked him, but she put up with him because she had to.

Bob sat atop of his horse and started up a conversation with Julia as she crossed his path, even though he knew that she would not be in the mood to talk to him. She was seemingly never in the mood to talk with him, and she always kept their interactions as short as possible. Julia usually did her best to keep her distance from him. He had a thick Southern accent and bad breath because of his tobacco habit. He was never seen without a wad of chewing tobacco tucked under his lip or protruding from his jaw. This turned his teeth brown, and to Julia, that added to his creepiness. She was disgusted by the guy with his strange demeanor and wiry figure. He was the closest thing to a lunatic that she had seen, but he served his purpose on the land.

"Hello, purty lady." Bob stopped her as he turned his head to spit out a blob of dark, coffee-colored saliva. Julia watched in disgust as she eyed the spit until it splattered against the grass.

"Hi, Bob." Julia's lips were twisted with the displeasure of the moment. She tried to brush past him without a lengthy exchange.

"Ah-ah, not so fast, purty lady." He suddenly took a jump from the horse and landed right in front of her. The heels of his old leather cowboy boots made a thud as they hit the ground. He put his hand on her shoulder with pressure to prohibit her from leaving, and that's when she became annoyed.

"What do you think you're doing? Get out of my way, Bob. I'll have you fired. I have business to attend to."

Julia made another attempt to shove him out of her path and continue on her way.

"What's a purty girl like you doin' in such a rush? Are you headed to find that nigger who you seem to take quite a lakin' to? How come you so nice to that nigger but you so mean to a good ol' white man lak myself?"

"Don't be ridiculous. Now get out of my way!" Julia insisted as she tried to push past him again with her small frame.

"Or else what? What you gonna do if I don't, Miss Julia?" Bob began to taunt her. "You gonna tell yo' husband? He ain't much of a man. He can't 'ford no house for ya, and you married him. He still got ya livin' with ol' Jackson. Then again, you could tell that powerful li'l poppa of yourn's, but I got somethin' that'll keep ya from that, my dear."

She was stunned by Bob's behavior and started to become more uncomfortable. She had never been spoken to in such a manner, especially not by Bob Jenkins, who had been working on the plantation for years.

"You must be out of your wits to speak to me like this. I'll have you know that if you keep this up, this will be your last day working on this land. If you're lucky, you might be able to find another job here in town, but I can see to it that nobody else in the state of Mississippi ever hire you again!"

"Is dat right, Miss Julia?" Bob came even closer to her. He came so close that their noses were nearly touching. "You see, Miss Julia, I have a li'l bit of dirt on ya friend. She ain't the perfect li'l nigger she pretend to be."

Julia stood gravely still and didn't take her eyes off of him. She stared him down as he stared back at her.

"I know what ya li'l friend been up tuh. Believe me, if word got out about it, she could be in a whole lotta trouba."

"What are you talking about, Bob?" Julia asked.

"The Bible. George Washington's Bible. Ya' li'l friend stole it from the house, and I know for sure she took it because I found it by her sleepin' cabin buried out back. That is a family heirloom, and it's worth a whole lotta money. Grandpa Jackson wouldn't let a soul touch it, especially not one of them no-good niggers!"

Julia was frozen like a statue, and all of the color left her face until she was pale as sheep's wool. She gulped her saliva in the moment of receiving this information.

"I saw her makin' her way home lookin' strange with her bag unusually heavy lookin'," he continued. "I followed her and watched her place da whole night, and that's when I saw her burry it along with the other readin' stuff she ain't suppose tuh have. I saw everythang, and I know that's ya' li'l friend. I been watchin' y'all two for a long time."

"Don't be crazy. I have no nigger friends. She's nothing to me." Julia told him this to absolve herself from any personal connection with Bertha out of fear, but Bob wasn't buying it.

"I know that's a lie." Bob Jenkins got closer to Julia. He was so close that she could now smell the strong tobacco scent of his breath, and she felt the hot moisture of it on her face with each word.

"Now, I haven't tol' nobody about this, and nobody have to find out if—"

"What do you want from me, Bob?"

Julia knew that he would want some form of payment to keep quiet. She wanted to save Bertha, and he knew she did. To him, this was great leverage for making demands.

"Mighty glad that you asked me that. Ever since you developed into a fine young lady, I've had my eye on you. I think you know exactly what I want." Bob adjusted his crotch, which was stuffed in a tight pair of dirty trousers.

"Mighty funny how you say you don't care nothin' about her, but you so willin' to keep me quiet. Maybe you know how bad it will be if folks found out that a nigger got a hold of such a thang."

"All right, Bob. I think that she deserves a break.

She's not a bad person. That's why I'm willing to stop this. What do you want?"

Julia's desperation was clear on her face, and Bob fed off of this.

"Yep, emm ... hmm. You know what I want from you, pretty li'l thang." He reached out and touched Julia's cheek with one of his callused hands, and she turned her head.

"I'm married!" she gasped in disgust.

"Nobody gotta find out about this, li'l thang. We can keep it between you and me." Bob's husky and unattractive voice always made Julia's skin crawl, and this time was no different.

She clenched her jaw as she turned her head away to escape Bob's hand. Then she grimaced at the disgusting thought of sexual activity with someone who she thought was the creepiest guy in the state. She knew that Bertha could be whipped or maybe even worse if anyone found out. Disgusting intercourse with Bob was the only thing that could save Bertha now, but Julia just couldn't bring herself to do it. After pausing a minute to contemplate her next move, she spoke up without further hesitation.

"Never. Go to hell!"

She stood up straight and looked him right in the eyes as his expression dropped. He had backed her into a corner, but she had not given in. All of the air had been let out of his blackmail bubble.

"That sound fine to me, Miss Julia. A few lashes for yo' li'l friend it is, and I ain't gonna go easy on her. Now, carry on."

He tilted his black cowboy hat to her, mocking her decision as he hopped back on his horse. The horse galloped off at his demand.

Chapter 26

The Whipping

Three adult white men stood in a semicircle staring at a shirtless Bertha. She was suspended from a post on the ceiling, hanging there by a thick rope that was tied around her wrists. She didn't know that she was in the same barn where Bubba had been murdered. The one holding the whip was Bob Jenkins. The other two men were nobodies in the community; they were just there for their own entertainment. One of the men smoked a cigar that filled the room with thick, potent smoke. He puffed on it as it dangled from his lips when he spoke.

"She sure is purty, boss. This should be somethin' to see," he spoke as he gazed on. The cigar moved with his lips.

There was a small amount of daylight seeping through that lit the place. It was the most powerless that Bertha had ever been in her life, but she knew that this day would come sooner or later. All the servants her age had been whipped at least once in their lives. She was very concerned about the pain to come, but she was not afraid. She knew that whippings were usually short and quick with a designated amount of healing time afterward. She was ready to take her whipping and later show off the scars to the other girls who worked in the field as a badge of honor. The field girls always questioned her toughness because she worked inside of the house and had never taken a beating. She hung there with only her thoughts to comfort her. Bob Jenkins stepped forward.

"Do you know why you here?" he asked, flashing a smile that displayed his discolored teeth. He could not wait to put a few lashes across her smooth and sculpted back.

"You know, ya back is too purty for a slave girl," he whispered in her ear and erotically caressed the skin of her back with his rough and unclean hands.

Bertha slightly turned her head to escape the foul odor of his breath. She was utterly disgusted with his hands being anywhere on her body. She was as disgusted by him as Julia was, and she would have gladly traded that intimately close moment with him for three lashes from the whip that he was holding.

Julia sat in her room that day while Bertha was in the barn awaiting her whipping. She was curled up in the corner on the floor. There were quiet tears streaming down her face, and she was ashamed that she couldn't go through with the sexual act with Bob to save Bertha from what was to come. The door of her room was locked, and no one else in the house knew what was going on with her. She had told Sage she wasn't feeling well and asked her to look after Margaret for a while. Logan was not in town. He had traveled to the North to attend to business and start the beginning process of looking for a home for them to buy when they moved back to Philadelphia.

There was outrage and concern around the plantation once people found out that Bertha had been accused of stealing a costly piece of property from the master's house. Even the field slaves who used to have animosity toward Bertha knew her not to be a thief. As a matter of fact, they knew her to be one of the most honest and trustworthy people who worked on the plantation. She was always fair and did whatever she said she would do. They felt that Bertha must have been framed, and many of them blamed Julia because they knew the two girls were forced to spend time together and had a volatile history.

It was high noon, and the plantation was in full operation. People around the field were busy at work, but in the back of all their minds, they knew that this day was the day that Bertha would face the whip for the first time.

"Well, seems to me like we found a little something in yo' possession that don't belong. You wanna tell me how it got there? Bob asked."

Bertha did not respond.

"What, is you deaf? I asked you a question. How did you get that Bible outta the Jacksons' house?"

Bertha said nothing and just hung there with the expression of a stone on her face.

Bob Jenkins didn't have a lot of patience, and he realized that Bertha was being stubborn and would never talk, so he turned his head to spit. Then he stepped back a couple of feet to create a good whipping distance between his whip and Bertha. He pulled up his slightly oversized trousers and suddenly started the punishment. The first crack of the whip crashed against Bertha's bare back, and the pain ran through her body like a bolt of lightning. She screeched loud enough that the workers in the field could hear her holler from yards away. There was another crack of the whip seconds later as the leather met Bertha's skin once more. She yelled out with every ounce of wind that she had in her lungs. The pain spread through her body. This was the second time that she had felt this sort of physical pain. She was reminded of the pain she felt during the childhood accident that caused her lung injury, and it became tougher and tougher for her to catch her breath as the pain became sharper. Then there was another blow landing across Bertha's back. It created a thick welt that immediately bled.

"Hit her across the other side, boss!" One of the onlookers yelled out without any regard. They laughed and cheered as Bertha hung there in a pain that no twenty-one-year-old woman should ever face. It was a pain that would break the most macho of men. A defenseless Bertha began to weep as all of her tenacity and will had been robbed of her at the hands of a callous man empowered by a whip.

She was only three strikes into a punishment that required twelve lashes. With two more quick lashes, she was down to seven more remaining. The seventh and eighth strikes made a swooshing noise through the air and ripped her delicate skin, creating two long lacerations about a tenth of an inch thick. Bertha began bleeding profusely and lost the strength to scream for mercy. Now, with each blow, her body jerked from the pain, and the muscles in her face drooped with exhaustion but tightened with each following blow.

There was a deathly stare in her eyes as her sight became blurry. She was overcome with delirium and salt-laden sweat rolled from her forehead and dripped into her eyes where they were then diluted with the tears of her agony. Her head dropped down and was suspended merely by the bone in her neck as she continued to bleed and sweat. She soon became too weak to lift her head as she hung there by the rope.

"Please stop," she cried out, barely able to speak with her weak voice full of muffled air.

Aunt Lola and Zeke stood waiting at the edge of the cotton field that was in sight of the barn. They were accompanied by another field worker who was new on the land named Melvin. He stood alongside of them for moral support. They embraced and sobbed for Bertha the whole time she was in the barn. When they stopped hearing her shrills and screams, they became terrified as to her physical state. There had been many slaves who went into the barn for their turn at the whip—sometimes for insignificant infractions—who had not returned from the whipping alive.

Usually if a slave died on the whipping post, it was because of his backtalk and was considered suicide by whipping. The ones that did not make it out alive usually were foolish and stubborn young men or proud old men who taunted the whipping master. Most slaves knew that there was a proper protocol for taking whippings. They kept your mouth shut the whole way through, unless the whipping master asked a question. Other than that, they were to, silently as possible, take their whipping and then return their battered body to the fields, where they were celebrated for their survival and nursed back to good health by the field women, who used home remedies and techniques that were passed down from generation to generation.

Cousin Zeke was now about seventeen years old.

He had the size and nearly the strength of an adult male. Zeke had had enough of waiting and made a break toward the barn, figuring that he would rush in and rescue Bertha at all cost. He only made it a few feet before Aunt Lola yelled out, pleading for him to stop.

"Stop, don't you go! Stop!"

Lola screamed at her son and reached out as tears streamed from her face, but he took off. She was too grief stricken to stand up in time to grab him. Melvin took off after him, and before Zeke knew it, he was being tackled to the dusty, gravel-covered ground. Melvin pinned him down using all of the strength that he had as a strong, full-grown man in an effort to keep him from bursting into the barn and putting himself in danger. Other field slaves watched things unfold from an even farther distance from where Lola, Zeke, and Melvin had watched. They saw Zeke being tackled to the ground. Many of them cried, and many others were enraged, but nobody had the power to do anything about the injustice taking place. When they saw the hopeless attempt that Zeke made to help Bertha, many of them became emotionally overwhelmed. Some of them stood at a distance praying, and others just watched with a burning fury in their eyes.

From inside the barn at that time, in her delirium, Bertha heard the large barn door burst open, and a familiar voiced yelled, "Stop now!"

It was a demand that came from the pit of her stomach. It was Julia.

"Let her down right now, Bob Jenkins, and get these scoundrels off of my uncle's property!"

"Not so fast, purty lady," Bob replied. "You see, I

have the right tuh go about this nigger's whippin', and your uncle approved. There ain't a thang you can do about it."

Master Jackson trusted Bertha, but the evidence that Bob had against her was damning. He did not know why or how Bertha got the Bible. He wanted to brush the whole thing under the rug, but this would not go over well and would cause too much outrage in the community. Although he cared for Bertha, because of executive and managerial reasons, he had to let her see the whipping post this time. If he didn't, he knew that there would have been internal chaos among some of the slaves who still resented Bertha, and people around the town would shun him for "letting niggers get away with too much" on his land. They would say that the niggers were running his plantation, and some of them might even have stopped doing business with him.

Before Julia had burst through the barn door, the field slaves saw her running over. She ran toward the barn moments after Zeke had been pinned to the ground by Melvin. As Zeke was on the ground wrestling with Melvin to break free, Julia nearly kicked open the barn door. The field slaves continued to watch, now even more captivated than they had been before. Inside the barn, Julia tried to impose her will on the situation. Her face turned apathetically red when she looked up and saw the ailing and helpless Bertha dangling there.

When Bertha heard Julia's voice, she mustered up enough energy to lift her head. Julia would not be denied, and she was determined to stop the whipping with every ounce of her five-foot frame.

When she did not get the answer that she wanted

from Bob, she launched at Bertha in a desperate moment. She was carrying a small knife that she planned to use to cut the rope to get Bertha down herself. Immediately, the guy with the cigar rushed over to her then grabbed and restrained her. She struggled to free herself from his grasp. However, she couldn't get loose. At that moment, Bob struck Bertha with the whip, and Julia wailed and screamed at the horror of seeing blood flow down Bertha's back, which was now raw with broken flesh. Then there was the twelfth and final lash. Bertha was nearly unconscious as she let out a final plea to Julia who was still struggling to break free.

"Help me!" Her airy and weakened voice carried through the room.

Julia was still being restrained but reached her arm out to Bertha as if she were close enough to grab her.

"What do you care so much about this nigger for?" Bob had rage in his voice, and his eyes were dripping with contemp. He looked over at Julia who was helpless under the power of the man who had easily stopped any effort she made to break free.

"Stop it!" Julia yelled and cried as she became exhausted from the struggle to get free and save Bertha.

Although Bertha had endured her twelve lashes, Bob became angrier when he saw how much Julia cared about Bertha's well-being because Julia had always treated him so rudely. As a result, Bob decided to continue to strike Bertha with the whip just for the sake of torturing Julia, whose shirt had become soaked in her own tears. She screamed and cried for Bertha with the same passion and urgency of a wailing newborn. Julia could do nothing. Bob continued to whip Bertha, creating more lacerations on her back, and Bertha bled even more. Her bright red blood leaked out of her body and fell to the ground where it stained the barn floor beneath her. With more blows from the whip, at the force of a grown man putting all of his strength into each crack, Bertha nearly passed out. In her barely conscious state, she heard the cigar-less man say something to Bob.

"Ain't this the same one you shot that Bubba boy in, boss?" The guy's question was accompanied by a chuckle.

Bertha became furious, because just then, even in her wooziness, she found out for the first time that Bubba was dead and had been shot in the same barn that she was now being beaten in. She knew then that he had not been sold. She found out the truth and realized that there was no hope of ever seeing him again. That's when despair and anger became concentrated in her, and she reached into the depths of her soul to speak in her airy, exhausted shell of a voice. Very surly, she struggled to slowly lift her head and look at Bob.

"Is that all you got?" she asked.

The spectators looked at each other and then looked at Bob, who had put everything he had into the whipping. He was out of breath and sweating. Her words cut him deeper than any lash he could give her with the whip. He was teased and picked on all of his life for being scrawny and physically weak, and this upbringing had done irreversible damage to his self-esteem as a man. Bertha had taken all that he had and was taunting him for more. He was humiliated.

In that moment, Bob lost control and struck her with the whip again and again and again, landing vicious blows on her. Her head slumped down with her chin resting limply on her chest, and she passed out. Julia kept fighting to break free, knowing that Bertha was in trouble. She managed to bend down to pick up the knife that had been knocked out of her hand. She grabbed it and stuck it right into the thigh of the man restraining her. The cigar fell from his mouth and onto the barn floor as he yelled out in pain, turning her loose.

Julia then rushed toward Bob and jumped right on him, grabbing hold of the whip. She slapped and scratched him. Bob instinctively reacted to Julia's attack, and slapped her. She fell to the ground, holding her face and crying. The barn door opened again, this time slowly. They all turned to look at the door being pushed open, which brought with it a passage for more sunlight to enter and created a distraction from the turn of events inside. It was an emaciated Margaret who walked with the help of a walking stick. The man who Julia had stabbed in the thigh ran out of the barn in pain. The cigar-less guy, who had been watching, quickly followed behind him exiting the barn.

"Let the girl down now, Bob. Those are orders." Margaret looked over at Julia who was slowly getting up off the floor. "You've whipped the girl more than her allotted punishment, and you struck a superior. Your job here is done. Julia, help the Negro boy down and get her back to the cabin and patch her up," she ordered Julia.

Margaret then turned around and weakly made her way out of the door before Bob could even answer. Master Jackson came through the door as his wife was leaving. They crossed paths, but Margaret didn't acknowledge her husband and continued on her way. Out of concern for the whereabouts of his sick wife and Julia, Master Jackson had rushed to the barn. He headed there because he knew it was the most likely place where they would be, and he was right.

Bob stood there dumbfounded. He quickly came to his senses and started to cut Bertha down as fast as he could, lowering her softly to the ground. When she got to the ground, Julia ran over and dragged Bertha away from the spills of her own blood. She began to cry again as she grabbed Bertha and cuddled her head. Bertha slowly regained consciousness and tried to speak, but Julia told her to be quiet because she had to save her energy for healing. Master Jackson watched all of this speechless until he told Bob to leave.

"We'll deal with you later," he said. "Get the hell out of my sight."

It was all over. Bertha had survived her ordeal, although she nearly died hanging there that day in the barn. She had no idea that her physical health would never be the same, and they spent months trying to nurse her to good health with limited resources. The wounds created by the beating were worse than any wounds that the women who worked the field, that usually tended to the wounds of the beaten, had ever seen on the plantation. No doctor would or could prescribe a Negro slave any medication or needed care. Bertha was bedridden for months as she tried to recover. Meanwhile, the war outside the plantation raged on.

Very soon after Bob had nearly beaten Bertha to death and slapped Julia to the ground, he was fired from his job. Julia confessed to her dad, Rufus, about Bob's blackmail. Soon after that, Julia's politically powerful dad secretly called for Bob's demise. Bob was found dead in the woods from a shotgun blast to the chest that came from the same shotgun that had been used on Bubba. The murder was never solved, and no one was ever arrested for killing Bob Jenkins. The day the slaves found out the news of Bob's death, there was a joyful jubilee in the slave quarters that lasted throughout the night.

Chapter 27

Garden Treasures

After Bob's death that year, the fall harvest came and went, and Bertha was too sick and battered to ever go to the garden and witness or appreciate the work that she and Julia had put in. Julia was disappointed about this and tried her best to help Bertha be a part of the joy that she felt about how well the garden had turned out. She made Bertha some soup with fresh vegetables that came from their garden. Bertha loved the soup and felt good that Julia was nice enough to bring it to her.

During Bertha's recovery, she was excused from her duties of working in the house. Most days she stayed in the cabin and read books, and she began to spend more time with Zeke and continued to teach him to read, even in her weakened state. The war continued, and tension was high around the plantation. Zeke would keep Bertha updated on the latest gossip, which is how they passed some of the time, as work around the plantation became slower and slower with each passing day of the war.

"You know, Bertha," Zeke began, "they say Betsy goin' behind Todd with another man. She pregnant again, but we don't know if it's really Todd baby. She been seen late night with Tiny Toe at least once."

"That Betsy is something else ain't she?" Bertha responded. "How she have the nerve to do that when she know how things get around this place?"

"That's the same thing I say, Bertha."

Zeke and Bertha were in the cabin together, and he was waiting on her hand and foot as she lay on her cot while they talked. Zeke walked over near the door to look outside at his mom, who was hanging laundry up to dry, and Melvin was with her. It was dark out, but in the darkness was when the field slaves on Master Jackson's plantation got their personal work done. Zeke noticed that Lola and Melvin seemed to be overly congenial.

"You know what, Bertha? I don't know how I feel about this Melvin. He been pushin' his way, tryin' get close to Momma. They say he got a family back at the place he came from, but he been here for a while now. They said he was gettin' out of line with his old masta, and he got shipped here. They gave him the choice of leavin' or gettin' shot. He only got a choice because we heard he had some kind of connections. I don't know what I think about him."

"Zeke, what you worried somebody gonna take ya li'l ol' momma away from ya?" Bertha teased. "Look, you almost a full-grown man now, and soon you gonna be runnin' around with some girl. Don't worry about what Aunt Lola doin'. She ya momma, but she still a woman."

"Bertha, what you know about bein' a woman? Don't Mrs. Margaret call you a boy anyway?" Zeke laughed as he teased his cousin. "And besides, I don't plan on runnin' around here anytime soon with none of these baboons around this here plantation."

"Here, Zeke, shut ya mouth and take this." Bertha threw a book at him, and it landed at his feet.

He bent down and picked it up, walked over to his cot, and sat down and opened it. Then he started to read it silently. He had finally picked up the skill of reading. Bertha was proud that he learned, but he only did it to make her happy. He liked building things with his hands far better than reading.

Bertha was trying to recover from her beating from several months before, Julia and her husband were waiting out the war in the South but were preparing to move to the North and buy a home. Logan planned to finish school and start work at the family business soon after the war was over. They both began to feel out of place in the South and longed for the lifestyle of the North.

During the last fall harvest before the war was over, Bertha's condition worsened because of the poor quality of medical attention and the lack of medication that she needed to heal properly. It had been over a year since the beating, and the war was nearing an end. Julia knew that there wouldn't be much more time to show Bertha the garden they had started together. She knew that she and her husband would be heading north one day soon. She wanted to share the joy of the garden with Bertha because they had worked in it together and had shared many great moments there.

On a bright sunny day in the fall, when Bertha was not up to it at all, Julia dragged her out of the cabin and brought her to the garden.

"What in the world you doin', Julia?" Bertha questioned. "I told you that I don't want to come. Let go of my arm."

"I will not let go of your arm until you come with me for five minutes to look at the garden. Come on, Bertha. You won't be disappointed. You can't just lie here every day and let time pass you by."

"If I go for five minutes, will you leave me alone for good? Why don't you go hassle Logan, Miss Julia?"

At the insult, Julia poked Bertha in one of her bandaged, infected wounds, and she screamed out in pain.

"What you do that for?"

"If you don't come with me, I'll stand here in this stinking old place all day and poke you to death," Julia threatened.

"Oh all right, I guess you ain't never gonna learn to take no for a answer, Jewels."

"I never plan to."

They headed out of the door, destined for the garden.

"Wait a second," Julia said. "Let me put this around your eyes, Bertha."

"There is no need to blindfold me." Bertha protested. "How am I supposed to see my way if you put a blindfold over me, Julia?"

"Oh just take my hand, and I'll guide you there. Don't be a whiner. Just come on—now."

Julia placed the blindfold over Bertha's eyes. Then she grabbed her hand and slowly led the limping Bertha to the garden. When Bertha realized that they had stopped walking, she was ready to untie the blindfold.

"Can I take this thing off now?" Bertha asked as she pulled at it impatiently.

"No, no, allow me to do it."

Julia untied the cloth, and Bertha was exposed to the breathtaking view of the expanded garden. By then, the garden was fully grown and fully complete. The section that the two of them had worked on a time ago was just a small section of the garden, and

Bertha remembered the painstaking hours they had both put in just for the small section. There were beautiful hues of purples, oranges, reds, and greens, and Bertha loved the mixture of all of the different hues of plants and vegetables. She was astonished.

"Whoa, who helped you do all this?" Bertha's tough façade melted away. She turned into a little girl right before Julia's eyes as she slowly limped through the large garden, exploring each of the different planted goods.

"My husband helped me with the garden a lot, and eventually, he got tired of putting up with me and paid a few guys from the town to come down and help."

"This is nice, Julia." Bertha displayed her huge smile. Julia would miss that smile so dearly.

"Being a Negro like you, I thought that this might impress you, Bertha."

"This is somethin', Miss Julia."

"Thank you, Bertha."

After about thirty minutes of touching, feelings, and picking up some of the flowers and sniffing them, Bertha began to cough uncontrollably, and her eyes began to water from the force of the coughing.

"You okay, Bertha?" Julia saw that Bertha was struggling with her breathing. "Let me get you back home to rest."

She reached out and grabbed Bertha's hand.

"All right." Bertha agreed. "Yeah, I should probably get back, but I'll make it on my own, Julia."

"I know, but let me help you. I think you can use some help, Bertha. And besides, you stink. Maybe they'll wash you when you get back."

"Yeah, let's get back; besides, I'm really tired and could use somethin' to eat."

They slowly made their way back to Bertha's cabin. Bertha's limp had gotten worse, so Julia placed her arm around her neck and helped her walk back home.

"Ain't this how we use to walk with Margaret, Jewels?"

Julia's eyes watered a bit from the memory of those days. Bertha noticed this, so she tried to stay away from that subject. Margaret had passed away only a couple of months before and had been buried with dignity.

"Goodness sake, Julia, you got me feelin' like a old woman. I don't need ya help. I can walk on my own."

Bertha scolded Julia, but Julia just looked at her and shook her head. She knew that Bertha was ailing, so she continued to help her.

Chapter 20

Aftermath of the War/Finally Free

The girls who worked in the house made it part of their daily routine to visit Bertha's cabin home. She was usually sick in bed, and they would tell her all of the stories they had heard about the war. Once they told Bertha a story about a man who had gotten his body blown in half while he was retreating from attacks. They said that when his upper body was blown away from his lower body, his eyeballs continued moving and he could still blink. This was the most shocking thing that Bertha had ever heard, but there were many other gory stories about the war. Bertha knew that some of the stories were probably exaggerated. She thought that this had to be true about the guy who had gotten his body blown into two pieces, but she didn't know for sure because she had never seen anyone get their body blown up.

Most times when the girls would visit Bertha, they would bring her food and try to make her laugh. There was an ongoing charade on the plantation among all the field slaves and even the house workers. When they would speak amongst themselves, they would tell each other to stay silent around white folks while the war was going on.

Miss Mattie would say, "Pretend that you don't even know what's goin' on. Not only pretend, but look sad, sick, and tired every chance you get, even if you happy."

There were reporters who would come and take photographs of different plantations and write stories about Negros. One of them even stopped by Master Jackson's plantation to take pictures and report on the war. That particular day the sun was shining bright and the folks around the plantation were in high spirits because they heard that the war could be ending soon. They hadn't even heard any firing of artillery in the distance for a long while. However, they were up to their normal routine of looking sympathetic and broken spirited in order to sway opinions about slavery and the war. Even the babies and young children had caught on to the routine. They called it the sad game. To them, it was so fun to look sympathetic while holding in hysterical laughter. That's what they did the day that the news reporter came to Master Jackson's land. When he was done taking pictures and had left the land that day, they laughed and laughed.

The sympathetic routine had worked, because the young reporter left the Jackson plantation mentally drained and more compassionate to the abolitionists' cause. He later came across this way in the newspaper article that followed. This was one of the stories the girls told Bertha on one of their visits, and she got a good laugh from it.

One day Lucille came to visit Bertha alone. The girls in the house were busy that day, and they all couldn't come together like they usually did. Mattie let Lucille go alone to visit just so Bertha would have a bit of company while Zeke and Aunt Lola worked. Lucille slowly opened the door to Bertha's cabin.

"Hey, Bertha. How you feelin' today?" Lucille asked.

Bertha was so sick that day she couldn't even speak. She merely turned her head and gave Lucille a forced grin while she lay on her cot.

"I brought you some soup. We startin' to get real busy around the house again, and Mattie sent me by myself."

Bertha listened but didn't respond. She lay there staring at the ceiling.

"I know you ain't got much energy or feel like talkin', but don't worry about a thing. You ain't gotta worry about talkin' to me today, I'm just here to keep ya company."

After that, there was silence as Lucille scrambled for the right words. She had something she wanted to say to Bertha, and it was eating her up inside. Lucille knew that this was the only chance that she might get to speak to her in private. She talked aimlessly for a while until she had the courage to say what she wanted.

"The girls around the house been changin' since you been gone. They been fightin' more and more. And guess who got into a fight, Bertha? Ol' scary Isabelle." Lucille laughed at the thought.

"Yeah, she got into a slug match with Beatrice. I don't know where she got the gumption from lately, but she seem to have had enough of them girls' mess. She smacked Beatrice right across the face, and neither one of them sisters have bothered her since."

Lucille laughed and then there was more silence. "You know what, Bertha? I got somethin' that I need to tell you. I wants to tell you just in case I don't get another chance like this, because like I said, we been gettin' busy around here with the war 'bout over.

"You know that day you got drunk at the weddin' and fell on the kitchen floor? We stood back hidin' in the pantry watchin' you and laughin'."

Lucille started to cry out of guilt. "I wanted to come and get you up and help you, but I didn't. I just went along with the others. When I finally got the nerve to come out and help you, I saw ol' Jewels comin' in, and I ran my tail back to hide in the pantry. I been thinkin' of that ever since then, and I just wanted to say that I'm sorry. We all are. I know the girls would want me to tell you so. We should have helped ya that night. We should have helped you. We just stood in that pantry and watched Jewels try to pull ya up off that floor. We just knew that she was gonna kill you, but she didn't. She didn't. Bertha, I don't know how you got that Bible, but I don't think Jewels got ya in trouble."

Lucille started to sob uncontrollably, and Bertha slowly reached out her weak hand and grabbed Lucille's hand. She squeezed it as tight as her limp arm could and let go after a short moment. Soon, Bertha started to fall asleep. Lucille sat at her bedside. She realized that Bertha was tired.

"Bertha, you get ya rest, and I'm gonna get back to the house. I'm leavin' this soup by ya bed. You get better now."

Lucille slid the bowl of soup right next to Bertha's bed, close enough for her to reach it when she woke up. Then she quietly and slowly left the cabin.

The saga of Bertha's health was like a roller coaster. Some days she would feel better than other days, and most days it would be a surprise how she would feel that day. When Bertha was not in too much pain, she would lay there and worry about the war and if it would ever end. She was absolutely terrified that the plantation could be blown up and pillaged. Whatever side would win the war, she just wanted it to be over.

The American Civil War was fought all over the region where Master Jackson's plantation was located, but it never came within twenty miles of his land. It was like God had a special shield of protection over that area. However, late at night, before the end of the war neared, when nobody was stirring, the people on Master Jackson's plantation could hear loud cannons and gunshots going off in the distance.

The end of this war in America came with joy for all of the slaves around the South who had been bound to the chains of nothingness since the time they'd been born and who came from generations of their families who shared the same fate. The North had won, and slavery was soon abolished. On Master Jackson's plantation, the joy of freedom came with a pinch of bitterness. Bertha's condition was not improving in the time after the beating. Her wounds began to reek with the scent of infection that began to take over her body. Bertha had turned twenty-three under the shadow of pain and illness, and for her twenty-third birthday, Julia conned her way into retrieving some pain medication and ointment for Bertha from a highly respected physician in the area.

Everyone around the plantation loved Bertha. She had always offered them hope even before they began to like her. She was blessed with the gift of optimism, and it was refreshing for such a hopeless group of people to witness her existence. She was beauty on the outside and inside. She was brave, and she had a smile that could brighten up the day. She was caring and kind, but she also had an edge, similar to the angst and attack of a wild animal if threatened.

Bertha hung on to her life long enough to see her people freed, people whom she had told all the time that prayer and God would bring justice and freedom, and it did. The words that she had spoken became truth. However, she would not live long enough to enjoy the freedom that she had professed to so many of them. She told them that better days lay ahead, and it happened. This was the beginning of a new life for them even though many more struggles loomed for the newly freed people. This was the end of the road for Bertha Oliver. She passed away on May 20, 1865, a date that marked eleven days after the American Civil War had ended.

Chapter 29

The Letter

Twenty-three-year-old Bertha perished on a bright sunny day, and Julia was not at her side this time as she had always been. Two days before Bertha died, Julia and Logan had taken off for the North to escape the ruins of the South. Southerners would spend years recovering from the wreckage and rebuilding.

Before Julia left, she secretly met with Zeke to make a secret exchange. She was careful that no one would see them. She gave Zeke the Bible that Bertha had been beaten for and told him to auction it off once he and Lola were granted their freedom. For Julia, this was an act of rebellion out of the anger she felt for what had happened to Bertha. On Zeke's part, to meet with Julia and accept what she had given him was also an act of rebellion because of what had been done to his cousin. He had no care as to the risk of the situation, and he soon realized that the money that could be gained from it would give generations of his family true freedom.

They could buy land and build on it and live financially free. In return, he gave Julia a letter that he had found and read. Had it not been for Bertha teaching him to read those days in the past, he wouldn't have known how important the letter was, and he may not have trusted Julia enough to meet with her. He found the letter strange, but he knew that he should give it to her. When she came to him to ask him to secretly meet with her, he knew that he would have the perfect moment to give her the letter that Bertha had written, and that's what he did. On the train ride to the North, with her husband asleep next to her, Julia thought about Bertha and went into her bag and pulled out the letter. She unfolded it and read it silently.

Bertha had written the letter knowing that one day Julia and Logan would move away. As she wrote it, she nostalgically thought about those days spent laughing and joking around with Julia. One day Margaret had awakened while the two of them were goofing around in the mirror with one of her wigs. Margaret shouted out at them, and both of their faces went pale. She grabbed the wig out of Julia's hand when she brought it over to her, and then she slapped it onto her head, crooked and backward. While the wig dangled loosely on Margaret's head, she fell back asleep. The girls had to run out of the room because they could not hold in their laughter any longer. Bertha wrote the letter suspended in the memory of those types of moments of joy.

Immersed in the bliss of their newfound bond, which neither of them would admit to, Bertha was losing all sense of reality. She felt loved, and she knew the feeling. She was a slave, but she had found hope in their bond. She had an instinctive feeling that she would one day be free and that everything would be just fine. The happiness that she felt was a familiar feeling that she had experienced once before in her young life. She was joyful, and it complimented her hope. She was carefree, and it was displayed in her smile. She finally felt something she had been missing. She didn't understand it, but she knew that she would never forget the feeling or forget Julia.

Julia had given her water when she didn't even want to admit that she needed a drink. She had pulled her off of the kitchen floor in her drunkenness without any judgment and an understanding and compassion that was sent from heaven. Julia had taught her about how to care for a person in a circumstance where it was prohibited and should have been impossible to care. Julia was abrasive, but she had been there and had reminded Bertha of the power of love through her actions. That was all that Bertha needed to blossom and keep pushing against the walls of slavery that had held her mentality hostage. Bertha could not forget the small gestures that Julia had done for her and had no real way to express her feelings and to show her gratitude, and so, she decided to write her a letter. This was forbidden and dangerous but Bertha knew that Julia and Logan would move away and their time living on the plantation was coming to an end.

She didn't want to let Julia's bravery and courage to love go unappreciated or unacknowledged. She knew that if she missed the moment, she would always regret it, so she took the chance. She took the chance in a short letter that she hadn't even considered how she would find the courage to give it to Julia. She decided to write it in the quiet of the night. She lay on her cot and waited for Aunt Lola and Zeke to go to sleep. When she was sure that they were asleep, she went to her outdoor hiding spot in the back of the cabin. Buried in the ground with two old wooden boards covering the spot were her writing paper and the pen Julia had given her.

Julia knew that Bertha was somewhat literate. One day when Julia made Bertha help her with cleaning, they came across a pen. The pen was one of the best writing utensils of its day, but Julia told Bertha she had no use for it. Julia insisted that she was tired of the old thing and had a much better one. She knew that Bertha would love to keep it. Bertha kept it and cherished it.

The night Bertha went to retrieve the pen with the other things, she quietly crept out of the door and into the night air that was cold and brisk but yet comforting from the hot air inside of the cabin. She looked up, and a full moon was beautifully shining bright in the black midnight sky. It was almost as if God had been waiting for her to come outside that night and placed the moon in the right place at the right time in order to light the way for her. She quietly crept around to the back of the cabin and removed the two wooden boards. She stuck her hand in the loose dirt to retrieve the goods. She grabbed what she needed, replaced the boards, and quickly scurried back into the cabin before she could be seen. The fear of being seen made Bertha's heart beat fast. She knew that getting caught outside at that time was very dangerous for her. She made it back into the house and quickly hopped back onto her cot. She paused a moment to make sure that things stayed silent. When the coast was clear, she crawled into the far corner of the cabin where a fraction of the moonlight had made its way through the small window, just enough for her eyes to see the pen and paper.

From her heart, she wrote a letter that could possibly doom her if it was found by the wrong person. It was a letter that was more than a letter to her, because within it was a piece of her. It was a letter that she could not resist writing. This was the letter that, by fate, made its way into the hands of Julia as she rode on the train that was destined for the North. During this time, an ailing Bertha lay dying on the plantation, and the distance of the road between them continued to increase.

It was a poorly written letter with rampant misspellings and writing mistakes of an undereducated slave who worked inside of the home of Master Jackson. It was written by a girl with a bright smile and infectious laugh. Julia stared at the letter for a while and began to feel like she was sinking into her seat on the train. She began to read it. It started with a common salutation.

Dearest friend Jewls,

Tonite I waited up real late untill they was sleep to write this letter to you. I do not no if I will ever have that much fun agin and I hope this letter get to you. Only if I could be brave enough to get it to you. You been a great friend and I know that everything you done for me come from the heart. I feel a connection to you that I can't tell in words and I thank you for it. You told me that if it were different me and you could have a real friendship and spend more time together around other folks. Remember you said that? I'm laughing now in my head. That seem riduculus to think about. You taught me that word riduculus and I can't spell it good but I think I did good enough for you to no what I mean. I just feel a good feeling everytime I think about you. It's like a strange smile that come on my face when I do and I giggle many times like that. I felt that feeling that come over a person when you know that some one care about you. You a person that truly care about anothers well being and I know it. I know you care about mine becus I can see it in you. That time when I fell down in the feild you turned round quik to see if I was okay then you turned away when you saw me get back up. I saw that and I felt some kind of way about it. Like the time when my spirits was down working out in the field and you came around the corner wearing that silly hat over Miss Margaret wig. You put a smile on my face and that is the real you. I wish I had more of a chance to learn about you and look into your eyes just to figure you out. I just feel some kind of way about you. Your eyes really do shine like jewels. I think Miss May was right. I don't know what it is. I just feel some kind of way about you and my heart tends to race. I guess what I want to say is that I loved before, but this is something different. I know I loved before becus I know what that feel like. I felt it with Bubba. I have surely loved before but not like this. Thank you Jewels.

Bertha Oliver

July 19, 1863

Chapter 30

Sage's Epiphany

Before Bertha passed away in the cabin, she lay there sick on her cot, made of scrap fabric and blankets that Master Jackson had given her, that rested on the floor that was steps away from the door. There was Aunt Lola and Zeke at her side, all of the girls who worked inside of the house were there, and Sage was there too. They were all there to be with Bertha in her final moments, and a young Sage faced the moment with the zeal of a wise adult.

Sage encouraged Bertha to go home. She sat next to her as Bertha lay there transitioning to the point of death. She talked very softly to Bertha. She knew that Bertha could hear her even in her very frail and barely conscious state. Sage knew how much Bertha had suffered through her illness, and she knew how much the place where they lived wasn't fit for a soul as beautiful as Bertha's. She sat on the floor next to Bertha's cot, holding her hand and whispering softly to her as everyone else stood around with tears falling down their faces and occasionally wiping them away.

"Bertha, I know how stubborn you can be," Sage whispered. "I know how strong you are. You don't have to be strong anymore. It's time for you to go home." She spoke without one quiver in her voice as she held Bertha's hand. "Go home, Bertha."

Sage had been upset over Bertha's condition

since she first found out about the whipping. She, like all the slaves around the plantation, thought that Bertha was innocent. Sage spent many nights crying and feeling terrible about what had happened. She wished that there was something she could have done to stop it, and sometimes she even blamed herself for being too caught up in her own life to keep an eye out around the plantation. The day before she held Bertha's hand as Bertha lay there dying, she miraculously found peace. It came over her that morning, and she was no longer torn apart inside.

She thought about the kind of person Bertha was and how Bertha had a beautiful heart with courage beyond her years. She knew Bertha had a great spirit and an immaculate soul. She knew Bertha did not belong in a world where someone like her could be tied up and nearly beaten to death at the hands of a man who had a heart of coal. She thought that Bob could have learned a thing or two from Bertha about what it meant to be a good human being, but all he saw was the color of her skin when he looked at her. Sage knew that Bertha deserved better than the suffering she was going through.

Bertha died holding Sage's hand, and it was the first day Sage had built up enough courage to come to Bertha's bedside when she had become sicker. Sage had lost her mom, and at that point, she was losing someone who she saw as more than a servant her family owned under the law. She was losing a great friend.

Before Julia left town with Logan, she begged Sage to go visit Bertha before it was too late. Sage never thought she would have the guts to stomach seeing Bertha in such a condition, but with peace of mind she found herself there with Bertha and the others during the last moments of Bertha's life. With Sage there holding her hand tightly, Bertha's grip slowly loosened, and she faded away to a place out of this world. Bertha went home.

Chapter 31

Julia's Confession

Julia lay in bed staring at the ceiling. The year was 1920, and Father Time had taken his toll on her body, despite her childhood dream of never getting old and her strong will and stubbornness not to do so. She made a long career out of taking care of the frail and sick, and now she had become one of those who needed care. Logan sat at her bedside. His body was also wrecked and ravished by coming face-to-face with gravity during his eighty-three years of life. At that time he was in a better condition than Julia, so he was there to take care of her the best that he could. In a few short years, he too would be met with the undefeated champions, time and old age, and become senile and bedridden while clinging to life.

Throughout the years, some of the things that Julia saw or did would remind her of Bertha. She never stopped thinking about Bertha, and she kept the letter that Bertha had written her in a safe place. Decades ago, Julia read in the paper that a forty-four-year-old freed Negro man from the South, who wished to remain anonymous, had traveled to the North and auctioned off a Bible that was once one of the few Bibles owned by President George Washington. He received forty thousand dollars for it. She knew that it was Zeke, and her effort to help his family was finally complete. However, not even that brought her peace. She always felt guilty about Bertha's death.

Julia and Logan's marriage had been rocky, as all marriages see their own ups and downs. They had many more happy times than bad, and over the years, they found joy in being together and raising their family. In their old age, Julia would talk, and Logan would try his best to hear what she was saying. On rare occasions, when the two could actually hear each other, they would reminisce about their marriage and the times they had spent together. Those became Julia's favorite moments late in life, because it engaged her mind and reminded her of life's lessons that she had learned.

Julia remembered that as a young adult in her twenties, she would often get upset and even furious at things that now seemed so small. Conversations reminiscing with Logan gave her a new perspective on life and new insight. She wanted to teach all of her life's lessons to her granddaughter, Bobbie, who she had named and who was the child of her son Logan Jr. She knew, however, that this would be futile. In her old age, she had learned that some things in life you just have to learn the hard way. She knew that Bobbie was too much like her when she was that age to listen, and because of this, she rarely tried to force those lessons on Bobbie.

Julia's skin sagged, and her bones ached. She hardly ever got out of bed, and she often lay there dreaming, either in a deep sleep or wide-awake daydreaming. Her eyes would often focus on a spot on the wall or on the ceiling, but her glare would remain in a faraway place far back in time—a time she could remember making the toughest decision of her life. Her mind would go to the time when she had experienced the purest form of love that she ever had known at that time in her life.

As she lay there staring at the ceiling, she began to tell her husband the story about why Bertha had been whipped long ago. This was a subject that they had never before spoken about, and he never asked. During the years after they settled in the North, Logan would sometimes find Julia with her eyes soaked in sorrow, a sorrow that he didn't fully understand. He would not force her to speak about it. Her burden was his burden, and his silence was the way that he helped carry it. On this day, as her decrepit body lay there, she began to speak, not even caring if he was listening. She had to hear the words come out of her own mouth.

"It was cold and raining heavily outside that day. This was not typical for the summer months in Mississippi back then. A storm was passing through the area, and it seemed to get more intense with every minute. Pretty soon it began to thunder and lightning. The sky was gloomy and blanketed with a thick grey hue that seemed to suck the life out of the town. The girls' area of the house was too damp, and shallow puddles of water had built up in crevices on the floor down there."

Julia suddenly dived into her story. She spoke through lips thinned from the passing of her youth long ago. She continued, and Logan listened.

"Uncle let all of the servants ride out storms in the large den, which had a fireplace. He would light it to keep them warm. The den had just enough seating for all of them to sit down and rest. They all worked really hard back then.

"They had been busy all day cleaning up after the party that uncle had thrown in celebration of closing a deal with a very prominent businessman who was new to the area. His name was Mr. Clay, and he had made millions of dollars in the North and saw the South as a prime opportunity to increase his wealth. As successful as he was, he should have known that the war would break out in a short time and damper the flow of goods. Free slave labor, along with the cotton gin, which cranked out a bunch of cotton, and the strength of the agriculture economy lured him to the South. Mr. Clay had envisioned the South would becoming the dominant region by out-earning the North. He supposedly had insiders in government who predicted a strong hold on policy favoring Southern issues. When the time came, he made his move and headed south. He eventually came into contact with Uncle, who was glad to accept his money, knowing it was a win-win situation for him.

"Anyway, at the party, there was the best wine and champagne served and live music. Everyone that mattered in the area was there, and they had the freshest seafood brought in from Louisiana. It was an extravagant party. Available women in the area showed up in droves, trying to get a shot with Uncle to become his next wife; they knew that he would soon be a widower. The news about Margaret's worsening condition had quickly made its way around that small town. I didn't attend the party because I wanted to stay inside at Margaret's bedside, even though Uncle wanted me to join them outside for a while. I didn't go, but I did glare out occasionally from the window that was in view of the outdoor festivities.

"Margaret was lying in bed under heavy dosages of pain medicine the night of the party, and I think that it soon made its way to her brain, causing her to become a bit loopy. She heard the trumpets and piano playing through the walls of the bedroom and cracked window. She began to speak to me. At first I couldn't even understand what she was saying, so I turned around and got closer to listen, taking my focus off of people watching through the window.

"'Frank,' she yelled at me. I said, 'I'm not Frank, Margaret.'

"She kept saying, 'Frank, what's that music I hear?' Frank was her brother who had died when he was twenty years old from an infection that started in his lungs. He had been dead for nearly thirty years, but Margaret insisted that I was Frank.

"She yelled out, 'Frank, is there a party going on out there Frank?'"

Ironically, in her old age, Julia imitated Margaret's shaky and weakened voice back then.

"'Yes there is,' I told her.

"'Well get me down to the party now! Get me dressed.' She was trying to get out of bed the whole time. You know, that Margaret was known to be a highly social person, and she would never miss a party in her healthier days. So I guess even under the influence of the medication, she knew that if there was a party going on, she had to be there. I insisted that she lie down, and I gave her a slight push. The soft push was all it took to get her back down on the mattress. Then I slammed the window shut and pulled the curtain.

"I said, 'Trust me, you're not missing anything,' and that's when she finally relaxed a bit. Of course, soon she was off to sleep and the party went on in the late hours of the night.

"By the next morning, Margaret must have slept well, because she had a different look on her face more relaxed and coherent. She had a dream that night, and she wanted to make a difference in the world and do something great for somebody who really deserved it before it was too late for her. She knew that she might not have much longer to live, and she wanted to bless somebody with something before she died.

"Because of the party, the house was trashed, and the girls worked all day on their hands and knees getting it back into shape. There was broken glass, spilled cocktail sauce, bottles of wines, and everything else that could be imagined laying everywhere around the house, from inside to the outdoor area where the party was set up. Bernadette found a woman's undergarment that had somehow been forgotten. She passed it around to the other girls, and they all got a good laugh, but I took it from them and tossed them in the trash.

"Even in their foolery, Mattie's hardworking crew had the house tidy by the time the storm set in that day. As it rumbled on outside, you could hear the heavy rain against the windows. The girls all sat quietly in the cozy room and waited it out. Mattie's rule back then was that when it's storming outside, God is working, and when God is working, people needed to sit still and wait quietly out respect for God and for good fortune. They were all quiet in the den until Bertha asked to be excused to use the outhouse. When she got permission to go, I heard Miss May tell her to hurry up and get back quickly. I then heard Bertha run outside into the heavy rain. She was an adventurous girl and dared to go out into the elements. I looked out of the window and saw her run through the rain and go into the outhouse out back. I exited the house so nobody could see that I had followed her and was hiding on the side of it getting soaked. When she emerged through the door and saw me she froze up.

"I said, 'What are you doing Bertha?' in my snobby little tone of voice that I used back then.

"She hesitated and stuttered for a moment. She said 'I-I'm ... I was using the outhouse, Miss Julia.' She was probably worried that I would rip her head off, because I was often mean to that poor girl. She quickly went into a long explanation about why she was in there, but I wasn't listening to a word that she said.

"'So, I got to get to goin' now. Bye, Miss Julia,' was all I heard.

"She was talking so quickly that I could hardly understand her. She was quite frantic. She was a tough girl, but I scared the living daylights out of her sometimes. I was the only one who knew how to offend her or make her so mad that it would knock her out of her comfort zone. Back then, I took pride in that. I felt like it was proof that she cared about what I thought of her, and that was not like her. Bertha never cared about what anybody thought about her. You could hardly get to her, but I could."

The aged Julia went on as her old, thin lips continued to ramble.

"She tried to make an effort to walk away from

me, but I stopped her. I said 'Bertha, I'm not going to yell at you if that's what you think.' I must have had an ominous demeanor about myself at that time, and I think that she began to notice this because the expression on her face changed. She really wanted to know what I wanted.

"I said, 'I have to give you something.' Her eyebrows were to the ceiling, and she was looking at me trying to figure out what I meant. You should have seen the look on her face." The elderly Julia chuckled in the memory, but then she continued.

"I pushed Bertha back into the outhouse so that we were both out of sight and explained my plan to her. I told her that I had a book to give her, and it was a Bible.

"She said, 'The Bible. Is that all?' I told her to quiet down. Then I asked her if she had one. She told me in the most innocent voice, 'No. I can't have one, Miss Julia.'

"I said, 'It won't be the only book that you have if I give you one. Will it?' She paused and looked at me. I had to cut the crap, so I said, 'Bertha, I know that you can read. I know how smart you are, so you can stop the dumb slave girl act. I know about the other books.'"

The elderly Julia was really into her story at that point as she looked over at the gray-haired Logan.

"I told Bertha that the night when we first met I felt really bad about what I had said to her at dinner. I was really mean to her. I sat there in my room until I was sure that she had made it back and was all settled in at the cabin. Against all sensibility, I walked over to apologize in what seemed to be the darkest night of the year. I told her that's when

I'd seen her go to her secret stash and grab the books. I let her know that I waited for her to go back inside, and I crept up along the side of the house and listened there a long while.

"I said, 'Bertha, I heard you reading to Zeke and teaching him new words.' I told her that I was touched that day, and at that moment, I was proud of her."

Julia's gaze became lost in the memory but she continued.

"Bertha stood there and didn't say a word. I told her that her intelligence was a gift from God—that no man had given it to her, and no one could take it away. I let her know that Margaret was probably going to die soon, and this was her last wish ... to pass on a gift to someone. I had to do it for her.

"I said, 'Bertha, she wants me to give you the Bible—and I have to do it—and it's a special Bible.'"

At that moment Julia had rambled almost all the way through her lengthy story, and she turned her wrinkled neck to look at Logan, who was lying down next to her. By the time she had come to that point, Logan was lying on his back, and Julia thought that he was asleep because he had been so quiet. However, he wasn't asleep. His eyes were open, and he was staring out into space, but he was listening the whole time.

Julia continued. "She trusted me completely, and she wanted to know when this was to happen, with little hesitation. I told her on her way home that night.

"I told her that I would meet her halfway to her home and put it in her bag. She was always talking about God back then, so I told her that God would be with her to encourage her even more.

"When the storm had subsided and Bertha's day was over, she nervously headed home. The air was damp, and you could smell the scent of wet mud and moistened flowers. She didn't know exactly where we would be meeting, so she tried to look unsuspecting as she made her way home. When she was past the garden, nearing the toolshed, she must have heard my whisper. I was standing in the cracked door of the shed waving my arms for her to come over. She ran over to me, looking over her shoulders to make sure that no one was around.

"She came inside. It was dimly lit and smelled of rusted metals and rotting wood. She must have realized that it had been her first time inside of it, because she looked out of place. Part of the ceiling was dripping, so we had to dodge leaking areas of the roof as we made our way to the back of the shed. That's where I opened up the cabinet that was nearly bare, except for two hammers and a box of nails. I reached inside all the way to the back and pulled out the Bible. Bertha just stood by and watched.

"I told her to open up the bag, and I hurried to throw the Bible in. Bertha could tell by the look in my eyes that this was an odd moment, and she seemed to become afraid. Even so, she opened up her bag, and I dropped it in.

"She turned and said to me, 'Why you doin this, Julia? What's so important about this old thing?' She held up the heavy bag and shook it in my face.

"I let her know that what I had just given her was worth more than she could imagine and that it belonged to George Washington. I explained that he was once the president of the country.

"She said 'Why you givin' it to me, Miss Julia?' She was so confused. I can still hear her naïve little voice in my head. She had no idea what she was getting herself into, but she still wanted to know more, so I went on with my brash explanation. I didn't want her to know the full extent of the trouble she would be in if she got caught with it because I wanted her to accept it.

"I said, 'Consider yourself lucky, Bertha. Margaret comes from a family of abolitionists. She never liked the idea of owning another human being, but she married into the Jackson family, and our prestige comes with the reality of it.'

"She said, 'Jewels, I'm startin' to think you crackin' up. You ain't makin' much sense to me.'

"I explained that Margaret married into the life of owning people, and she didn't like it and made me promise that I would give one of the slaves this gift. I said, 'Bertha, this may be the key to a better life for you and your family one day.' I told her that slavery would one day end.

"That may have been hard for any one of the others to believe, but not her. That's why I chose her. She had heard the rumors of the war, but when I mentioned it to her, it seemed to soak in. She yelled at me with her eyes bulging. She said, 'A war? So it's true.' I had to calm her down.

"I told her that I didn't want to believe it either until I overheard my father one night saying that the Yankees were trying to crumble the prosperity of the South and that it would not be tolerated. He said that Southerners were considering planning a new government.

"I said, 'Bertha, the Yanks are going to great lengths to stop Southerners. They're using slavery as a ploy to bate us into a war. They want it to end, and they are willing to pay all costs to get what they want. I told her that there was definitely going be a war. She was one of the first Negros in the area to know for sure.

"I could see that she was still trying to wrap her mind around the situation. I looked her in the eye and said, 'I believe in you, and I think that you're a great person. I know that you can take this gift and use it the way Margaret would want it to be used, but you have to hide it until the time is right.'

"She became afraid, and her eyes were so vulnerable. She was in disbelief. I told her, 'Hide it until you're freed—when it happens. That thing is worth at least forty acres of land, and that could do so much for your family.

"Of course, she wanted to know what would happen if she ever got caught with it, and at that moment, there was a pause. Both of us stood there in the damp toolshed, and I tried to answer her, but I pussyfooted again. Both of us had a gloss of perspiration on our faces. I looked into Bertha's eyes, searching for the right words.

"I said, 'I reckon that these folks will be mighty unhappy if they found out I've given you this. Please don't get caught with it.' She asked me who knew about it besides Margaret, and her expression had become more serious than I had ever seen the jovial girl get. I told her that we were the only ones who knew and that not even Uncle knew that Margaret had done this.

"I'm sure that Bertha had to do some quick thinking. She knew that accepting the Bible was very dangerous. I think that she felt as if she had nothing to lose and much to gain. She had been hiding books all of her life, and I'm sure she thought that this would not be any different. She probably thought that the worst that could happen to her was a whipping, and she knew that she had one coming after all of the years of avoiding them. By then, she was ready for it if she ever got put on the post. After taking a few moments to think about the situation, she seemed to have no more doubts about it."

Julia stopped talking and began to cry as tears seeped into the wrinkled crevices of her face.

"She was doing a brave thing." Julia was determined to continue, so she did. "Neither she nor I knew that the decision that we made at that moment would lead to her death."

As an elderly woman, Julia still remembered the noise that she and Bertha had heard that night outside of the toolshed after the exchange. She continued to be haunted by the feeling she had when Bob Jenkins approached her the day he attempted to blackmail her. She knew right away that Bob had probably been listening outside of the toolshed or had seen Bertha leaving with the Bible in her bag. He had made the noise outside that day. They thought the noise was made by a wild animal. Even after so many years, this memory still made her sick to her stomach.

Logan lay by her side and listened to the whole story without one word until she was finished. Then he spoke from a place of comfort that came across in his voice. He only had one thing to say.

"You loved her, didn't you?"

He asked, so she responded "I loved her. I still love her."

Now an elderly woman, Julia had finally told her husband the story surrounding her sadness and guilt about what had happened to Bertha. After all of the long years of her keeping it inside, after all of the guilt and pain that she felt about Bertha's death, she purged herself of its weight, which had been holding her down. At that moment, she was free.

Julia's youth had long faded and she had raised children who were now adults. When the first nursing school was founded, she enrolled in it and became a nurse. She had worked a long and successful career, and she was proud of that. She had lived in the country during historic and volatile times. She had done all that she could do in life, and she was proud of that as well. The guilt behind the circumstances of Bertha's death was the last thing that she needed to gain peace with, and after telling her husband the story, she could let it go.

———————

I am the great-grandson of Logan and Julia Thompson. I choose to remain nameless. I am a white male of upper middle class social status. I am nearly fifty years old. It is I who has narrated this story based on stories passed down from generations of my family. I have told this story for all to read and for all to understand how great a woman my great-grandmother Julia was. As a young man growing up in this country, you become focused on and distracted by gaining material things and achieving great wealth and success. You forget about the value of love. Bertha loved my great-grandmother, and my great-grandmother loved her. They loved with the purest love, a blind love that not even their circumstance, their skin color, or their time could erase. My great-grandmother Julia was my hero, and Bertha was hers.

That day my great-grandmother had finally unleashed her story without hesitation. It was the last important thing that she had left to do in life. At that moment, as an old and fragile woman, she was finally complete; she was ready to face death.

About the Author

Matrinna Woods was born and raised in Milwaukee, Wisconsin. She attended Milwaukee Public Schools and graduated from Riverside University High School, located on the eastside of Milwaukee. She is an alumnus of The University of Wisconsin-Milwaukee, where she graduated with a Bachelor's degree in Political Science in May 2012. *I've Loved Before* is her first fictional publication, and she spent more than a year crafting the story while working full time as an environmental service worker at a hospital located near downtown Waukesha, Wisconsin, a small town located thirty-five miles west of Milwaukee.

In the near future, she plans on continuing her education and crafting more fictional novels. She is already busy at work crafting her second fictional work.